FLAME AGAIN

RALEIGH DAMSON

This book is a work of fiction. Names, characters, places and incidents are the product of the author's imagination or are used fictitiously. Any resemblance to actual events, locales, companies, or persons, living or dead, is coincidental.

Copyright
© 2022 by Raleigh Damson

All rights reserved. This copy is intended for the original purchaser of this eBook only.

No part of this eBook may be reproduced, scanned or distributed in any manner whatsoever without the prior written permission from the author, except in the case of brief quotations embodied in critical articles and reviews.

Thank you for respecting the hardwork of this author.

Warning: This book contains sexually explicit scenes and adult language and may be considered offensive to some readers.

This book is for sale to adults only, as defined by the laws of the country in which you made your purchase.

The author is not responsible for any loss, harm, injury, or death resulting from using the information contained in this book.

Ebook
ISBN: 978-1-7780254-7-1

Print
ISBN: 978-1-7780254-8-8

raleigh@raleighdamson.com

ACKNOWLEDGEMENTS

To my mate and cubs, thank you for giving me time and space to wrangle the words.

Thanks to my dearest, just put it on my tab.

Thanks to my writing friend, Author K.S. Ellis, for pulling Gabe and Ivy
out of the fire so many times when I wanted to leave them to burn. Thank you
for cheering me on and reading all the things.

Thanks to Author Morgan Eliot and Author Ivy Whitacker for their support and
encouragement.

Thank you to my beta and ARC readers. I appreciate you so much!

And thanks to you, for reading!

To keep up with the Bandit Brothers Series and to know when *Flame True* is going to be released, visit raleighdamson.com

To grab a bonus scene of Ivy and Gabe, visit here https://BookHip.com/KRLZHSW

To holding on and getting through.

Contents

1. PART ONE AUGUST- BEFORE — 1
2. CHAPTER ONE – GABE — 2
3. CHAPTER TWO – IVY — 13
4. CHAPTER THREE – IVY — 21
5. CHAPTER FOUR - GABE — 34
6. CHAPTER FIVE – IVY — 44
7. CHAPTER SIX – IVY — 51
8. CHAPTER SEVEN – GABE — 59
9. PART TWO APRIL - AFTER — 63
10. CHAPTER EIGHT – IVY — 64
11. CHAPTER NINE – GABE — 71
12. CHAPTER TEN – IVY — 80
13. CHAPTER ELEVEN – GABE — 88
14. CHAPTER TWELVE – IVY — 96
15. CHAPTER THIRTEEN – GABE — 106

16.	CHAPTER FOURTEEN – IVY	118
17.	CHAPTER FIFTEEN – GABE	125
18.	CHAPTER SIXTEEN – IVY	131
19.	CHAPTER SEVENTEEN - GABE	141
20.	CHAPTER EIGHTEEN – IVY	151
21.	CHAPTER NINETEEN – GABE	158
22.	CHAPTER TWENTY – IVY	170
23.	CHAPTER TWENTY-ONE – GABE	181
24.	CHAPTER TWENTY-TWO – IVY	189
25.	CHAPTER TWENTY-THREE - GABE	197
26.	CHAPTER TWENTY-FOUR - IVY	205
27.	CHAPTER TWENTY-FIVE – GABE	212
28.	CHAPTER TWENTY-SIX – IVY	216
29.	CHAPTER TWENTY-SEVEN - GABE	228
30.	CHAPTER TWENTY-EIGHT - IVY	235
31.	CHAPTER TWENTY-NINE – GABE	242
32.	CHAPTER THIRTY – IVY	250
33.	EPILOGUE	260

PART ONE AUGUST- BEFORE

CHAPTER ONE – GABE

As a former medic, Gabe Arthur had been in many tough spots. Gabe thrived on any situation that called for the use of his skills and training. But sitting here, waiting for his brother? He'd rather jump out of a plane.

And flying? *Not* his thing.

He squinted in the bright sunshine as he rubbed his temples. Seeing his older brother, Cole, always triggered his migraines.

Glancing at his watch, he wished he was home, waking up Ivy, his submissive. He had just returned from a job that took him away for three days. Ivy had a music gala to attend last night, so they hadn't had time to reconnect.

He thought of calling her and commanding her to orgasm. How delicious it'd be to start her day that way. For him and her.

As part of their D/s, he controlled her orgasms. When she could come, if she could come, how many times she could come, was all up to him. Her orgasms were his. He'd spent hours edging her, learning her body to get to that point. He'd stop and start her, make her masturbate at set times and trained her to come on his command.

CHAPTER ONE – GABE

And after all that, he added in a cue word and got her to the point where she could orgasm by hearing the word and his tone of voice. His cock pulsed, thinking about it.

His thumb hovered over her number, but the squealing tires caught his attention as a sleek black Mercedes-Benz AMG S 65 stopped at the curb in front of the café.

His brother, a former superstar defenceman, had arrived.

Cole's towering frame emerged from the car. He stopped to shake hands with people and pose for pics as he ambled over to Gabe's table at the back of the patio.

"Hey, Shrimp," Cole said, taking the chair across from him.

Gabe was six foot one. Cole was six foot three. Gabe snorted, hating the nickname. "Hey. I don't think you can park there. What do you want?"

"Like they're going to tow me?" Cole flicked a salt packet at him. "Nice to see you, too. Why so rushed? Have to get back to your video games?"

Gabe shook his head, not bothering to reply to his brother. He couldn't tell anyone about being an elite private security operative for Axis Management.

His brother and his dad rode him hard about being unemployed.

"I don't game, Cole, you know that." And even if he did, so what?

"I saw you had dinner at *Le Cerf* the other night. How fancy. Did your cash cow girlfriend pay for that?"

Gabe bit the inside of his cheek, getting to his feet. He didn't need this. Cole should think better about Ivy. After all, she had made his brother a ton of money through Metric, the PR firm she worked for.

"Gabe, no c'mon. Look, she's coming to take our order now. I'll have the California lettuce wrap and an orange juice on ice." Cole smiled at the server. She blushed and looked at Gabe.

Gabe sighed, the chair scraping on concrete as he sat. "Just a coffee for me."

"You got it." The server skipped off.

Cole stared at him and smirked.

Gabe wanted to wipe that expression off his brother's face. It was the same expression he had when he locked Gabe in the closet when they were kids. Or when he broke their dad's collectable RC plane and blamed it on Gabe.

"How did you even know about the dinner?"

"She posted about it."

The pulsing in his temples picked up the tempo. Ivy needed social media for her job, and she loved it. But he hated it, and they had many heated discussions about her tendency to overshare. He didn't want his life online, and she loved posting all kinds of shit.

The dinner had been a week ago. They had gone with coworkers of Ivy's to celebrate a new contract Ivy brought to Metric.

"What do you want, Cole?"

"Are you working?" His brother put so much venom in that comment.

"I have some jobs here and there."

Cole scoffed. "Yeah, maybe you're content to have a sugar momma, but if you want an actual job, I have something."

"What, you want me to wash your cars?"

"You're so funny. Seriously, man, this is legit. Do you want to hear it?"

Gabe sighed. He'd hear his brother out and blow him off later. "Go ahead."

"How very gracious of you," Cole said. "A couple of months ago, this charity, Ribbon of Aid, asked me to meet with them."

"You get approached by a lot of charities."

"Yes, but this one was interesting." Cole raised an eyebrow. "They fund excursions to drop off medical aid into places damaged by the environment or war. They want former military."

"Yeah?"

CHAPTER ONE – GABE

"Yeah. And I thought of my bro, the army medic. They have a job coming up in a couple of weeks. Do you want in?"

Gabe tried to read his brother's expression, but Cole's poker face was pretty solid.

Cole didn't do anything out of the goodness of his heart. But Gabe wanted in on this. He loved working for Axis Management, but this job he had just come off had been the first in almost two months. The first one since his buddy Jordan died.

Gabe eyed his brother, trying to figure out his angle. The server brought their orders.

"The pay is pretty good," Cole said.

Cole didn't have to bring this to him. Ever since his retirement from the pro league, his brother had called him more often. Maybe he was trying to be a better big brother.

"C'mon, Gabe. Unless you're too scared?"

Gabe scoffed. He needed to work; he craved the rush. But since June, things at Axis Management had been slow. Gabe wasn't sure if they'd ever be the same. They were all recovering from Jordan's death. He'd battled nightmares for weeks after, but they stopped once he had a job to keep him focused.

"Yes, I want in. Send me the details."

"If you sign on, you need to do a good job, you know what I mean? It's my reputation on the line." Cole bit into his wrap and stared him down.

"I won't do anything to tarnish your rep," Gabe said.

"Are you and Ivy coming to Dad's on Saturday?"

He'd rather skip the weekly dinners. Ivy always asked him why he went when they were so terrible. Gabe didn't know. His dad had always told him that family was everything, and Gabe clung to that after his mom left. Damn, he was lucky to have Ivy by his side.

His dad would spend most of the evening asking Gabe how much money he had or when Gabe would start his own business or get a job.

Gabe shook his head, trying to clear his thoughts. His dad would point out how successful Cole was. How Cole is stronger and smarter than he was as if Gabe's time as an army medic didn't count, and to his dad, it didn't. He didn't understand why Gabe joined the military.

To get away from you, Gabe had stopped himself from saying many times. Ivy told Gabe to ignore his brother and father, but it was like an earworm he couldn't shake; their voices were rooted in his brain.

Working for Axis Management helped. One reason Gabe signed on for their Team Stealth as a private operative was the money. The other part was Logan, Quinn and Jordan, Erik and his best buddy Nick. Guys he knew and trusted.

The pay that came with Axis Management would be enough, even for his father, and for the first time in their history together, he was making more than Ivy. She had stayed with him throughout his army years, money never bothering her.

She worked hard to become a senior PR Strategist, and Gabe knew she was good at her job, even though he felt she lied for a living.

Even if Ivy reassured him over and over that money didn't matter to her, it bothered him that she earned more in the early years of their relationship. And even when she surrendered to him as his submissive, the inequity still bothered him.

"Yes, we'll be at Dad's. I got to get going."

"Glad we had this chat. Don't worry, I'll get the bill," Cole said. His brother waved to a couple of fans who stopped to take a picture of him over the restaurant railing.

Gabe clenched his hands into fists and exhaled. He wasn't going to quibble over a buck twenty-five.

"Thanks."

He waved bye to his brother and started walking toward their condo, stopping by the bakery to buy Ivy her favourite blueberry scones.

CHAPTER ONE – GABE

As he entered the lobby of their condo, he waved to their neighbours. He loved this place, minutes from the trendy shops, cafes, and restaurants and ten minutes to the beach. The view of the ocean and the North Shore Mountains was amazing.

Ivy had wanted this place so much. The only reason he had to say no to it was because he couldn't afford the down payment on his own. In the end, he shared her love for their home and was happy he didn't stop her from buying this place.

He shook his head, clearing away the thoughts as he unlocked their front door.

"Princess, I'm home."

"Finally! Come and ravish me already!"

Gabe grinned. Ivy was never shy about what she wanted when it came to sex, and he loved that about her. Putting down the box of pastries on the counter, he kicked off his shoes and strode down the hall to their bedroom.

Her short blonde hair was mussed from sleep, and he needed to run his hands through it. She sat cross-legged, naked on the bed, her phone in hand. Her green eyes lit up as he came closer, dropping a kiss on her pouty lips.

"Give it to me," he held out his hand.

"I need it!" Ivy batted her eyes dramatically. Her phone buzzed in her hand, and she glanced at it, her expression focused and intense.

"Nope. You're off the clock." He plucked the phone out of her hand and set it on the nightstand.

She squealed. "No! I had to check the feeds from last night's gala. It got good press, and everyone's happy. I did my job."

"You want a cookie?" Gabe smiled at her.

"No, but I'm hoping you brought home blueberry scones."

"You know I did." This woman made him feel like a million bucks, despite what his dad and brother thought of him. She grabbed his shirt pulling him closer.

"I've missed you." Gabe dropped a kiss behind her ear.

"Not as much as I've missed you. I haven't orgasmed in five days."

"Has it only been that long? We could try for another record. Or you can be good."

"Where's the fun in that?" She returned his kiss with fervour, her sweet taste familiar and needed.

Her velvet lips met his, her mouth opening for him, urging his kiss deeper. Her hands swept down his abs to the waistband of his t-shirt.

"You are insatiable." And he fucking loved that about her. His girl made everything better, washed his brother's voice from his mind with her touch. He threw off his t-shirt.

Their lips met again, and he deepened the kiss, swallowing her soft moans of pleasure. Ivy had opened his eyes to sex being something more than the clinical experience he had before her.

Then there was the kink.

She had no shame about expressing her kinks, and they had a collection of toys that would rival any BDSM club.

When Ivy first asked him to spank her, Gabe balked at her and said he knew nothing about kink.

"Ask Logan," she had said. He learned that most of his buddies were in the D/s scene. They had seemed so young then, so hopeful.

Over the years, they explored all the kinks until they found what worked for them. Yeah, life was fun, and he had few complaints.

He broke off the kiss. Sitting beside her on the bed, he reached out and out and traced the delicate gold chain that served as her collar. Ivy would have loved something flashier, a traditional collar with a D ring, but he liked the subtlety of this. He liked that even though she was strong and didn't need him to take care of her, she was his.

CHAPTER ONE – GABE

"Come here, Princess." He turned her towards him, leaving a trail of hungry, insistent kisses from her collarbone to the swell of her breasts. She urged him on, her hands on the back of his neck.

His mouth came around her large, juicy nipple. Ivy's moan vibrated through his mouth as he lapped and sucked, tugging at her nipple with his teeth. Her hand drummed on his shoulders, her attempt at telling him to hurry.

His hands roamed over her stomach to her waist. He squeezed her wrist, cueing her to stop it, and bit her nipple lightly.

"Ouch!"

"Impatient, are we?"

"Always."

He scored her wrist lightly with his nail, enjoying how she closed her eyes against his infliction. Gabe took the other nipple in his mouth, sucking until she squealed with a mix of pleasure and protest.

"Okay! Too much!"

He smiled, flicked his tongue around her areola, and dragged his teeth along her beaded nipple before switching sides.

"Damn you!"

Gabe laughed, squeezing her right breast as he feasted on her left. Her legs opened as he pinched her nipple.

"I call the shots in here, Princess."

"Yes, Sir."

Her leaf green eyes were glassy. His hands slid down to her thighs. She spread her legs for him, pushing her hips towards him.

Slowly, he lapped her pussy, the taste of her calming the angst in his brain. Ever so softly, he took her clit between his teeth and pulled oh so gently.

"More! Dammit, more!" Her fingers threaded through his hair.

With the barest of touches, Gabe rolled his tongue over her clit. That was the fun thing with Ivy. She wanted sex; she loved sex, and he absolutely loved being in control of her orgasm.

"Gabe!"

He lifted his head from her pussy, and dropped his hands from her thighs.

"I don't know if you're ready, Princess." He stood, giving her his best Dom glare.

"You know I am!" Ivy clutched his shoulders.

"I'm not sure I'm convinced." Gabe smiled while shucking off his pants.

"Please feel my pussy, Sir. Feel how wet I am for you."

"Let's see. Are you wet and ready?" Gabe sunk one finger into her and then another, and Ivy grabbed his arm, her nails digging into him.

"I am *so* wet."

"I don't know if you've earned an orgasm." Gabe plunged two fingers into her pussy, working them back and forth. "I think I'm in the mood to fuck you and leave you."

She bit down on her lip and shook her head from side to side, but she gushed at his words, her juices covering his fingers. He knew how much she loved this type of play.

"No! Why?"

Gabe grabbed her and shifted her position so she was horizontal across the bed.

"I heard you posted where we were last Friday," He grabbed her legs, spreading them as he stepped in between her thighs.

Her eyes went wide, her foot drumming on his back. "Ah! You're so mean."

Easing his cock into her pussy, his lips brushed hers. "I can be meaner."

Her pussy gripped his cock, inviting him into her warm core further.

CHAPTER ONE – GABE

He wrapped his arms around her, bringing her almost chest to chest as he drilled into her, deep and fast.

"Sir! Yes!"

Ivy panted, the flush creeping up her neck, so gorgeous. He slowed his pace right now, captured her lips and felt her angst through how her body trembled. She kissed him back as if he was her favourite thing.

He bit her bottom lip. And her pussy clenched around his cock.

Gabe grinned and tangled his hand in her silky blonde hair. With fast and quick strokes, he hammered into her so hard that her hips bounced on the mattress. Her eyes closed, her hands pressed on his back, driving him for more.

His balls drew tight, fire trailing down his spine. "I'm going to come in you, now, Princess, and you're going to say 'thank you,'" Gabe gritted in her ear as his orgasm rolled over him.

"No! Damn you!"

"Going to come right *now*."

The release was so good that he trembled. He stayed in her warmth a moment longer, feeling her muscles coil tight. He kissed her as he eased out of her, pulling her against him as he lay on the bed, catching his breath.

His fingers went to her clit, wet and swollen. "Still ready?"

"Yes," Ivy said.

"I didn't hear a 'thank-you?'"

"That's because I was going to say, 'Please, Sir, can I have an orgasm?'" she whispered the words into his chest, her cheeks red.

"Were you?"

"Yes."

"Let's hear it." He pulled her hair, tipping her face to him.

"Please, Sir, Can I have an orgasm?"

So damn heady. He kissed her, flicking her clit. Her hips jerked off the mattress.

"Please!" She clutched his arm.

"Open." He held his fingers covered in her juices to her mouth.

She glared at him, but her velvet tongue slowly glided over his fingers, cleaning herself off of him.

"Want your vibe?"

"No! I want your cock."

"Too bad, Princess. I meant what I said. Vibe or nothing."

She scrunched her face at him. He raised an eyebrow, waiting.

"Yes, vibe, please!"

Gabe reached into the nightstand drawer and set her favourite vibe against her clit. He turned it on.

"Ahh!" Ivy flung her head back.

He increased the speed. Her eyes closed, her brow furrowed, and she grabbed his hand. "God, it's so much."

"Do you want me to stop?"

"No!"

Gabe kissed her collarbone, nuzzling her ear. "*Babylon.*"

Her face scrunched up, her eyes closed, and Ivy screamed.

"Good girl," he said, kissing her nape. He removed the vibe and brushed the hair out of her eyes.

"Don't touch me now!" Ivy said, batting his hands away.

She hated being touched after a scene or sex, preferring to have space for her to come back down to reality.

He stretched as he got off the bed. Ivy curled on her side, a small smile on her face. He was one lucky bastard to have this woman.

Gabe leaned down, meeting her eyes. "Who do your orgasms belong to?"

"You, Sir."

"That's my girl. I'm going to make some lunch."

He slapped her ass, whistling as he strode into the kitchen, hearing her phone ring as he started pulling out pans.

CHAPTER TWO – IVY

"No luck?" Ivy looked up from scrolling on her phone as she heard the patio door slide open.

Gabe's pinched expression and hunched shoulders told her it hadn't been the answer he wanted. He crossed his arms, his thick biceps rippling, and shrugged.

"No. Xander says work is coming. I feel so restless."

Gabe hadn't worked for two weeks, and it was wearing on him. Ivy frowned; she didn't like seeing Gabe go so hard, but ever since Jordan died, it's like he needed work as if he could fix what he couldn't that day in June.

He ran a hand through his auburn hair, sitting next to her. He brought her legs on his lap. "What are you looking at?"

Ivy turned her phone to show Gabe the pictures of her cousin Alice's baby, then a photo of her mom standing on stage in front of the new set at the community theatre. "Wendy looks happy."

"Mom is always happy," Ivy said. A wave of homesickness crashed around her for her parents' berry farm, forty minutes outside Edmonton.

Reaching for her French-pressed coffee, Ivy sighed.

When she left their berry farm for UBC, she was determined to make a good life here, and she had. As much as she sometimes missed her family, she wouldn't want to leave here.

"Must be nice to have a mom."

Ivy rubbed Gabe's arm, knowing it was hard for him. His mother took off when he was eight, and his brother was ten.

"Kiss me?"

He took her coffee mug, set it down, and leaned down. His brown eyes glowed as his lips met hers. He kissed her slowly, exploring her tongue, tasting her, and she moaned as he bit her lower lip, a promise for later.

Her phone rang beside her, and she broke off the kiss. "Hello?"

"Hey! Do you guys want to come to Club Bandit with Logan and me tonight? We're going to try the chair suspension."

"Hey, Clara." Ivy loved the private BDSM club, and they hadn't had much time to get over to it lately.

"I'll run it by Sir and get back to you."

"Okay! Hope to see you tonight."

"Bye."

"What's Clara up to?"

"She just asked if we can come to Club Bandit with her and Logan tonight. It's not usually busy on Sundays, and I have tomorrow morning off."

"Sounds good." Gabe placed his hand on her leg. "Can't wait to torment you, Princess." His tone dropped, and Ivy squirmed in her chair.

"Yes!" Ivy leaned forward, kissing him, breathing in his familiar scent. Gabe enjoyed hanging out with his friends, but crowds weren't always his thing, so when he agreed to go to Club Bandit, it felt like it was something he was doing more for her than for him, and it made her feel so loved.

"Okay. Nick asked me to swing by his place to help move a pool table or something. You want to come?"

CHAPTER TWO – IVY

Ivy's phone buzzed on the table. "It's work."

"Ivy, this was supposed to be your day off." Gabe's perfectly formed lips frowned.

"I know. I'll be quick," Ivy smiled. "Hi, Flint, what's up?"

"Ivy, sorry to pull you in, but I need a couple of hours of your time. News just broke up that Riley Maddison is getting a divorce."

Riley Maddison was a top ten pop star and her client. "I'll be in twenty, Flint," Ivy said to her boss.

"Thanks, Ivy, you're the best."

"You could have said no," Gabe squeezed her hand

"You know I have to go in if something breaks."

"For you to smooth it out, I know." Gabe's tight expression said he knew but didn't like it. Her stomach twisted in a knot.

Ivy grabbed the empty coffee cups and kissed him on the cheek. "That's what I do."

He followed her inside, and Ivy put the empty coffee cups in the dishwasher.

"Will you only be there for a couple of hours?"

"I don't know, Gabe. You know how these things go."

His jaw tightened. She hated seeing that worried expression, but his anger was always just below the surface, and though he rarely directed it at her and never physically, it took little to brush against it. The one place he seemed to gather it and use it was in their play in the bedroom. That was fine with Ivy, and sometimes she pushed to be his target. She liked that she didn't just give in... Even if she loved being a submissive. She wanted him to work for her submission, and she loved that he had taken control of her orgasms. But for them, their D/s didn't extend to outside of play or being sexual. Sometimes she wanted more.

"Yeah."

"Go hang with Nick, then meet me at Club Bandit." Ivy wrapped her arms around his waist.

He kissed her mouth so hard it felt like it was going to bruise. "Okay. I don't like you working so much."

"But you like working so much."

He blinked at her and took her hand in his. "I know it's stupid to be bothered by it when you never complain about my work."

"At least you know it." Ivy kissed his cheek, grinning.

"Do you want me to drop you off?"

Ivy paused, running her fingertips through his just past regulation haircut. His warm brown eyes had lost the tension. Ivy placed her palm on his chest. This man loved her. He knew she didn't like driving, but she wanted the car, in case she finished later than she hoped.

"I'll drive."

"Okay."

She let go of Gabe, changed into office clothes, and gathered her work bag. She slipped on a pair of pink pearl-coloured heels and kissed Gabe goodbye.

"See you later."

"You say that, but will you be there?" His tone stopped her.

"Gabe, you know I will."

"Yeah, I know, Princess." He kissed her and held the door open for her. Ivy blew him a kiss goodbye. "Sorry, I'm just restless."

"Go chill with Nick."

"Good luck with the crisis."

"Thanks." Ivy smiled.

As she heard the door close behind her, she exhaled.

Ever since June, Gabe had been more withdrawn, which is understandable. What happened to Jordan was a terrible thing, affecting Gabe's circle of friends. She thought he was coming out of his grief, out of the bubble he had himself in, but he seemed to retreat more whenever she had to work, and he didn't.

CHAPTER TWO – IVY

Maybe seeing Nick would help, and a play session at Club Bandit would ease some of the tension he's been storing.

And try as she might, Ivy couldn't get out of work until four hours later. Riley Maddison sobbed in her office for two hours. Ivy patted her back and ushered her into her comfy seating arrangement of yellow and red club chairs and her chaise lounge. Ivy loved that chaise. She spent a lot of late nights stretched out on it.

"I still love him," Riley sobbed.

"Of course you do."

Flint had tapped on the door. "Ivy, we need Riley to sign off on the press release."

"We'll do it whenever Riley is ready." Ivy smiled, holding Riley's hands. For the next three hours, Ivy brought out her store of candy, kept Riley's glass filled with sparkling water, and looked at every photo on her phone of her dog, Marley.

"I want Marley. He can have the rights to all my songs I made while with him, but I want Marley," Riley wailed, clutching her phone to her chest.

"What is Marley's favourite treat?"

"He loves, loves the organic double-baked bones. I send them to the groomer with him each time he goes." Riley's face cleared. "Oh, I am not letting that fucker have anything. Marley needs his treats!"

"Right! I bet Marley loves that bedazzled collar. Does he have any others?"

"Oh, yes!" Riley started flipping through her phone again. "Look, here he is in his Christmas ones."

Finally, now that she had her client's emotions on the level for the moment, Ivy grabbed her iPad. "Let's mention how upset Marley is in the press release. What else should we say?"

It took another hour for Riley to sign off on a release she was happy with.

As Riley left the office, Ivy realized the time.

"Crap," she muttered. It was her idea to go to Club Bandit tonight. For a brief moment, she considered calling Gabe's friend Logan and asking him to... what? Run interference for her? Ivy didn't know.

She rinsed off her face and grabbed an outfit from her work closet. Her car was the only one in the parking lot.

Driving to Club Bandit, she put all the work stuff in a mental box and shut the lid with an effort. She loved that kink turned off her brain for a while. Gabe could make her a complete puddle. That was the kind of release she wanted tonight.

The clock on her dashboard read 9 PM when she finally made her way through the black iron gates with the initials of CB stylized on the centre.

She parked her car behind Logan's motorcycle and hurried, buzzing at the door for the entrance.

Beyond the double doors of the club, soft, warm light greeted her, the waterfall feature tinkling. Ivy brushed her hand through the water, shrugging off the work events.

She rounded the corner into the vast space. The golden textured walls shined, somehow making it cozy and elegant. Usually, the club hummed with people, the sounds of leather hitting flesh, the cries of passion, but tonight it felt oddly empty. About twenty people stood in front of the stage. She smiled, seeing Clara tied to a chair and the unmistakable physique of Logan holding ropes in his hand, lifting the chair off the stage.

No wonder the place was quiet. She spotted Gabe standing next to Nick in the crowd and made her way to him.

CHAPTER TWO – IVY

On stage, Clara's eyes were closed, and Ivy could hear her breathing hard.

"Hi, Princess." Gabe's breath tickled her ear. "They are so close to pulling off this suspension."

"Clara isn't comfortable."

"She's not far off," Gabe muttered.

"I can't! Let me down!" Clara sobbed.

"Getting you down nice and easy." Logan did something with the ropes that brought the chair down to the stage floor.

"Yes, I want to do this. I just don't like heights."

"Many people don't," Logan soothed, a hand on his rope bunny. He knelt in front of her, quickly getting her out of the ropes.

"We'll get there," Logan said. "When this suspension happens, it's going to be epic."

"Yeah, if it works," Nick said.

"It'll work, right, Zee?"

"If anyone can pull it off, it's you," the grey-haired goatee owner of Club Bandit said from the front of the crowd.

The group dispersed as Logan held Clara. Ivy sent her friend a thumbs-up. Gabe draped an arm across her shoulders.

"Hey Princess, let's go play."

"Sorry, I'm late. I tried calling you."

"Left my phone at home. It's okay. I knew you would be." Gabe cupped the back of her neck, and Ivy closed her eyes against his warm touch. Yeah, this is what she needed.

He leaned in and kissed her, and he hugged her to his muscular chest. "I missed you." He kissed her hard, his tongue twirling with hers, and Ivy closed her eyes. This was her man. This was her Dom.

When he wasn't stressed, when his nightmares didn't plague him, Gabe was attentive and thoughtful and made her feel treasured and loved.

"Princess, I have a surprise for you." Gabe slipped his hand into hers and took his toy bag off a bench.

"Is it a pony?"

"Do you want to be a ponygirl? I'd love to see you with a bit in your mouth, a bridle on your head." He turned her slightly towards him, stuck his thumb and index fingers in her mouth and stretched her cheeks. "Just like this."

Her insides went gooey, and she snuggled into Gabe's arm as her cheeks heated at the thought. "Maybe," she said around his fingers.

"No, it's not a pony." Gabe removed his fingers and spanked her ass, making her squeal. "But I do have plans for you."

Her pelvic floor clenched at the heat in his eyes.

"Can't wait, Sir."

CHAPTER THREE — IVY

"Remember, you said that."

Ivy swallowed. The heat in his eyes lit her nerve endings with anticipation. He guided her past the bar, down the hallway and held his thumb against the scanner to one of the private rooms.

He tugged her inside, and as soon as the door closed, he grabbed her hands, pinning them above her head.

"Remember when I had you in that bondage contraption?"

Ivy closed her eyes as the memory washed over her. The memory was so tactile that she could feel the ring's metal around her neck, as it kept her in position, buckles around her feet, attached to a metal platform on the floor. She remembered the sweet erotic humiliation, standing in the club naked, as others touched her body, as Gabe wrote "cum slut" across her chest. He urged her to give in, bringing her to the edge, then he'd tell her, "Don't you dare come," while fingering her mercilessly. The fight she had to keep going against the orgasm trembling through her body because the moment she gave in, she'd impale herself on the waiting dildo.

How Gabe's voice broke when he said, "good girl" to her, his dominant pride seeping into her soul.

God, they were so in sync that night.

"Yeah."

"Let's make another memory, just like that."

That night had been so special. Ivy couldn't recall when Gabe had been that open since. These last couple of months had been so tough.

"Sounds perfect."

His tongue swept across her bottom lip. Ivy moaned, her lips parted for him, and he kissed her with so much force that the coolness of the wall grew warm against her back. Heat radiated through her body. Whatever his plan was for tonight, she was ready.

"You're perfect, Princess." He dropped her hands and stroked his palm against her cheek.

He took her hand, guiding her across the honey-hued hardwood floor between the two wooden posts.

Other than the cupboards at the back of the room, next to the sink and the massage table over to the side, there was nothing else in the room except for these wooden posts. The pale textured walls gave the room a warm feel despite its starkness.

"Love this." Ivy stood on her tiptoes to touch the dangling chains with her fingertips.

Gabe laughed. "I don't want you to stress too much. Let's adjust that."

She admired how his biceps rippled as he adjusted the chains, setting them so she wouldn't feel stress in her joints when she was cuffed between the posts.

"Thank you, Sir." Ivy smiled, brushing a hand along his arm. He kissed her hand.

"Strip for me, Princess." Gabe stood in front of her, an eyebrow cocked.

Excitement rolled through her. She licked her lips. "Yes, Sir."

Ivy kicked off her heels, her bare feet pressed into the smooth wooden floors. She took off her skirt and her nylons. Her fingers trembled as she undid her black silk blouse, meeting his amber eyes. His gaze held hers. She rolled down her emerald lace panties, kicking them off.

"Help, please, Sir?"

He stalked slowly toward her like a predator. Ivy shivered from the blaze in his eyes.

"I told you to strip. You can't handle that?"

He grabbed the fabric of her silky emerald bra between her cleavage. She gasped. "Sir I...no Sir." She rasped but couldn't keep the smile off her face.

He yanked hard, his knuckle pressing against her breasts. The fabric ripped. "There. Better?"

She glared at him, throwing the bra across the room.

He smiled, slow and sultry.

"Careful what you ask for, Princess. I'm in a giving mood."

His tone of steel arrowed right to her pussy. She shivered slightly as his hands roamed under her breasts. His hands swept over her folds, around her tummy, and over her ass.

He didn't care that her body was size large, he never brought up her weight, and that was one of the things that made her fall in love with him: his acceptance of her.

"Close your eyes. I have a surprise for you," he said against her ear.

Ivy exhaled and kept her hands at her sides. She heard the zipper of his toy bag, and she tried to centre her thoughts as the anticipation buzzed through her.

She felt cool leather draped around her shoulders against her neck a moment later.

"Open."

Ivy brushed her hands along the tails. "Florentines?"

"Yes." Gabe smiled. "Do you like?"

"They're gorgeous."

"Wrists, Princess." From his pocket, Gabe took out her favourite pair of pink faux leather cuffs lined with faux fur. He slapped the cuff on her right wrist and attached it to the chain from the post.

"Move your arm."

Ivy flexed, seeing how there was too much slack in the chain. Gabe tightened it from the post.

"Comfortable?"

Ivy flexed her fingers and raised and lowered her arm. She had circulation, and it was a comfortable hold.

"Yes, Sir."

Gabe grabbed her left wrist and repeated the process, adjusting the length of the chain until it was precisely the same.

"Gorgeous." Gabe lifted the floggers off her shoulders, pulling them across her breasts.

Ivy licked her lips as he walked around her, slow and steady. He threw the floggers through the air.

Ivy jumped at the whistling, biting her lip. She jumped as the strands landed on the back of her calves. "Ahh."

"Yeah, this is going to be good."

And then the only sound in the room was leather striking her calves, her back, her ass. Ivy breathed, keeping herself as relaxed as she could, and leaned into the hot blasts of pain.

Leather fell on her back, crisscrossing, falling in rhythm.

So, *so* good.

And he threw them again, hitting exactly the same area.

She fell forward with the next bite of leather, the chains holding her taut. Gabe threw again, softly this time, on her back.

Ivy exhaled, her limbs heavy and infused with warmth.

She heard Gabe step twice behind her, and the leather cracked hard along her sides.

"Fuck, *ow*."

CHAPTER THREE – IVY

"You love it."

"Yes, I do!" Ivy yelped out the words as the strand caught her on the shoulders.

As the beat of the floggers hit her skin repeatedly, she closed her eyes, her muscles relaxed, except for her pelvic floor, which was clenched, needy and waiting.

She rocked forward as the tips of the strands brushed against her ass.

"Ahh! Yes, more!"

The strands caught her across her lower back.

Her skin was hot, and her hands clammy. The pain rocketed through her mind, firing all her nerve endings.

The lashes fell like a steady rainfall, and her usually crowded headspace stopped, coming to a place of stillness.

Only the slap of leather on her flesh. Only her Dom's voice.

"That's a good girl. Look how you hunger for my lash."

She moaned low in her throat, arching back.

And his floggers landed. One, two and three, hard and fast, so hard that it took her breath away. Five, six and seven, making her hiss through her teeth.

"So fucking pretty." Gabe's fingertips traced the raised stripes on her back. Ivy shuddered. Walking in front of her, he dropped a kiss on her forehead. "Good girl. I love the marks these have left."

Ivy grew warm, loving how he looked at her. Leaning into his touch as his hand glided along her cheek.

"Now your front."

"Sir! I can't."

"I say you *can*. Are you wet for me, Princess?"

"Find out." She wiggled her hips at him, spreading her feet apart.

He dragged the flogger around her shoulder, over the swell of her breasts. "Hold these for me."

Ivy opened, clamping her lips over the flogger's handle. He settled the other between her chin and shoulder.

"There's a useful submissive," Gabe purred.

Ivy gushed. Gabe made her so happy, and he knew exactly what she needed when he wasn't stuck in his head.

She sucked in a breath, watching as he went to his toy bag, took something out and strode back to her.

He smiled, plucking the flogger from her mouth.

"Give me that tongue."

Ivy stuck her tongue out.

He snapped on a clothespin. "That's better. Can't sass now, can we?"

She glared at him, a thrill of delight and desire churning low in her pelvic floor.

"Answer me."

She swallowed, knowing wetness ran between her thighs. "No, Sir," she spat out, mumbled and intelligible because of the clothespin on her tongue.

He took the other flogger from under her chin. Ivy closed her eyes at the relief.

"And a matching pair." He opened one clothespin and set it around her areola.

"Fuck." The damned things hurt.

He took the other clothespin, smiling like the Dom that had his submissive exactly where he wanted her and placed it on her other breast.

Hot damn, they pinched. She'd much prefer nipple clamps.

"Look at my pretty sub." He trailed his fingers between her breasts, down along her hips, stopping where she wanted them most. "I'm going to see if I can flog off these clothespins."

Sometimes, she regretted telling Gabe she liked kink. Sometimes. Not now. This is exactly what she wanted.

CHAPTER THREE – IVY

He stood back and threw the floggers. They figured eight through the air in a beautiful pattern too fast to follow.

Her breath hitched in her throat. And the strands landed on the top of her breasts.

She screamed in delight, in pleasure.

And they came down hard again, the tips hitting the clothespin on her left breast.

"Close enough." He marched over and took the clothespin off her nipple.

"Dammit!" The blood rushed back painfully to her nipple.

"Nothing you can't take, Princess." Gabe tugged and rolled her nipple in his fingers. He fisted his hand in her hair, half in praise and half too roughly for that and stepped back.

Her heart danced as the floggers flew. She closed her eyes as the tips landed on her breast.

He struck again.

The leather burned now where it landed, her skin on fire. She knew she was soaked between her legs.

"Sir!" The leather stripe landed right on the tip of the clothespin.

"Got it." The satisfied look on his face sent a shudder of delight through her.

"Ready? I want to hear, 'thank you, Sir,' as soon as I take this off."

Ivy nodded.

He ripped the clothespin off her nipple.

"Fuck! Thank you, Sir." Her pussy clenched as drool slid down her face.

"Good girl," Gabe said, his hand cupping the back of her neck.

He took the clothespin off her tongue. Ivy swallowed, exhaling.

Gabe massaged her shoulders and kissed her hungrily, his lips gobbling hers.

The taste of him, against the heated, pleasured pain on her back, left her wanting.

"I'm going to uncuff you now, and then I want you to stand by the table."

"Yes, Sir," she whispered, her tongue taking a moment to form the words.

He freed her right wrist, took it between his strong hands, and massaged it. "Good, Princess?"

"Yes, Sir."

He did the same with the left, gliding his hands from her wrist to her arm and shoulder, then he massaged her shoulders while kissing her again, gently this time.

"Good girl," he said.

Ivy smiled and stretched her arms, feeling the heaviness in her body. As she walked across the floor to the table, she felt the heated pain in her back in a good pleasurable way.

Gabe uncapped a bottle of water and passed it to her.

"Good girl." He set the water down on the back table. "How are you feeling?"

"Achy but good, Sir."

"Great." His gaze took her all in. He grabbed her right breast in his hand and squeezed.

Ivy gasped at the zap of pleasure.

Her breast spilled over his palm, and he slapped it with the other hand. One. She drew in her breath, hissing. Two. She flinched at his slap hard on her bare flesh.

"Who do these belong to?" He grabbed both her breasts so hard Ivy stood on her toes.

So damn delicious, wetness pooled between her legs.

"You, Sir."

"That's right."

CHAPTER THREE – IVY

He slapped the left breast. Ivy closed her eyes, listening to his palm hitting her flesh, lost in the blissful sensation. She loved not too much, but just the right amount of pain, and Gabe knew precisely how much; it had come throughout the years of trying different things.

"You're going to be so wet you will leave a puddle on this table. Then I'm going to make you lick it clean."

"Sir!"

"Yes?" Gabe slipped his hand between her parted legs pressing hard, grabbing her pussy lips between his fingers. He flicked her pussy with his other hand.

She didn't think he'd actually make her do it, but the mindfuck turned her on.

"Up on the table, Princess. I'm going to cool you down and send you flying."

"Yes, Sir," Ivy mumbled. She felt like she was halfway there, out of her mind into the altered state of subspace.

She laid down on the table, the leather comfortable on her sore nipples.

He settled the Earpods on her ears, and a moment later, her favourite playlist started.

Gabe massaged her shoulders, his firm, warm hands working out the knots, his fingers carefully skimping along the fresh welts. Ivy murmured in approval as the tension left her. She tried to stay in the moment, only focusing on his touch as his hands moved down to her back, but briefly, her mind floated back to work and what was on her desk for the next day. Before her boss left for the night, he mentioned a new not-for-profit that had hired Metric to oversee a recruitment campaign.

"Ouch!" It didn't hurt. The snap of suede on her ass jarred her out of her thoughts.

"You're thinking. I can see the thoughts flutter across your face. Stay with me, Princess."

Ivy settled back down, relaxing as Gabe worked his deerskin flogger across her claves, over her back.

After the harshness of the leather strips, this was so good, like a thuddy massage.

Thuds fell over her shoulder blades.

Heavy, measured strands fell across her back, landing on her ass.

The soft strands fell on her calves and back to her shoulders. Ivy closed her eyes, her thoughts taking a backseat again.

Her body relaxed, suffused with pleasure, endorphins swimming through her body. She closed her eyes, lost in the hot sensations.

Yes, this is what she needed, the perfect thing to turn off her brain. Her body grew heavy. She started to float, lost in her head in a whole different way, her pussy soaked with wetness.

It took Ivy a moment to realize the soft rubbing on the back of her neck. "Hey Princess, going to wake you up now. Bring you back."

"Nooo," Ivy half-heartily protested.

Gabe smiled, that particular *"you don't know what's coming"* expression that made her brace and, at the same time, want whatever he was going to do to her.

"No! Ahhh!"

The handle of the flogger came down across the middle of her bare foot. Ivy laughed and squealed, the sensation both pain and pleasure. Her fingers came into fists as Gabe kept striking the soles of her feet.

"Okay, you had fun. Stop now."

"Why? It's so much fun to make you squirm." Gabe laughed at her. As he swept his hand along her foot, Ivy squealed as he started tickling her toes. She squealed and kicked, and Gabe slapped her calves.

"Now, let's see how wet you are, Princess." He kissed the base of her spine. Ivy bit her lip as his fingers dove into her folds.

Ivy flexed her feet, squirming under his rough touch. "Ahh, Sir! Gabe!"

"Yeah, you're going to scream for me now."

CHAPTER THREE – IVY

Ivy lifted her head, bit her lip, and shook her head at him.

"Funny, Princess." His fingers pinched her clit, she yelped. He leaned over her and captured her mouth, his tongue dominating hers.

His warmth, his controlling touch, made her arousal spark. His fingers curled, finding the right spot.

"*Babylon.*"

"Sir! Gabe!"

She couldn't hold back. Pleasure mounted too high and big to contain, leaving her gasping and shuddering in one big, blissful heap.

"Yeah, that's my Princess." Gabe wiped the hair out of her face. His pleased expression made her glow from the inside out.

"Don't touch me right now."

"I know, Princess." Gabe's amber eyes glowed with caring. "You need time to come back to me." Ivy nodded, closing her eyes. Being touched after a scene was like hot prickles against her skin; it was like making a sudden movement when she just found her peace. In the early days, Gabe used to insist on cuddling her before he learned the type of aftercare she needed.

"I'm here when you're ready."

She sent him a smile, watching as he tidied up his toys.

It warmed her heart to see him like this: confident, in charge, sure of his Dom self. A session at Club Bandit affirmed their roles.

"I'm good now." Ivy slowly got herself to a sitting position and slid off the table.

"Come here." His arms folded around her, and he kissed her slowly, tasting every inch of her. "Beautiful, Princess. You gave me so much tonight."

Ivy smiled at him, her tummy flip-flopping. She had tried. Even if her thoughts returned to work, she had stayed in the scene with him.

As he guided her out of the room, she realized the music was off in the club, and only Logan and Clara were in the sitting area, sharing an oversized gold fabric chair.

"Hey," Clara said from Logan's lap.

"Hey. How long were we playing?" Ivy asked Gabe.

"Couple of hours."

"Hi guys," Ivy said. "Saw some of your suspension scene."

"It's not a suspension scene. It's a 'Clara is freaking out scene.'"

"We'll get it," Logan said. "Just need to practice."

Clara frowned. "If you say so. I should call it a night."

"Let me know how your date goes on Tuesday. He better be good to you." Logan kissed his rope bunny, and Clara smiled. "I'll call you, and you." Clara squeezed Ivy's arm.

"Text me when you get home, darling," Logan said.

"Sorry I didn't catch up."

Clara flashed her a smile. "It's okay. You look so blissed out. I hope you had a pleasant scene."

"I did."

Ivy hugged her goodbye and then sat beside Gabe, leaning her head against his shoulder.

"So, what's your week looking like?" Gabe asked Logan.

"Going to take Hana to Vancouver Island on Friday," Logan said. "You?"

"I'm going on a gig for a private contractor."

Logan raised his eyebrows. "Hope you're not leaving Axis Management, Doc."

"No, need something to fill the time."

Ivy lifted her head from his shoulder. This was the first she had heard of Gabe taking on work from a private contractor.

"Some of those outfits are nasty. You make sure they're legit," Logan said.

"Yeah. My brother got me this one. It's called Ribbon of Aid."

"An NGO?"

"Yeah."

Logan shrugged. "As long as it checks out. But I have the feeling we're going to be busy on Team Stealth soon."

"Yeah, but until it's more than a feeling, I got to do something. I'm going stir crazy waiting at home."

"I hear you. Let's get out of here," Logan said.

Gabe nodded and held out his hand to Ivy, holding him up. Ivy bit her lip, knowing she had heard the name of the NGO before. Still feeling blissed out from the scene, she couldn't place where.

"You okay, Princess?"

"Just tired." Ivy smiled at Gabe. He slipped his hand in hers, and they followed Logan, exiting Club Bandit.

CHAPTER FOUR - GABE

"Yes! I'm going to beat your ass."

The basketball hit the side of the rim but dropped in, and his brother pointed his finger to the sky.

"It's not a championship," Gabe mumbled, dribbling the ball. He lined up his throw and missed.

"Sorry about your luck there, bro." Cole swiped at the ball and fired it over his head, landing the next basket. "I win!" His brother punched the air.

Gabe grabbed his beer from the deck, taking a long pull. For his brother, everything was a competition. Who could run furthest, who could ride their bike the fastest, and who could date the most girls. When they were kids, he was always out to prove that he was better than Gabe. As he got more into playing hockey, it was all about being the best.

Gabe was longer, leaner, and never cared about sports. His dad and brother called him a wuss. Gabe was good at school and didn't want to bring any attention to himself, so he kept quiet while Cole loved the spotlight.

His brother and father never understood why he didn't chase fame or money, but Gabe was comfortable in his skin, and the chase of the mission was fulfilling enough to him.

CHAPTER FOUR - GABE

"So, was the ice cream any good?" Cole towelled off the sweat on his brow.

"What are you talking about?" Gabe turned away from the view of the water, cursing as his palm skimmed a splinter on the deck railing.

"Yesterday morning, you were eating ice cream with that cow on the beach. You haven't broken up with her yet?"

Gabe glared at his brother, his skin heated by the anger humming through his body at that smirk on his face. He crossed his arms over his chest.

"How did you know?"

"You're such a Luddite. She posted it, obviously." Cole held his phone out to him, and Gabe snatched it out of his hand. His jaw clenched as he saw Ivy sitting on a bench, holding her tiger lily ice cream cone. She had captioned the photo with, *'This is the sweet life.'*

Gabe grunted and passed the phone back to Cole.

What was his Princess thinking? He told her he hated her posting about them on social media, and she kept doing it.

They were kinky in the bedroom, and he controlled her orgasms, but they didn't have a set of rules to follow beyond that, even though Ivy had brought up how she wanted more structure.

He didn't see how she could follow rules if she couldn't respect his wish of not posting about their life every moment.

"Where is she? Why wouldn't she come to your send-off dinner?"

"Ivy's at work."

"Hey, leave him alone, Cole. If he wants a sugar mama, that's his own business." Their dad joined them on the deck. "Your mother made money and left with it."

Gabe turned his back on them, looking over to where kids were building sandcastles. He clenched his jaw and tried to breathe. His dad claimed their mother was selfish and only wanted to make money. That's exactly what his dad cared about, so it was an odd argument.

It wasn't until Gabe met Jordan and his friend pointed out how false the narrative his dad had spewed all these years that Gabe realized how toxic his dad was. Things were still tense between him and his mom. He hadn't seen her in years.

"The chick also made me money," Cole said. "So I guess if you're happy sitting at home gaming, that's fine." He and his Dad laughed as if that was the funniest thing, but the tension climbed up to Gabe's neck.

Gabe never understood his brother's dislike of Ivy, other than Cole was just that superficial of a person. His dad didn't like how opinionated she was, and Ivy reminded him too much of their mother. Gabe frowned, realizing that Ivy had a lot in common with his mom for the first time.

"I signed on with Ribbon of Aid today."

"Good." His brother crossed and stood right beside him. "See that you don't screw this up. Did you meet the whole team?"

"No." He checked his watch. Ivy said she'd be here.

"Yeah, I'm putting my name on this. It's going to bring me more connections."

"I wish you all the happiness," Gabe said sarcastically.

"All right, boys, I'm putting on the steaks. Is she coming or not?"

"I don't know, Dad. We can cook something for her when she gets here."

"If she gets here," Cole said. "She never misses an appointment at work. I guess her work is more important than you."

"Yeah, she's busy making some other asshole money," Gabe sneered.

Cole slapped him on the shoulder. "How long have you shacked up with Ivy? Seven years?"

"Looks like your beer is empty," Gabe said. He went into the house, trying to block out his brother's taunting. Where the hell was Ivy?

He tried to be understanding. Ivy had stayed with him through his time as a medic. He understood putting work first, and he didn't want to dis-value her work, but she was skipping out on him more frequently. Gabe checked his phone. Not even a text.

Gabe got to his feet the instant he heard the click of the clock in the door.

"Hi! You didn't have to wait up for me." Ivy hung her bag on the hook and took off her heels.

"Leave them on, Princess. Where were you?" His hand flung out, grabbing her throat. He crowded her space, pinning her against the door. The flash of confusion on her face didn't sway him.

"Work, where else?" The annoyance in her tone made him more pissed off. He wrapped her hair in his hand and tugged, squeezing her throat lightly.

"Gabe!"

"That's *Sir*," Gabe said. "What was so important to you at work?"

"The Cherry Nails people. I was tied up with them all day, and then they took me to dinner afterwards as a thank you. What's wrong?"

Gabe took her chin in his fingers. "I'm so mad at you, Ivy. I don't know whether to cane you, deny you orgasms for the next month, or make you sleep on the couch."

Her eyes glowed. "You want to *punish* me?"

Gabe yanked her hair. She gasped. "You didn't hear me, Princess. I'm upset with you. It's not the fun kind of punishment. You forgot about the dinner again."

He watched the thoughts flutter behind her eyes. Yeah, it took her a moment.

"Oh my god, Sir. I am so sorry." Her hands came out, and she hugged him, and he couldn't help but embrace her back. She knew what his family did to him. This was the woman who stood by him during his deployments, who didn't believe a word of what came out of his brother's mouth and told him over and over not to let him and his dad get to them. "Was it awful?"

"The usual. You didn't even call."

"No, I was just so caught up in the meetings. I should have. I'm sorry."

"Don't you care I am leaving in four days?"

"Yes, I do. But you don't have to. You have a job here."

He turned away from her, exhaling a pent-up breath. They had been over this so many times.

"Sir, I'm sorry."

He turned to see her on the floor, with her knees parted, her palms up, resting on her thighs.

She had taken off her skirt. With her pink heels and black nylons and the dark pink shirt that somehow complemented her fair colouring, she was a sexy picture of contrition.

"This doesn't make me any less mad at you."

"Not even a little, Sir?"

Gabe stalked over to her, stood in front of her, reached down and grabbed her lips with his fingers, pinching them slightly.

"No. Go get the cane and your clit vibrator. Come back here naked except for the heels."

"Yes, Sir."

Gabe strode to the balcony doors. Throwing them open, he took in a gulp of the cool air. They didn't have punishment as part of their D/s. But he wanted to get through to her, needed to remind her that she was his while he was gone.

He closed the doors. Ivy walked towards him with his fibreglass cane held out in her hands, her gaze down.

"Thank you." He took the cane from her. She stood with her arms behind her back, her gaze on the floor. Damn, she looked gorgeous. He spotted the small smile around her lips.

"I hated you weren't there tonight. Why is work taking up so much of your time lately?"

"It's nothing new," Ivy mumbled.

He flicked the cane through the air. She jumped at the wispy noise, then he laid it across her breasts. She crumpled forward.

"You usually share with me what's going on. You at least check in with me, and the last few weeks, you haven't."

Her eyes flashed with annoyance. "You don't share the details of what you do at Axis Management."

He flicked his wrist. Her face scrunched up, and a red stripe appeared across her breasts.

"Enough talking, sub of mine. Now, get your face to the wall, hands above your head."

Ivy huffed as she walked by him but took up position beside the balcony door. She put her hands above her head.

"Thank you. Count these for me."

Gabe sent the cane flying across her ass.

"One, Sir."

Ivy standing still, her gaze on the wall, her legs spread, her arms stretched, by his command, was so damn gorgeous.

"Two, Sir." Her voice caught.

Gabe brought the next three down hard and fast, not giving her time to recover.

"God! That hurts. Six, Sir," Ivy moved her legs close together.

Gabe tapped the back of her calves.

She got the hint and spread her feet.

Gabe struck her ass again, keeping a steady rhythm of the cane, watching as the red stripes appeared over each other, pushing aside all thoughts other than this, of giving her a break, of helping her find a submissive headspace, to turn off her work gear.

The cane swished through the air, her ass a picture of angry red stripes.

"Twelve," Ivy whimpered out.

Gabe paused, running his hand along her shoulders. "Are you okay with continuing?"

"Yes, Sir," Ivy whispered.

He rubbed her shoulders, then stood back, throwing the cane on her left ass cheek.

"Thirteen, Sir."

Her tone had lost the snark, her voice slightly above a whisper.

The next stroke of the cane landed right across the top of her thighs.

"Fourteen, Sir!"

He loved how she was taking this punishment. Damn, he loved her so much. But he didn't love her freezing him out. And not showing up when she said she would.

"Fifteen, Sir!" Ivy shrieked but kept in position.

Gabe smiled, his heart swelling. She had always accepted him as he was, and he strived to do the same for her.

"Sixteen, Sir."

Her voice hitched, and he knew she was struggling. But damn, he wanted to push her.

On the next strike, he landed the cane right on top of the angry stripe with the lightest flick.

"God, that hurts! Seventeen, Sir."

And before she could recover, he sent the cane flying.

"Eighteen, nineteen, Sir!"

Her head hung down, and her arms trembled slightly, but she kept them above her head.

Gabe took a step closer to her, swished the cane through the air once, twice, and then landed it right across her ass.

"Twenty, Sir!" Ivy yelled.

Gabe dropped the cane on the table. Then his hands glided to Ivy's waist. "Good girl for taking that caning."

CHAPTER FOUR - GABE

He touched the red stripes, and she hissed, her shoulder blades flexing with tension. "Beautiful marks, Princess."

He cupped the back of her neck and turned her towards him. Damn, he loved the tears streaking down her cheeks. "Good girl."

He kissed her tears away, gently sealing his mouth against hers.

She let out a sob, and he swallowed it, kissing her deeply, imprinting her with praise by the touch of his lips to hers. He took her over to the couch and settled her on his lap.

"I am proud of you for obeying."

She closed her eyes and snuggled into him. He wrapped his arms around her, holding her, breathing in her familiar scent.

"I liked it, Sir. I felt put in place, and I got how disjointed you were by my actions."

His cock throbbed as he held her. She wanted this kind of structure, and he'd always been hesitant, preferring to keep their D/s in the bedroom and at the club. He loved she was a strong, independent woman, and he knew how much her work meant to her. He didn't want to be forgotten as she climbed the next ladder.

"Spread those legs for me."

Gabe squirted lube into his palm, then reached for the vibrator, flicking it on.

Ivy moaned as it pulsed against her.

"Who do your orgasms belong to?"

"You, Sir." Her voice was thick with desire.

Waiting until he saw her toes curl, he turned off the vibe.

"Sir!" Her eyes flew open.

"No masturbating while I'm away."

She opened her mouth as if to protest, then thought better of it. "Yes, Sir."

"Show me how sorry you are, Princess."

She slid off his lap, between his feet, and Gabe undid his fly. Gabe pressed lightly on her shoulders as her warm hands slid down his jeans. He stepped out of them. He moved his hands to either side of her face and brought her nose to his cock. "Open and suck it good, Princess."

She wrapped her lips around the head of his penis. Her tongue slowly rolled down the length of his dick, her mouth moving to his balls.

Gabe hissed as he palmed her cheeks. She took his cock back in her mouth, licking it from root to tip.

"More," he grunted.

His balls were heavy with cum. Her big green eyes met his as she swallowed down on him, so far he felt the tightness of her throat.

The fiery hot pleasure of her mouth made him bite his lip to hold back a groan. He knew other Doms thought this was a reward, but he needed her like this, on her knees servicing him.

Gabe wrapped his hand in her hair as her tongue glided on the underside of his hard dick, controlling her speed. He couldn't help the moan that escaped his lips as she turned her head, pulling slightly down on his cock.

"Suck deeper, Princess."

She took all of him in, hollowing her cheeks, her fingers cool under his balls.

"Faster." Gabe pulled her hair up, and her head moved rhythmically as he pulled on her strands.

Fuck, yes!

He pounded into her sizzling mouth, and her lips kept sealed on his cock. His cock throbbed. He was going to burst.

"Swallow every drop, Princess." He slowed her down for a moment, pulling at her hair and then sped up, faster and faster, her lips pressed around his cock, trying to hold on. As he exploded into her mouth, he closed his eyes. He fought to stay upright as he felt her jaw muscles work to drink in every drop of his cum.

"I'm sorry, Sir." She licked her lipstick red lips. Damn this woman. She had his entire heart.

Extending a hand to her, he helped her up and crushed his lips to hers, tasting himself on her pouty lips.

"I know." He stroked her cheek with the back of his knuckles. He took her by the arm and led her to their bedroom. He pulled down the sheets.

"Come on, I know you have an early meeting."

Ivy laid down on her side, and Gabe lay next to her, pulling her head on his chest.

"I guess it's three days till you leave now."

Gabe glanced at the alarm clock on the nightstand, half-past twelve. "Yeah. I'll be there and back before you know it. Why don't you invite Alice to come and stay for a few days?"

"I can't take time off work to spend time with her, and she'll tell me it's too much with her four-month-old."

"Okay." He knew him being gone was hard on her.

"You like what they said when you signed the contract?"

"Yeah. They seem to have experienced people here, and they are focused on running medical supplies, nothing else."

"Did they go over their emergency extraction plan?"

His stomach clenched. They hadn't, and when he asked, they said it was in the contract, and further details would come. "Ivy."

"Gabe, I'm worried. Much of my worry has to do with Cole bringing this to you, but I can't find anything on them other than a sparse website."

"They want to fly under the radar."

"Weird choice for an NGO."

"Ivy, leave it, okay?"

"Okay." She kissed him and didn't say anything more about it, but the churning anxiety in his stomach didn't go away.

CHAPTER FIVE – IVY

"I've arranged an interview for you with Joanne from Eco News. She's eager to talk to you about how Cherry Nails is changing to an eco-company."

"We're not there yet." Yvette Marksom tapped her long bright red nail on Ivy's desk.

"That's why you talk about how you are changing and the steps you are taking. Here, I have drafted some key points for you to mention. This will get the environment rights people off your case because you are coming out and refuting them."

Yvette flashed her a cover-worthy grin. "Thanks, Ivy. You're the best." She stood and flipped her long black hair over her shoulder. "I don't need to tell them about my stepfather's shares in oil, right?"

Ivy smiled. "Keyword being stepfather. Do you like him?"

"That old prick? No."

"If they ever uncover that, you add it to your story as your source of motivation."

"My only real motivation is to make money."

"Nothing wrong with that." Ivy smiled, walking Yvette out.

Okay, so sometimes her work was as shallow as Gabe said.

CHAPTER FIVE – IVY

But she loved it, and she was good at it, and she needed to make money too. Nothing was wrong with having a job and being good at it.

Sometimes she thought Gabe would fit in with her parents' berry farm.

"Hey Ivy, I have a meeting with Paula Gibson at one. Can you sit in?"

Ivy smiled at her friend and junior associate, Emery. "I can, but you'll do fine. You got this."

"It'll be my first major client I handle by myself."

"Hey, you're not out there alone. I got your back."

Her friend's dark eyes sparkled, and she tapped her tablet. "You're right. I'm going to be great!"

"Keep saying that."

"Do you give yourself a pep talk?"

"Every day." Ivy grinned.

Emery made a face, and they burst out laughing. Ivy finished making her coffee, looking at her phone as she walked down the tiled hallway to her office, passing the photos of Metric's famous clients on the wall.

Back in her office, she looked over her calendar. Good, it was packed. She wanted to be busy the first week Gabe was gone.

Last night when he had punished her had been *so* good. She didn't know how much she needed it until it happened. With his attention entirely on her, she felt wholly connected to him. And she loved that he showed her how angry he was with her.

She shifted on her chair, the stripe marks of the cane still smarting.

The knock on her door startled her out of her reprieve.

"Hey, Ivy. Can you come with me to the conference room? I want your take on this campaign before we publish it."

"Sure, Flint." Ivy smiled, but butterflies danced in her stomach.

Flint and she had disagreed on many campaigns, but her boss, Flint's father, had often taken her side. As Ivy landed more prominent clients and saved Metric face, Flint had warmed to her.

There was even talk of her name being next for an executive position.

And this, she thought, following Flint into the conference room, is why she put in the long hours. She wanted to know if she was good enough to earn that next executive position.

"Vince, thanks for coming in. Meet Ivy Powell. She is one of our newest senior staffers. We're very pleased with her work and, if I recall correctly, she had a boyfriend in the army."

"I know you're the best in the business, Flint. Ivy, nice to meet you." Vince Winston's bushy eyebrows and thick silver hair were familiar from being on an investor TV reality show. If Winston was investing in this, it was serious.

"Nice to meet you, Mr. Winston."

"Is your boyfriend still active?"

"No. He's moved on to other things," Ivy said.

"Come sit, Ivy, and we'll catch you up. Ribbon of Aid is a new NGO that will take medical supplies to hard-hit targets that need them the most. What's unique about us is we aren't like the other private contractors. We only hire former military."

Ribbon of Aid. Ivy swallowed over the lump in her throat. It's the NGO Gabe had signed on with. In two days, he'd be on the job for them.

Private contractors hire former military all the time. She wondered briefly how much Mr. Winston actually knew about this organization.

"I'd love to hear more," Ivy said.

Flint pulled out a chair for her, and Mr. Winston flipped open a portfolio. "Our team on the ground has worked with locals to make sure they can deliver these medical supplies into even the most hostile territory, and I guess that's what's unique about us. Check out our mock-up ads."

Ivy flipped through the pages in the book of guys Gabe would fit right in with, delivering boxes while men in tactical uniforms stood around.

"So we need a new story to attract former military members. What do you think, Ivy?" Flint asked.

CHAPTER FIVE – IVY

"Well, from what I see here, the emphasis is on the supplies, but if you're going to attract former military, you need to tell them what's in it for them, how they can use their skills."

"Are they really so altruistic? Look at the pay we're offering them."

Ivy took the contract from Mr. Winston. She nodded. "Yes, that's a very generous amount, but it's not that much more than other contractors. I think what they want to know the most is this is an ongoing gig."

Mr. Winston grinned. "Yes, here at Ribbon of Aid, you're a member of the family. That kind of thing?"

"Yes. For a lot of guys, it's the family they miss as well as the purpose," Ivy said.

Flint stared at her from across the table. "I knew you were the right one to have on this, Ivy. Vince, I'll get the ad guys on it, with Ivy looking it over before it goes to you. How's that?"

"Great. I'm glad to go forward with this. Thank you, Flint. Ivy, nice meeting you." Mr. Winston stood, shook her hand and exited the building.

"Mr. Fitzgerald? Carly Edwards is in your office crying her eyes out," Steph, their receptionist, poked her head in. "I told her to wait in reception, but she insisted."

"Damn, I hate it when they cry," Flint said. "Thanks, Ivy."

"Happy to help. I'll get those copy notes over to you today."

"No need. Send them on to the ad people. I trust you."

Ivy glowed at the compliment.

Flint waved and rushed out of the room. Ivy gathered the portfolio and the literature Mr. Winston had left on the table.

She noticed a flat black wallet and raced down to reception. "Hey Steph, did Mr. Winston leave? I think he forgot his wallet."

"He always forgets something." Steph smiled. "I might be able to catch him. He just left."

The phones on Steph's desk buzzed.

"No, that's okay, I got it." Ivy raced into the hallway, throwing the door to the stairwell open.

"Yeah, these six guys aren't going to come back. They think they are dropping off medical supplies into the hostile territory, but it's not." Mr. Winston's voice echoed off the walls in the empty stairwell.

Ivy swallowed bile, carefully backing up against the door so it didn't slam shut. "They've been told not to check the inventory. No one will know it's us. They'll think it's an ambush or something. You know how people believe anything. That's why we're paying good money for this PR firm. Yeah, I'll be there in twenty."

Ivy closed her eyes, willing herself not to move or breathe. She waited, hearing footsteps on the stairs and the outside door slamming shut.

Finally, she closed the door to the stairwell, took a deep breath and walked back into Metric's main office.

"Did you find him?"

"No, must have just missed him." Ivy handed Steph the wallet. "Can you send it over to him?"

"Of course. You okay? You're looking a little pale."

"Just tired." Ivy smiled.

"Ivy! The meeting with Paula went so good" Emery appeared in front of her.

"I knew you had it!"

"Are you okay?"

"Yes, I just need to focus on getting these notes over to the ad department before I leave tonight. I'm going to shut my door for a while." Ivy smiled while her heart beat in double time.

"Okay, I'll talk to you later."

"Looking forward to hearing the details." Ivy squeezed her friend's arm, walked into her office and closed the door.

She pulled the blinds, so no one could look in, and then she slumped to the floor against her door, trembling.

CHAPTER FIVE – IVY

God, this couldn't be happening.

Taking out her cell, her hands shaking, she dialled Nick.

"Hello, Ivy." Nick's twangy accent calmed her for a moment.

"Nick, how are you?"

"All fine. What's up?"

Ivy exhaled. Nick was a good guy, and he was tech-savvy. "So you know Gabe signed on for contractor work?"

"Yeah."

"Can you check these guys out? Their website is so sparse, and I don't know. I have a bad feeling about it."

Nick was quiet for a long moment. "Gabe told me how you didn't show up at the dinner by his dad's last night. I know they aren't the nicest people, but you got to support him, you know?"

She shot to her feet, annoyed by Nick's comment. "That's rich, Nick. That's *one* dinner I missed. I have had years of them."

"If you were my sub, I would call you out for being disrespectful to another Dom."

"Good thing my Dom doesn't care about stupid protocols like that," Ivy gritted through her teeth, wondering what was up with Nick.

"Ivy, the man needs to work. Step back and let him work."

"Right, talk to you later." So much for reaching out to him.

Ivy opened the desk drawer and took out a granola bar. She chewed it in two bites and drank water, and, for the next half hour, tried to convince herself that the conversation she had just overheard wasn't real.

Even though it made her feel sick to her stomach, she finished the copy notes and sent them to the ad people.

Then she worked her way through phone calls and emails, and when she couldn't write anything for the pitch, she was putting together for a supermodel rumoured to spend the winter in the city, she shut down her work laptop.

And called Quinn Walsh. His phone rang and rang.

Ivy pressed end on the call, feeling awful for bothering him. He had the most challenging time with Jordan's death and wasn't doing well. She barely saw him all summer.

She fired a quick text off to Logan Marrock. ***Hey Logan, please call me ASAP*** and stuck a piece of gum in her mouth, willing herself not to throw up.

CHAPTER SIX – IVY

"Remember when we first came here?" Gabe pulled her close to him.

She smiled, placing a hand on his freshly shaved face.

"Yeah, it was our third date. You told me you loved their shakes."

"And you didn't believe me." His eyes twinkled.

"Would you if one of your buddies said the best milkshakes in the city are at the seafood place?"

"My buddies know where the best drinks in town are."

Ivy laughed, threading her hands through his. This was her Gabe. Each time he had a job to go on, it relaxed him. He teased more, and Ivy loved this carefree side of him. "After you, Princess." Gabe held the door for her, and they went into the seafood restaurant.

After the server seated them and took their drink orders, Gabe pulled her hand into his.

"I know me leaving is always hard on you."

"It's not that."

"But you didn't want me to stay in the military."

"Not true. I wondered if you wanted to apply for another position."

"Yeah, one that would have me at the base, not where the action was." Gabe smiled at the server as she came around to take their orders.

"She'll have the scallops-"

"Actually, I want to try the Moqucea."

Gabe raised his eyebrow at her. "You always have the scallops."

Ivy shrugged. "I want to try something new."

"It's one of my favourites." The server smiled at her.

"Okay, I'll have the scallops." Gabe grinned.

The server smiled and left.

Her stomach still felt queasy. She didn't think she could handle eating anything too heavy.

"Gabe, many medics go on to be physician's assistants." Ivy sighed, not wanting to rehash this again. She was only trying to express concern for his nightmares, for how wound up he was every time he came back home.

His face softened for a moment. "You're right. You're the only one who told me I could play guitar."

"And you can."

Gabe gently made a strumming motion across her knuckles, hooking his foot between hers. "I'm going to strum you all night long."

"I can't wait." Ivy forced herself to smile, to concentrate on Gabe, but she couldn't shake her queasiness.

"Here we are," the server said.

"That looks delicious," Ivy said as the bowl of Moqueca landed in front of her.

"Are you sure you don't want a scallop?"

"I'm good." Ivy dragged her spoon through the soup.

"So, what are your plans for the first night I'm gone?"

Ivy glanced around the restaurant, seeing if she could spot any clients of Metric's. Her shoulders hunched, and she refrained from rolling her eyes. She didn't know why Gabe thought being on her own was a problem. She called her parents, zoomed with Alice, listened to her audiobooks, painted her nails, and worked too many hours like usual.

And she missed him so much she ached, but she didn't need him to get her through the day.

"I'm going to invite a hot guy over."

Gabe paused with his fork to his mouth, his eyes narrowing at her. "Princess, we've never discussed that."

"And would you be up for it?"

"No. I'm not Logan. I can't have a sub be someone else's wife."

"Clara isn't someone else's wife."

"Answer the question."

"I'm going to soak with my favourite bath bomb, eat a carton of ice cream, put on a chick flick and miss you."

"Yeah, glad you have plans."

"Yep."

"Princess, you know I have to do this."

"Can we just eat, please, and enjoy tonight? You're leaving tomorrow?"

"Before the sun goes up. It should only be ten days."

Ivy put down her spoon, not feeling hungry. For the rest of the day, she had convinced herself that the conversation she had overheard wasn't real. It was a made-up thing they were talking about, but she couldn't shake it. What if Gabe went on this trip and didn't come back?

Once they were home, lounging on the couch together, Ivy snuggled against Gabe. "Anything I can help with before you leave?"

"No. They wanted me to clean my social media. You should have seen their expressions when I told them I didn't have any social media accounts. They think this is going to be a good fit with them."

"Gabe, Metric is handling the recruitment for Ribbon of Aid."

"You're serious?" He shook his head.

"Yeah, just a coincidence. But you said Cole told you about this? Maybe he mentioned us." Ivy swallowed. She had reasons for disliking his brother, but before Flint took Cole off her client list, she netted Cole a lot of money with the sponsorship spots she found him.

"Yeah, maybe. So you can see how outstanding they are, right?"

Ivy squirmed under his arm. "I don't know, Gabe. Honestly, I don't think you should go. Call Xander or Ares tomorrow, and ask if they have anything."

"Ivy, c'mon, it's my last night home. I don't want to argue about this."

"I'm not arguing. I am more worried about this one than any of the jobs you went on with Axis Management."

Gabe took her chin in his hands and turned her face to his. "Stop worrying, Princess."

He kissed her, his tongue pressing into her mouth, urging her to open for him.

Ivy closed her eyes. It would be so easy to give in to this, to have kinky fun before he went, but she couldn't.

She pulled away from him. "Sorry, I think I have a headache coming on."

"I'll get you some water." Gabe dropped a kiss on her forehead.

She looked out at the city's lights, smiling as she remembered her mom standing at this window with her, with her hand on her hips, asking her where the grass was. Ivy shook her head at her mother and tried to explain how much she loved the city life, and as soon as she did, a horn blasted, and a car alarm went off.

"Yeah, I can see it's peaceful." She and her mom laughed.

"Here." Gabe brought the tray over. "What are you thinking?"

"Just of my parents. I didn't return my mom's call yet."

"Call her tomorrow. I'm going to double-check that I am all packed."

He hugged her and nuzzled her. She exhaled, trying to disperse some of the tension in her body. Ivy reached up and ran a hand through his hair. She didn't want to let him go.

"Gabe, stop for a moment. I overheard something at work."

"Like what?"

Ivy pulled back from him, wringing her hands. "I heard the guy who is the investor of Ribbon of Aid say that the six guys going on this trip weren't going to come back."

Gabe blinked, his brows knitting together. "Ivy... that can't be right. You must have misheard that."

"I didn't, Gabe."

"Does that even sound real to you?" He raised his voice.

"No. I tried to keep it out of my mind all day, but I couldn't."

"You knew about this all day, and you're just telling me now? Ivy, I think you're grasping at straws."

His words landed like a punch to her heart. He should know that she wasn't given to being overdramatic. "I'm not. That's what I heard."

"This is unbelievable. Why would you say this to me? Look, Ivy, if they were sure guys wouldn't return, they wouldn't send us. They're paying us decent money for this job."

Ivy bit her lip, blinking back tears. "I... I don't know what their reasons are for that, Gabe. But I heard what I heard."

"No, you're just making it up because you don't want me to work. You don't want me to provide."

"That's outrageous!" Now she was yelling. How could he think such an outlandish thing?

"No, it isn't. You want to take care of us for your self-esteem."

"You're wrong." Ivy stared at him, his hands in flinched, his nostrils flaring.

"I am? Then why is it every time I leave, you don't want me to?"

"That's not true! That's a story you have concocted in your head."

"Are you calling me crazy?"

"No! You're being... I don't know, but Gabe, I have supported you for years!"

"Exactly, and you like to do that. It makes you feel good." He spat out the words from across the room.

"Yeah, because I love you. And people who love you take care of you. You're letting your brother or dad get into your head, Gabe." She turned from the door, walked over to the corner, and snatched up his guitar from the stand. "I gave you this, remember? I have encouraged you to do something other than the army."

"Yeah, because you don't want me to be in it."

"Because it didn't seem like it was any longer healthy for you!" Ivy yelled. This man made her want to jump out of her skin.

Gabe turned the guitar over in his hands, his fingers plucking the strings gently. "You could admit that you don't want me to go."

"I have! I've told you *not* to go, and I just told you I heard a conversation saying the guys on this medical supply drop-off aren't going to make it back."

Gabe shook his head, putting the guitar back on the stand. "I'm going down to the gym. I need a run before I hit the sack."

He grabbed his keys off the hook, shoved his feet into runners and closed the door. Ivy marched into the kitchen and splashed water on her face.

She wanted to call her mom. Her mom was always cheerful and happy, and Ivy felt like the air was thick with gloominess.

Wiping the tears from her cheeks, she tried to think. She needed to make him see reason and not go on that job. But his mind was set on leaving.

She texted Logan again, hoping he'd call her. Of all the Bandit Brothers, he was the easiest to talk to.

Glancing at the clock on the kitchen wall, Ivy swallowed. Gabe was rolling out at four am. She only had hours to stop him, and she wasn't sure the plan in her head would work, but she had to try.

CHAPTER SIX – IVY

She was good at what she did. Really, damn good. Going over to her desk, she quickly scanned her social media, taking all the photos she had posted of her and Gabe and then copying them to a folder. She checked Cole's feeds for any pictures of him and Gabe. Then she activated a social media account Gabe had once but never used. She uploaded all the pictures.

It'd work if people didn't look too closely at the dates.

She saw that Gabe had a bunch of friend requests, and she quickly accepted all of them.

In their bedroom, she changed into a silver shirt and a leather skirt. She quickly did her make-up, and then from their toy box, she took out a pair of fuzzy black handcuffs. Taking a moment, she changed the settings to make sure her family won't see this post on their feeds.

Shaking, she kneeled on the bed. Closing her eyes, Ivy steadied her nerves.

She held up the handcuffs and snapped a selfie. A minute later, she had posted the picture all over social media, tagging Gabe.

The caption under the photo read, *"Looking forward to a night with my Dom @GabeArthur before he starts an exciting new job with Ribbon of Aid."*

Done.

She was counting on the fact that Ribbon of Aid didn't want attention on them, and because they asked the guys to scrub their social media, they'd be checking before go time tomorrow.

She broke out in a sweat, her stomach sinking. Gabe was going to be pissed at her. But he'd get over it, and then maybe Axis Management could look into Ribbon of Aid, and he'll realize she did this to protect him.

She loved him so much and wanted her Dom to be safe. He always made her feel loved and cared for, and this is how she cared for him by stopping him from going on a deadly job.

Ivy scrubbed her face, set her phone to do not disturb and climbed into bed, waiting for Gabe to come home.

CHAPTER SEVEN – GABE

Giving his bag one last check, Gabe zipped it and set it by the door. He wiped down the counters, emptied Ivy's forgotten coffee from last night, and then took out her favourite mug, leaving it on the counter against her ready-to-go French press. It was two-thirty in the morning. He was eager, pumped up. He didn't like leaving Ivy like this, with last night's argument fresh, but he wrote her a note, and he'd call her as soon as he could.

He was lucky to have her to put up with him. Grabbing his bag, his hand was on the door as his phone buzzed.

"Hello?"

"Arthur, I don't know what you're thinking violating our agreement. Do you know you could have jeopardized the entire job?"

"Mr. Winston?"

"Yeah, who else do you think it is?"

"Sorry, Mr. Winston. I don't know what you're talking about."

Winston laughed. "Then you better talk to your girlfriend. We asked you to wipe social media because we want to keep our drops off quiet until we are done. You should know it could put you in danger to have it branded about when you're going to leave. We also asked you not to post about us publicly because we don't want bad press coming for us.

What we're doing is very specific, and we're up against our competition. With that info, they can scan the flights leaving today and trace it back to us. Sorry Arthur, but you can't be on this flight out."

Gabe's mouth went dry. "I don't understand."

Gabe's stomach twisted. The throbbing in his head intensified.

"Check your girlfriend's social media post. Too bad. You would have been perfect for this job." With that, he hung up. Gabe rapt his knuckles hard on the counter.

He stalked over to Ivy's desk and flipped open her laptop. She was always logged in, so he quickly scrolled to her feeds.

What the fuck did she do?

He blinked, trying to make sense of what he saw. A profile he never created in his name. A post by Ivy that tagged him. His mouth went dry. A glossy selfie mocked him. She kneeled on the edge of the bed, holding a pair of fuzzy handcuffs.

The caption read, *"Looking forward to a night with my Dom @GabeArthur before he starts an exciting new job with Ribbon of Aid."*

His head buzzed, his hand curled into a fist. He was sure he'd sail it through the wall.

"Fuck."

What was she thinking? They just talked about how much he hated her posting anything personal online.

Unbelievable. He had signed on with Ribbon Aid, and she didn't like it, so she went and sabotaged it?

Was she so consumed with her job, crafting made-up narratives, that she couldn't separate them from reality? She had to mess about in his stuff, just for the hell of it?

His anger rolled through him like a pounding drum. His neck throbbed, the migraine pulsing at his temples. He thought of going into the bedroom, gripping her by the throat, demanding an explanation, but he knew his urge to do that was hollow.

She didn't put him before what she wanted and didn't respect him. How could he be her Dom? How could they even stay together?

The tap in the bathroom caught his attention, and he marched down the hall. Ivy opened the door, her face awash with surprise.

"Gabe, why are you still here? Did you oversleep?"

"No, I didn't oversleep. I'm here because you got what you wanted."

He crowded her, pushing her against the bathroom door.

"What do you mean?"

"I've been fired from Ribbon Aid because of your post."

Her face drained of colour; she placed a hand on his arm. He shook it off. "Gabe, I know you're upset right now, but you'll see it's for the best. I know you don't like me posting online..."

"Like it? I told you not to fucking do it. And you couldn't obey, could you?" His hand snagged at her gold chain, his collar around her throat.

"Gabe, you were so determined to go on this job. You didn't listen to me that these were bad people."

"Do you think I'm stupid? You don't think I would have done my research, read the contract and decided?" He pulled the chain. Her hands came over his, her eyes wide with shock.

"I don't think you're stupid. Of course not."

Ivy bit her lip, her fingers on his. He flung them off and unclasped the collar from her neck.

"Gabe!"

"So much for that commitment, Ivy. You couldn't even respect my privacy."

"I did it to save you!" Ivy's eyes flashed with anger, one hand clutching her empty neck. "Do you think I wanted to hurt you?"

"I don't know! Everyone else I have loved has, so why not you?"

"Because I never have!"

He turned from her, shaking his head.

"There isn't a fucking thing you can say to make this right. What part of *I need to work* didn't you understand?"

"I know you do, but it didn't have to be this place. I told you what I overheard."

"And I told you, people talk, people lie. You should know. That's what you do for a living."

"That's all you think I do." Ivy sobbed.

Gabe scoffed, wincing, grabbing the wall as his migraine took hold.

"You need the pills. I'll get them."

He shook a finger at her. "No, Ivy. Don't do me any *more* favours. I'm spending a few nights at Nick's. I don't want to see you here when I get back."

"What do you mean...Gabe." She placed her hand in between his shoulder blades.

He shook her off, stepping out of the bathroom. "I mean it, Ivy. I can't be around you right now."

"Gabe! You can't throw away everything we've been through. This is just a disagreement."

"You're the one who threw everything away, Ivy, when you did exactly what I told you not to. When you didn't respect what I wanted."

"We live here together. We share a home, a life."

He shook his head, leaning on the wall, closing his eyes against the pounding in his skull, against the pain in her voice.

"I can't live with someone who doesn't respect me. I don't want to see you, Ivy. Be gone when I get back."

"Gabe, you can't do this."

"Yes, I can. You showed me how important trust is to you, Ivy when you broke mine. Just get out before I come back."

Clutching his head, he grabbed his bag from the front door and slammed it on the way out. His heart shattered. Damn her for ruining it all.

PART TWO APRIL - AFTER

CHAPTER EIGHT – IVY

"Be ready this time, Ivy!"

Ivy grabbed the handrail and gripped her cellphone tightly in her other hand. She wanted to be anywhere else but here, seventy metres above the ground, on a suspension bridge. Her heart thundered in her chest.

She clicked a few photos of influencer and socialite Bethany Wilder, posing with the ruby red lipstick that had glitter, or "micro diamonds" as the product info the company sent over-claimed, that was so sparkly it almost glowed on its own.

A family of four and two elderly people walked by her, muttering something about being in their way, and Ivy blushed. They were right. But Bethany tended not to care about such trivialities. She needed the shot for her social media account.

The photo is meant to be a selfie, but it's one of about several hundred that Ivy has taken over the past few months.

"That one looks good!" Ivy called.

"Let's do it again. Crouch down this time, so you get my face on an angle."

CHAPTER EIGHT – IVY

Oh god, she couldn't. The bridge swayed slightly as she touched the floor. She swallowed, willing the contents of her stomach to stay in her body.

She quickly clicked off four shots and scrambled to her feet as thunder boomed in the sky.

"That's good. We should go before the rain gets harder," Ivy said.

"Yeah, I don't want my hair to get wet!"

The bridge felt like it swayed faster, with people speeding up to reach the exit before the skies opened. Ivy grabbed Bethany's hand.

"Ivy! Let go!" Bethany shrieked.

Ivy did, reluctantly, and concentrated on looking straight ahead. Not to either side of her, definitely not down below to the river. This is not what she envisioned when she finished her communications degree.

She swallowed, pushing thoughts of Metric from her mind. She had worked so hard there. But a day after she made that post, they fired her.

She knew the post rankled some people the wrong way, but she honestly thought the firm, which prides itself on being ground-breaking and ahead of the trends, wouldn't have such an over-the-top reaction to a post of a fuzzy pair of black handcuffs. It wasn't like she used the company account to post it on.

Ivy bit the inside of her cheek to stop the flood of emotion. She thought Gabe would be mad at her, but he'd calm down, listen to what she had overheard, and take that to Axis Management. Never did it cross her mind she'd lose both her job and her Dom over the post.

And even though it led to her taking stupid pictures and being single and lonely, she would do it again because she did it to save Gabe.

"Come on, Ivy!" Bethany yelled at her.

She tried to hurry up her careful steps.

At the end of the bridge, Ivy leaned against a tree, sucking in full breaths of air. She would never, ever do that again.

"Eww, I got another creepy text." Bethany shoved her phone in front of Ivy's nose.

Taking the phone, Ivy read it. For the past month, user max65 had been sending Bethany creepy messages. Stuff like he wants to see her naked. He can't wait to get her alone. He wants to mess her up.

Ivy thought she should report them to the police, but Bethany scoffed at her and did what she did every time something in life didn't work out for her: called her father.

Not trusting Bethany to screenshot it, Ivy took a picture of it with her phone and handed it back to Bethany.

"It's harmless, right? Just some troll."

The mask slipped for a moment, and a frightened nineteen-year-old woman stared at her.

"I'm sure it's nothing."

She didn't think that at all, but giving reassurance was a big part of her job, and she was tired of trying to convince Bethany to report it.

"Yeah. Let's go!" Bethany said, taking off at a gruelling pace again.

Finally, out of the park, drenched from head to toe, Ivy pulled a towel from her trunk and tried to sop up some water. She climbed in the car, Bethany following her.

"How many people do we have for Friday?"

"I updated the list this morning. We're at one hundred and fifty."

"I want two hundred and fifty," Bethany said. "Send out more invitations."

Of course, Bethany wanted more invitations to the product launch of a new stiletto by the well-known shoe company, Emergence.

"I'm on it," Ivy said. "See you tomorrow."

"Yep," Bethany said.

CHAPTER EIGHT – IVY

Ivy plugged her phone in to charge and started the hour drive home. She missed living in the West End condo she had shared with Gabe, her perfect home in the heart of the city, five minutes from the beach. She missed her morning yoga session, and she didn't get to see her friends as much.

Not that many friends stood by her after she made that post. Ivy chewed her lip. Her life sucked, and it was all her fault. But she didn't think it was fair. People posted stupid stuff on social media all the time. Why she was one of the few people to suffer consequences for it irked her.

Pulling into the parking lot of her apartment building, Ivy groaned, seeing Bethany's father, Mark's number flashing on her screen.

"Hello, Mr. Wilder."

"Ivy? You get another hundred people at the Grand Lake hotel on Friday, or we are firing you. We took a chance on you, and I expect better results."

"Mr. Wilder, of course. I am sending out a new set of invites tonight. I expect attendance to be great."

"Glad to hear it. Bethany would never let on, but these recent threats have shaken her. I don't like them. So I've hired a security firm for the evening."

"Oh?" Ivy's heart leapt into her mouth.

She wondered if it would be Axis Management, and she bit her lip. They handled security for celebrities. Not that Bethany was an A-lister. But Mr. Wilder had connections. She didn't want to see Gabe.

"Yes, Stone Security will oversee extra security measures at the event. I don't think there is anything to these threats, but it's better to be overcautious. Bethany is excited about this; don't let her down."

"It's going to be an exceptional event," Ivy promised.

"Okay, see you Friday." Mr. Wilder hung up.

In the lobby of her apartment building, she collected the mail and climbed the three flights of stairs. She missed the concierge service. She missed door-to-door mail and not having to drag the laundry to a laundromat.

Ivy sighed, hearing the music blaring from one neighbour and the daily domestic screaming match from the other. This wasn't the life she wanted. But it's where life brought her after Gabe told her to leave that night. Her friend Emery told her to put out resumes, but Ivy tried, and each time she went to job search, a ball of anxiety formed so tightly in her stomach that she couldn't get past it. It was hard to start over again.

She pushed her door open.

"Good, you're home!" Her roommate, Holton, grinned at her.

"Yes, I am, Mr. Birke. How was your day?"

Ivy shrugged off her rain jacket and kicked off her boots.

"It was glamorous as usual. But I have an audition tonight."

"You'll get it!"

In the tiny galley kitchen, she filled her French press with her favourite coffee and flipped on the electric kettle.

"Yes! But then you'll have to look for a roommate again!" Holton sang.

"You won't leave me." She grinned.

"You're right! But we'll move to something bigger and grander," Holton said.

Ivy smiled. The only person to still talk to her from her old work was her friend Emery, Holton's sister, and when Ivy said she needed a place to live fast, Emery suggested her brother. Ivy was grateful for the connection, she knew how hard it was to find a place on short notice, and she didn't want to move back home to Alberta.

Ivy tidied the dishes on the counter. She owed her parents a call. Telling them she had lost the job at Metric had been so hard. Her dad's gruff, "You know, you could come home." And her mother's fawning worry had sent her into a crying heap as soon as she hung up with them. Ivy had fibbed and told them her firing was due to staff changes, and then she bit her lip, realizing she was doing exactly what Gabe had often accused her of, lying.

She and Gabe hadn't discussed what would happen with the condo, so she was still automatically paying her half of the mortgage. She hadn't talked to Gabe since that awful morning. Other than sending him an email with her new address, she hadn't had contact with him at all. The day Metric fired her, she came home to most of her stuff boxed up, delivered by a courier company.

That reminded her that she had to do everything she could to keep her job.

"Holton?" Ivy stuck her head around the living room to see Holton folding up his double futon. "Are you free tomorrow night?"

"Maybe. Is there free booze?"

"And food." Ivy smiled. "Can you come and bring thirty or a hundred people? It's at the Grand Lake hotel. A launch party for a new shoe by Emergence. Free swag."

"Send me the deets, and I'll bring the biggest crowd I can."

A thumping on the wall made her jump. Her neighbours had progressed to the throwing stuff part of the evening.

"Thanks. You're the best."

Holton had been the friend she needed, getting her through many nights of crying her eyes out.

"You know it." Holton picked up his messenger bag, grabbed his keys and kissed her cheek. "Don't wait up. I'm hoping to get lucky tonight."

Ivy grinned. "Have fun."

"Bye."

When Holton left, Ivy changed into pj's, grabbed her tablet and went through every contact list she had, sending out invites for the product launch, and after okaying it with Mr. Wilder, she ran a last-minute ad on social media. It might be close.

She missed her old contact lists and the access to media she had with Metric. Ivy shook off a feeling of sentimentality and flipped through the mail, gasping as she saw a black and gold envelope with Club Bandit's logo on it. Being careful not to tear it, Ivy opened it. It was an invitation to apply for membership. Ivy grinned. Looks like Club Bandit was opening to the public. A thrill of excitement raced down her as she contemplated the invite. It said to send them an email, and they would arrange an interview. She grabbed her tablet and fired off the email.

It wasn't just access to a great play space; it was the contacts. Ever since the summer, she had been lonely. She lost her job, their mutual friends and her socialization. Maybe being a member of Club Bandit would give some of that back to her.

Feeling hopeful, Ivy set herself up with her old laptop and fired off a bunch of posts for the product launch. While she was at it, she made a new ad for clients and made it go live.

Maybe she had this after all.

CHAPTER NINE – GABE

Gabe turned his nose to his shoulder, trying to discreetly sniffle a sneeze. The room smelled like all the perfume counters that ever existed mixed up into one. As a medic, he had sniffed some funky things, but the aroma in this room rivalled them all.

He smiled at a brunette with a pink floppy bow in her hair, her cleavage barely contained in the sparkly little dress that clung to her body. "Good evening. What's your name?"

"Veronica Martin."

Gabe checked her name off the list on his iPad, and Erik stepped forward to check her just over the size of a wallet purse.

"Have a good night," Erik said.

Veronica flounced past them, through the doors to the ballroom, decked out with gold streamers everywhere.

On and on it went. Gabe didn't mind the tedious task. It was better than sitting at home in his condo, pacing the floors or working himself so hard at the gym he nearly collapsed.

Erik got him this gig with Stone Security, though it felt a little traitorous. Gabe tried to push that thought down. His boss, Xander Montague, called him a couple of weeks back and told him he was off rotation from

Team Stealth because he'd been working too many hours. Taking on each job that came his way, and he had been doing it since August.

Gabe knew he needed a break but keeping busy kept his mind off stuff he would rather not think about. Like one of his best friends dying. He chewed the inside of his lip. The other Bandit Brothers had moved on, even Quinn, since he met Simone Roberts. But Gabe hadn't. He, the medic, couldn't save Jordan. And then there was Ivy.

Ever since that morning in August, he had lost a part of himself. Everything felt heavier without Ivy around. She was his Princess, his ray of light in his miserable life, and without her, he became more of a working machine. He never expected her to hurt him as she did. Gabe shook off the thoughts. So he worked.

Erik also worked every job he could, and the guy was okay. Erik mostly kept to himself, but in Gabe's experience, the guy was solid. You could count on him. And his fellow Bandit Brother scored points for getting him this job tonight.

"Gentlemen, please close the doors," the deep voice of River Stone filtered through their earpiece.

River kept surveillance from outside in a van, monitoring tonight's event. A few months back, Axis Management had sold the bodyguarding side of their business to River Stone, but that wasn't why it felt disloyal. River and Xander weren't on the best terms, and Xander held loyalty as the highest tenant.

Gabe crossed his fingers that Xander would let this slide when he found out about it. And he would find out about it. There wasn't anything Xander didn't know about the people he hired.

He took his stance six feet away from Erik, and he scanned the room. Some top twenty pop song played, and servers with trays filled with appetizers circled the room. As if shoes were pieces of great art, women crowded around the glass display cases and the shelves on the back wall, taking pictures. In the middle of the room, there was a cube shape

CHAPTER NINE – GABE

covered with a sparkly gold cloth, with Emergence's logo in gold embroidery.

Gabe scoffed to himself, all this for a pair of shoes. People liked to waste their time and money. It was exactly the kind of event his brother's girlfriend, Chantal, would attend. The lights dimmed, and the music stopped and apparently, that was a signal for all the women and men to put away their phones. Loud pop music blasted through the room. Gabe could feel the beat through his steel toes. Flashing yellow, green and purple lights cascaded over the room.

Bethany, the influencer they were hired to watch tonight, literally tittering in heels, waved her hands above her head and danced on the platform beside the covered cube. She swayed and danced and spoke into her old-school microphone.

"Hello, Vancouver!" she shouted.

And the feedback blasted through the room because, of course, it did. "You being here means you're awesome! Thanks for coming out. I can't wait for you to see the brand new stilettos by Emergence! You're getting to see them first. Drum roll, please!"

A recorded drumroll echoed in the room, and the cheering increased by three decibels. Bethany pulled off the gold cloth. The audience screamed as a pair of golden heels were revealed, spinning on a disc inside their cube box.

"I know! They are *fabulous*. Who thinks I should try them on?"

Everyone in the entire room except him and Erik screamed "me."

With one quick motion, two guys in grey suits lifted the case off, and Bethany reached in and grabbed the shoes, setting them in the palm of her hand and holding them up above her head.

"These are stilettos every woman wants and maybe a few of the guys! They'll look good on anyone, and they go on sale tomorrow for only fifteen thousand dollars!"

Women jumped up and down and screamed and held each other's arms. Gabe scoffed. So much ridiculous fanfare for a pair of overpriced shoes. It took a lot to gross Gabe out, but at this moment, his stomach kind of dropped to the floor. His brother bought stupid shit all the time, but Ivy would call him a sexist or something.

Thinking about Ivy caused him to bite the inside of his cheek. There was no way she would be in this crowd clapping for a pair of shoes, and that's the first positive thing he had thought about the woman in months.

She stomped on his heart and cost him a job. He shouldn't be thinking about her at all. But part of why he was working so much was because he thought of her every time he went through the door of their condo, and she wasn't there.

"We need crowd control right by Bethany," River Stone's voice sounded in his ear. Gabe sighed, he wanted to be situated right by the case from the beginning, but the client, Mr. Wilder, thought it would detract from the display.

Seamlessly as possible, with Erik beside him, they made their way through the throng of people, dodging full drinks and ignoring the cries from the people who thought they were trying to get closer to the shoes.

"I can't wait to slip my foot right in!" Bethany said.

"Sorry!" A woman apologized and bumped into Gabe. He waved her off and continued until he was slightly behind the case, beside Bethany.

"Hold this," Bethany hissed. For a moment, Gabe thought she had given the order to him.

All the breath left him. He'd know those curves and that silky short golden hair anywhere. Ivy took the mike from Bethany, and Bethany held on to her arm as she tried to balance awkwardly and slipped the pricey shoes on her feet.

Ivy. His mouth went dry. She looked good. Damn.

He wondered if he wanted her to look bad. As if there was a single thing she could do to look ugly. A silky black dress hugged her hips and clung to her breasts.

With her ruby red lips and her green eyes illuminated by sparkly powder she had brushed on them, she was the most gorgeous creature in the room. She looked up, and Gabe saw her bare neck, which was another punch to his gut. He tried to look away. But couldn't.

He gave her that collar two days before Christmas Eve two years ago. He remembered the feel of her cheek against his jean-covered knee as he clasped it around her neck, and she promised to submit to him. It was just them in their condo. The lights were low, and their blinds were open to the cityscape. And then, the memory of him taking it off her neck after she made that post spiked a heated fury through him.

So much for promises, he scoffed.

"Oh my god, you guys! These are amazing! They feel like a giant hug for my feet, like I'm walking on air!" Lights flashed as cameras clicked away, people crowding closer to get a better look at the shoes.

"A million thanks to Emergence for letting me have these shoes! I'm going to slip them off so you can take even more pictures, but no touching!" Bethany said.

Bethany almost toppled Ivy to the floor as she grabbed her arm, and Gabe stopped himself from reaching out.

But he wanted to. He wanted to touch her, feel her, and reclaim her as his. And he didn't like that pulsing urge, one bit. This woman hurt him intentionally. He refocused on the crowd.

"One moment! Don't forget to hashtag golden shoes and Emergence!" Finally, Bethany got the shoes off her feet.

Suddenly, a woman from the crowd charged at Bethany, grabbing the shoe out of her hand.

"You stupid twit," the woman yelled.

Erik got between Bethany and the woman as the woman swung the shoe, hitting Ivy in the face. Gabe watched, his heart in his mouth, as she fell to the floor.

Erik hustled Bethany out of there while River Stone barked orders in his ear. Gabe didn't care.

He offered his hand to Ivy. "Going to get you out of here."

Ivy's perfectly shaped mouth formed an o, and her eyes blinked frantically.

The woman who charged Bethany was still screaming and waving the shoe about. Above the crowd, he saw two men from Stone Security; backup had arrived.

She put her hand in his, he hustled her out of there through the exit doors that led to the second-floor lobby.

He heard her raspy breathing and wanted to reassure her. As his fingers touched her flesh, he felt like throwing her against the wall. But his dick twitched.

Because the truth was, he wanted to throw her against the wall and fuck her brains out.

He tightened his grip.

"Ow," Ivy said.

"Oh please, you like it rough."

Yeah, that got her blushing and her eyes shooting lasers at him. He had spent many sleepless nights wondering why she had to destroy him.

He wanted to spend the rest of his life with this woman.

He noticed the cut on her cheek. "You're bleeding. Sit down."

"This is outrageous! She grabbed the shoe from me. I can press charges, right?" Bethany said.

"I'm not the person to ask about that," Erik said.

"What do you mean I'm bleeding?" Her voice shook.

He stopped her hand before she could touch the blood. In his experience, it made it worse the moment the person saw the blood.

CHAPTER NINE – GABE

"Need a first aid kit," Gabe said into his mic.

"Got it," River said.

"How long do I have to sit here?" Bethany said. "I need to get back to mingling. Ivy, do you have my phone?"

Ivy reached into her kitty purse and passed Bethany her phone.

"Eww, you're bleeding," Bethany said.

"How bad is it?" Ivy asked.

Her green eyes met his, and the hurt in them seared his heart, but he brushed it off. Why would she be hurt? He's the one she hurt.

"That depends on how long it takes to stop the bleeding. I'm giving it nine minutes before sending you to the hospital for stitches."

"Don't want stitches."

"You don't want a lot of things," Gabe bit out before he could stop himself.

"You're hurting me." Ivy wrenched her head away from his hold.

"You can take it." And he had missed giving it to her so damn much.

She bit her lip, and her gaze fell to the floor.

"Here, Gabe." He handed Gabe the first aid kit.

"Thanks." Gabe nodded at the former US Marine. River's dark eyes scanned the situation, his thick biceps rippling as he put a hand on Bethany's shoulder.

Silently, Gabe cleaned her wound, trying not to inhale the familiar scent of her that evoked memories of lazy Sunday mornings in bed and her favourite French-pressed coffee.

"Miss Wilder, I hear you had a scare this evening," River said.

"Yes, I did. It was awful, but that man here got me out of there in two seconds. Can I charge that woman for harassment or something?"

"You can file a police report," River said. "Have you had any threats tonight?"

"I don't know. Ivy?"

Ivy turned, and for a moment, Gabe saw her unguarded expression before she smiled. "No new threats tonight. One last night."

"You got to take those threats seriously, Miss Wilder. We don't want anything to happen to you."

"I'll take them seriously," Bethany said.

"Bethany! Thank god you're okay." A short man in a sports jacket hurried over to her.

"Daddy, it was so awful."

"Let's get you back in there. Tomorrow, I'll take you on a shopping spree. Thank you." Mr. Wilder nodded at them all as he ushered his daughter back to the fray.

"I'm going to grab the security feed to give to the police," River said. "Let me know when you're done here. Good work."

Gabe nodded. Erik followed River, leaving him alone with Ivy.

He finished cleaning her wound, placing a Band-Aid on her cheek. "At least keep the Band-Aid on for a day."

"It looks ridiculous," Ivy said.

"You could never look ridiculous." He threw out the alcohol wipes and closed the first aid kit. "You should take yourself home."

"Do you mean the home you kicked me out of?" Her eyes flared in anger.

His mouth went dry. Kicking her out of the condo was kind of an asshole move, and part of him regretted that. He should have sold it and split the profits with her.

"What did you want me to do, Ivy? You ruined my life."

"You kept your job at Axis Management, and it looks like you have another one. Your friends still speak to you, right?"

"Your actions have consequences," he snapped.

"I ruined my life by trying to save yours." She glanced away from him, but he caught the angry expression on her face.

CHAPTER NINE – GABE

"So you've said." It was the story she told him back in August. He had a hard time believing it. Ivy counted on that post having an effect. That's why she posted it, to cost him that job.

"So much for taking care of me," Ivy spat.

"Ivy, if you need..." Gabe said.

"I don't need anything from you. All I got from you was broken promises."

She walked by him, her head held high. Gabe paced to the window at the end of the hall and back again. The woman had a knack for goading him. Usually, it led to sexy times. Now it just made his rage bubble over with all the hurt he had stored inside.

But her barb landed. He let her down and should have taken care of her. Taking out his phone, he transferred money into her account. He tried not to think about what it meant, that the action soothed his rage. He took the stairs to the ground floor of the hotel, catching up with Erik and River. He needed to finish here quickly and not think about Ivy Powell.

CHAPTER TEN – IVY

Ivy squirmed in the office chair under the steely gaze of Zee Riddell, owner of Club Bandit. "I got the letter in the mail asking if I would like to apply for membership and schedule an interview. So I did. Here I am for an interview."

Zee rubbed a palm over his face, and gave her a small smile. "Those invites went out to everyone who has ever been a guest of a founding member."

Ivy chewed her lip. "Oh. So it wasn't a personal thing? I thought when you scheduled this interview... I had hoped I would be approved because you know me."

"Ivy, that's the problem. I don't think Gabe or our founding members would be comfortable with you playing at the club. You have a very public display of outing a member, and we must protect the privacy of everyone who plays here."

Ivy shook her head. "It's been over six months. Nobody believes me, but my reasons were good."

"The community has a long memory. Even if your reasons were noble, you still outed Gabe."

CHAPTER TEN – IVY

"Did I?" Ivy said. Her body heated. "I said I couldn't wait for my Dom to play with me tonight. I didn't say he was a member of this club."

The stare Zee sent her made her scoot to the edge of her seat.

"I'm sorry, Ivy, I can't offer you membership to Club Bandit."

"Okay," Ivy said. Another thing she had lost was because she tried to save Gabe.

"I'll walk you out," Zee said.

Ivy followed him out of his office through the gorgeous golden textured walls of the main space of Club Bandit. All the play equipment gleamed. Walking past the station with the wooden cross, she shook her head, not wanting to linger on the memory of Gabe tying her up and using the crop on her nipples that flooded her brain. God, that was a great night, a sweet night.

"Take care, Ivy," Zee said. He looked like he meant it, so Ivy tried to smile at him as she felt tears gather in the corners of her eyes.

Her mother told her life wasn't fair, but this sucked. In her car, she took a deep breath, trying to ward off the emotions. Fine, if Club Bandit didn't want her, she would just take herself to the other club in the city.

Maybe she could make new memories there, find a Dom to play with for a few hours, and forget about her life.

She didn't want a new Dom. Sighing, she drove through the gates, leaving Club Bandit behind.

Her phone rang, flashing Bethany's name.

Ivy pulled over. "Hi, Bethany!" Ivy said. "I got an email from Emergence this morning. They loved the results of the product launch."

"Yes, I know. They want me to do another shoot. Meet me at the Lions Bridge right away."

Ivy gritted her teeth. "Which part?"

"Obviously, the part where people take selfies? The underneath part in the park?"

"Got it."

"Be here soon! I'm going clubbing tonight."

At least it gave her something to do than feel sorry for herself. She wasn't going to give Gabe that kind of power, not like this. If the man wasn't so stubborn and he had listened to her, she wouldn't have had to make a post that ended her life.

The congested traffic didn't improve her mood. She clicked on a self-help audiobook and clicked it off again when it suggested she "envision the life she wanted."

The life she wanted was the one she had with Gabe. With her friends. She wanted to sit in bed naked on Sunday morning, drinking coffee and eating the pastries he brought back for her from his run. She wanted Christmas at her parents' house, with the chaos. Though she could pass on Christmas with his dad and brother and the awkward conversation that consisted of his father asking him when he was going to make some money.

Gabe never relaxed at her family home. Her mom and dad were always welcoming. They had a ton of family that peppered her with questions about marriage and the future. Gabe always looked slightly out of place until her dad asked him to go look at something in his workshop.

At Christmas Dinner this year, she excused herself and went for a walk around the neighbourhood, being there without Gabe hurt.

She hadn't exactly told her parents she had broken up with Gabe. Ivy figured telling her parents wouldn't be quite the truth, so she justified not bringing it up. She told her family that Gabe was on a job.

Ivy rested her head on the steering wheel for a moment. She hoped this would be quick. Mr. Wilder took forever to pay her, and it was starting to feel like she was working for more than she was getting paid. But she didn't have any other options. She had a mortgage and rent to pay. Following the directions Bethany sent to her phone, she passed runners and hikers on the path.

"No," Ivy breathed, catching sight of Bethany. The influencer had some bad ideas but standing on a paddleboard under the Lions Gate Bridge topped them. Signage along the shoreline told paddleboarders and kayakers not to enter this part of the water.

"Hi, Ivy! Come on in and take a few pics of me!"

As Ivy got closer, she saw Bethany holding a pair of golden shoes. She swayed on the paddleboard, fighting for her balance.

Groaning, Ivy kicked off her shoes and waded into her knees. Ivy pulled out her phone and quickly took a few pics, zooming in on Bethany's hands.

"Come back to shore!" Ivy called.

"In a minute! Isn't this going to look amazing?"

You couldn't beat the background, the still water, the sharpness of the bridge's slope. Ivy had to concede Bethany's risk would lead to more followers, and that's the goal when you're an influencer.

And she needed to eat.

"Woot!" Bethany shouted, raising her hands above her head.

"Bethany!" Ivy screamed, watching as her client landed headfirst on her paddleboard. Like a pebble skipping on the water, the shoes took two delicate tumbles, floated for a second and sunk.

"The shoes!" Bethany screamed. Straddling the paddleboard, she tried to reach for them.

"Ivy, get them!"

The cool water of the Burrard Inlet hit her thighs, and Ivy gasped. She caught one shoe by the strap.

"It's over there!" From her perch on the paddleboard, Bethany pointed behind her.

Over here, the water rose to Ivy's waist. Her teeth started chattering. She grabbed the shoe and marched back to the shore.

God, she couldn't believe this was her life.

"Hey! You left me," Bethany said.

"I'm cold," Ivy said. She held out the sodden pair of shoes.

"I don't want those. They're ruined! You are going to have to tell the company. I wouldn't be surprised if they made you pay for them."

"I didn't take them in the water!"

"Whatever. I'll tell them it was my brilliant PR Strategist's idea. They'll send you the bill. And Ivy? I don't like how you still have that bandage on your face. It's been like four days. I don't want to work with you anymore."

"What do you mean?"

"I don't feel that you are good for my confidence," Bethany said.

The influencer flipped her highlighted hair over her shoulder, threw the paddleboard down on the sand, and walked away.

Ivy looked toward her old condo. Her old life. Why did things keep getting worse?

The halls of the apartment building were quiet for once, except for the music blaring from their apartment.

Holton had company, and she wasn't in the mood for people. Ivy sighed.

"Ivy! Have a glass of bubbly!" Holton pressed a stemmed glass into her hand.

She gulped it almost without thinking. "What's the occasion?"

"Someone's gotten himself a lead!" Jerome, Holton's on-again, off-again boyfriend, said.

He opened the door for her. "You look wet in a bad way. Did you go swimming with your clothes on?"

"Long story," Ivy said.

Sipping the glass of champagne, she squeezed past a bundle of people by the door.

CHAPTER TEN – IVY

"Congrats Holton!"

"Isn't it fantastic?" Holton smiled, kissing her on the cheek.

"Hi Emery," Ivy said. She suddenly felt shy. It was the first time she had seen Emery since being fired. But Emery slung an arm around her.

"Isn't it amazing? I'm so proud of my brother. And horribly jealous. He leaves tomorrow morning to go film on location for six months."

"Holton, that's great!" Ivy said.

"Yeah, sorry to leave you in the lurch, but Amanda and Flo have agreed to take over my lease." Holton gestured to the two she had passed on her way in.

"Oh. That's nice." Placing the empty glass of champagne on the coffee table, she smiled at the guests and escaped to her room.

Behind the closed door, she hugged a pillow to her chest. Losing her job and the roof over her head in one day was too much.

Not wanting to shower with houseguests, she threw on a sweatshirt and yoga pants. She got in bed, pulling the blankets up to her chin.

A soft knock sounded on her door.

"Ivy, it's me. Can I come in?"

"Sure, Emery."

"Hey, I know this isn't great news for you." Emery sat on the end of the bed.

"I'm happy for Holton. He's a great guy and a talented actor. It's nice that someone saw that," Ivy said into the blankets.

"Yeah, but he should have waited instead of giving up the apartment to his friends. Ivy, you need to go home."

She shook her head. "Emery, I don't have a home. Gabe kicked me out."

Admitting what happened between her and Gabe had been hard, but Emery had been kind and a good friend to her.

"You bought that condo with your hard-earned money. Right now, *you* have nowhere to go. Gabe has family here and friends. He can find somewhere else to go if he doesn't want you home."

Ivy stared at Emery. "You're not mad at me?"

Emery shrugged. "I was afraid to take your side at work, and I should have stood up for you. It was on your personal account, and I've seen co-workers post worse. I'm mad about how Gabe has treated you."

"I saw him the other night at an event. He thawed towards me a bit." Ivy touched her bandaged cheek.

"Maybe he's cooled down enough to come to his senses. But as of Friday, you don't have a home. You look like you need a shower, and this party will go all night long. Want me to drive you?"

"No, I want my car if he doesn't let me in," Ivy said. "I wonder if he changed the locks."

"Ivy, if you can't get in, call me, and you can crash on my couch tonight. My roommate is at her boyfriend's. But it's your home."

"You're right. He shouldn't have kicked me out." She threw off the blankets.Someone saying it out loud lit a fuse in her. She grabbed a bag from her closet and started packing. Damn it. She shouldn't have suffered for trying to do the right thing. Gabe shouldn't have thrown her out of their condo. He promised to take care of her. She did something he didn't like, and suddenly all the promises became dust.

"That's a girl," Emery said. "And send your resume out. Metric needed to find more budget dollars. You were an easy target."

"Really?" Ivy squeaked.

All these months, she thought she wouldn't be a good hire because of the post she made and Metric's swift action in firing her. She had sent out an occasional resume, but she hadn't taken on a job search seriously.

"Yeah. Many clients left, Ivy. Like Cherry Nails."

She hated how much Gabe messed with her confidence.

"Thanks, Emery. I'll let you know how it goes."

CHAPTER TEN – IVY

"Go get them," Emery said, hugging her.

Ivy kissed Holton's cheek on the way out. "Good luck. I'm going home tonight. Party on."

Holton raised his eyebrows and gave her a high-five.

"Come on, Holton! Let's do shots!" Jerome called.

Smiling, Ivy left the party.

At her old building, the concierge waved at her. She pressed the button for her floor and, holding her breath, she put her key in the lock.

He hadn't changed the locks. "Thank god."

She had missed this place with its views and space. As if she was afraid of being kicked out, she raced down the hall, threw off her clothes and turned the taps on, starting the shower.

CHAPTER ELEVEN – GABE

Gabe grabbed the wall, swaying as the migraine grounded into his temples with force enough that he wondered if he'd stay on his feet. He unlocked the door to the condo, not bothering to turn on the lights. He gulped down a glass of water.

He had spent the last six hours as security for a web girl operation on the west side. Another gig Erik sent his way. He guarded the backdoor, making sure only people who belonged there entered and made sure each woman got to her car safely.

Afterwards, he hit the gym, weights, rowing machine, and treadmill. His muscles burned, but he needed to get Ivy out of his head, and ever since he saw her at the event, he couldn't. All the expressions on her diamond-shaped face floated through his mind like a slow-motion movie. Her surprise at seeing him, the look of stunned hurt on her face and the one that stabbed his heart, the flash of sadness in her eyes when she hurled the line about him breaking promises.

It didn't matter how hard he went at the gym. It didn't stop his thoughts from returning to Ivy.

CHAPTER ELEVEN – GABE

He placed the glass in the sink and strolled down the hall and into the dark bedroom. Shucking his pants, he tossed them on the chair in the corner and slid into bed.

The scent of the shampoo Ivy used flooded his nostrils, and his arm flung over a pile of blankets. He couldn't get that woman out of his head no matter what. He turned on his side, then flopped to his back as his brain made the connection.

"What the hell, Ivy?" He flicked on the bedside light, wincing,

Ivy murmured in her sleep.

He put a hand on her, rolling her towards him. She placed a hand on his arm, then pulled it back as if he was the forbidden hot stove.

"You weren't home. I needed to go to bed." Her husky voice brought to mind past morning wake-ups.

"Why. Are. You. Here?" he spat out the words.

Ivy clutched the blankets to her chest. "This is my home."

"It isn't. It hasn't been your home since you hit publish on that post." He rubbed his temples, the sharp pain making him hiss through his teeth.

"Gabe." Her voice wobbled, pulled at his heart, and suddenly, the tiredness he had felt all these months settled heavily on his shoulders. Not physically tired, but tired of being angry.

"Today, I waded in the water of Burrard Inlet to rescue a pair of overpriced shoes I am probably going to have to pay for. My one client fired me. My roommate sublet the apartment I've been living in since August. I was tired, cold, and had nowhere else to go. You didn't buy me out of this place. You just told me to get out."

He swallowed, his mouth dry at her words. The absolute hollowness in her voice cut through his anger. "You could have gone to a hotel or a friend's house."

"I don't have much money. I've still been paying my part of the mortgage here." Gabe glanced away. He should have called her. But maybe it was his way of holding on to a piece of her.

"And most of my friends stopped talking to me months ago. Emery said I could crash on her couch tonight if you were going to throw me out of my home again."

Geez, when she put it like that, he was a complete asshole. He should have handled the finances. The hurt she caused, the betrayal of trust, was too much for him to deal with.

"I sent you two thousand dollars." Only when he saw her at the product launch and realized he hadn't been taking care of her.

"Thanks," Ivy muttered.

"I'm so tired of being angry at you."

"I'm tired of that, too."

"But I don't know how to stop being mad at you."

"I never meant to hurt you!" Her voice rang with insistence.

"It's hard to believe that when your actions were calculated to hurt me." She wouldn't meet his eyes.

"Not to hurt you, to *stop* you from signing on with them and making a mistake."

"So you've said, Ivy." He clutched his head in his palms, wincing.

"I can get your pills for you?"

"Okay," Gabe said.

Ivy threw off the blankets and strolled out of the room, gloriously naked. He knew exactly how gorgeous she was, how soft her skin was, how sensitive her thick nipples were. He missed her. By the blood rushing to his cock, his body craved her, even as his emotions were trying to repeal her.

Ivy handed him a glass of water and his medication. He took it. Staring at her in the soft light of the bedroom from the outside lights, all the times they had in this room circled through his mind.

"What is it?" Ivy said. Her eyebrows furrowed. He saw the fear on her face, and it was like a punch to his gut. His anger caused him to be a jerk, and he didn't want that. Not right now.

CHAPTER ELEVEN – GABE

Her being here with him eased some of the pain he felt. He set the water glass on the nightstand and leaned back against the pillows.

"Do you think I can stop being mad at you for one night?" He reached out, lightly dancing his fingers along her arm.

She turned her head away from him at the question.

He knew he was being unfair. But right now, right here, it was impossible to resist her, and he didn't want to.

"I wish you would stop being mad at me forever."

"I want you so bad, and I know I can set it aside for tonight." He took, grabbed her hands and pulled her close to him. She dug in her heels. He pulled her harder. She giggled and fell into bed beside him.

She smiled, revealing her dimples, softening the hard angles of her face and making him feel like he won the game because she didn't give that smile to just anyone. He always thought of that expression as the smile she only gave him.

"If one night is all you'll give me, I'll take it," Ivy said.

He touched his forehead to hers, breathing in her scent, his eyes drinking in her familiar features. They had been through so much together. She was his. And he never thought she wouldn't be with him. As soon as his hands touched her hips, the hurt in him eased. Touching her was like coming home. His hands moved to her breasts, cupping them, squeezing.

Her soft cry urged him on.

He pushed her nipples in on themselves, and she threw her head back, her eyes closed in pleasure.

He scraped her nipples with this thumbnail and grinned as her hips bucked. "You like it so much." He grabbed her nipples and pulled them hard.

"Yes, please," Ivy said.

Her plea, the permission he needed.

He pulled her nipples, twisting them in his fingers. Ivy pushed down on his shoulders, tears leaking out of the corner of her eyes. Damn, it made him high. He wanted more tears. He pulled her to him roughly. His skin felt heated all over, next to her cool soft flesh.

He crushed his mouth to hers, and her lips parted, inviting him in. He kissed her, closing his eyes as her scent flooded him, her touch, and the rightness of how she felt in his hands. He cupped her neck, sweeping his hands over her back, massaging her shoulder blades. Damn, he knew this was unfair. It wasn't going to cease his anger, but right now, he needed her. He drank in her taste, feasting on her mouth.

"Gabe."

He tore his mouth from her, pushing her off him. Damn it. He couldn't do this. The way she said his name, with that mix of pain and love, was too much.

He clutched his head and jumped off the bed, trying to calm himself. To think he could just throw off all his anger for a night was laughable. Hearing his name from her sparked a fresh wave of anger, and what did that say?

"Please, Sir."

He turned back to the bed. "Fuck."

His heart and head were not in agreement. She was on her knees on the bed, her head on the pillow, holding her ass cheeks apart.

"Damn you." He stalked over and slapped her ass so hard that his palm stung. He spanked her, every hit of his palm against her flesh as if it were a drum he was trying to beat his emotions on.

And he landed his palm across her hot ass again. And again.

And every time he struck her flesh, she mewled. This woman was the damn devil, and he had missed drinking the sin.

He reached between her legs and roughly fingered her soaking wet pussy.

"So sloppy for me."

CHAPTER ELEVEN – GABE

"Yes! I've missed this," Ivy said.

Yeah, so had he, but admitting it would be giving up some of his anger, and he didn't want to do that.

She thrashed, twisting as he plunged two fingers into her wetness. Her cries of pleasure were an invisible line to his cock, making it lengthen and harden with every little whimper that left her mouth.

He pulled his fingers out of her cunt and jammed them into her mouth. "Clean these for me. I don't know where this pussy has been."

She trembled at his words, shaking her head, but she hollowed her cheeks and sucked his fingers cleaned.

Ivy had always been a target for his sea of raging emotions for whatever reason. *Because she's the one who never rejected you, asshole.* His brain threw up that thought mockingly.

She vibrated under him, pushing her hips towards his hand, demanding he give her more and give in.

Because she was hot and gorgeous, wet and willing, he couldn't resist. Oh god, how she was willing. He grabbed the lube from the nightstand. He climbed behind her and lubed his throbbing cock.

"Yes! Put your cock deep inside me, Sir. I want to know if it's as good as I remember."

He settled behind her, gripping her hips, and posed his cock's head at her entrance. Grabbing her shoulder, he bit into the soft flesh.

"God, that's too much." She thrust her ass back against him, telling him to continue.

Her hips rose off the bed, and he thrust, shallow and quick.

Ivy mewled.

How did he live without this? His anger had deprived him of it. Gabe knew deep in his heart that he had hurt this woman.

He grabbed her hair, yanking her head back and slung an arm around her shoulder, angling her up, so he got even deeper.

"Dammit, yes!"

"Take it, Princess," Gabe commanded.

His balls slapped against her mound; Gabe closed his eyes, feeling the sweat roll between his shoulders.

Dammit, this was so hot. He was going to come in her, any moment.

"Gabe."

He let go of her hair, his palm clamping over her mouth and nose. "Don't say my name."

By the new pool of liquid, he knew she loved that. He pressed his palm harder against her face, her saliva on his palm, feeling her pussy clench around his cock as she mewled, and he hammered hard and fast into her.

Each stroke in her wetness was like dipping into electric fire. All his nerve endings buzzed.

"Yes, whimper for it."

So damn good.

Her pussy drew him in deeper, fire licking up his spine.

He tilted her neck up, her eyes so dilated, so huge.

He pounded her mercilessly, his hips pushing into her, deeper and deeper. He felt her walls grip him, close around him, her body tense. Under his palm, she screamed, tears running down her face.

If she wanted him, she was going to take it. He drilled through her orgasm and kept going as she cried out, trying to bite his palm.

Ah! This was the rush of dominance he missed. The fucking power and control. Her pussy shook with aftershocks. He kept blazing through them, hearing her pant. Her sharp intake of breath made it sweeter.

"Please, Sir," came her mumbled plea. He brought his hand away from her mouth and pushed her face down on the pillow.

Fuck, yeah. He didn't know if her cry was for him to finish and let up on her, but that whisper of pain in her voice drove him over the edge. His orgasm yanked all his muscles, catapulting him into a blaze of pleasure.

Black spots danced behind his eyes as he released in her hot depth.

CHAPTER ELEVEN – GABE

He let out a groan of his own, releasing his grip on her as he removed himself from her warmth. Ivy shuffled, so her head laid on the pillow, and she looked up at him with her dewy green eyes, leaning forward to kiss him.

He turned his cheek, running his hand along her jaw.

"Now, can you say you're sorry?"

Like a light going out, she frowned. She threw the blankets off and glared at him.

"So much for putting it behind us for one night. No, Gabe, I am not sorry. I will not apologize for doing what I believed was right. I'll take the couch."

Damn her. Why couldn't she admit she was wrong? Why didn't she want what they had?

"No. I need to be out early. I'll take it." He didn't want to leave her. He wanted to cuddle her, stroke her, and tell her it would be okay. But she never wanted to be touched after sex, and by the anger in her tone, she didn't want that now.

Her harsh laser stare followed him as he grabbed the pillow and blanket and closed the bedroom door.

CHAPTER TWELVE – IVY

He said one night.

Yet he barely gave her that. Ivy closed her eyes, luxuriating in the jets in her much-missed shower. His anger was real and raw, and she wondered how he would have used that anger if he was at Club Bandit or if it wasn't a sleepy tumble-into-bed scene.

The thing was, she wasn't afraid of his fury. It was always there. Gabe Arthur wasn't chill.

It didn't scare her because he treated everyone around him with respect and courtesy. He wasn't violent. He never threw anything or hit her, and once they started D/s, it's like he found an outlet for his emotions. She took what he gave, and he expressed how proud he was of her for doing so and heaped her with praise. That's how it had always been between them.

She dried off and tiptoed down the hall to check on him, early morning light enough to see by from the opened curtains.

He was stretched out on the couch-the dark green one she had fallen in love with when they first moved into this condo-his knees kind of between the chaise part and the seat part.

The sex tonight, the raw push-pull sex, ripped her part. But it had felt so damn right to feel his muscles above her, the weight of his arm around

CHAPTER TWELVE – IVY

her shoulders, his palm over her mouth, to breathe in his familiar musky scent.

She stood back, knowing that if she touched him, he'd startle awake.

God, she wished things were different. That he would stop demanding from her something she wasn't going to give. He claimed it was only for a night, and he didn't want her, but his cock driving into her so hard she was still sore this morning said he did. Ivy climbed back into bed, remembering the heated touch and how the orgasm was so powerful that it left her wanting more.

She tossed and turned for another half hour. Then Ivy reached into her nightstand drawer and found her favourite vibe. Gabe hadn't thrown it out. Closing her eyes, she switched it to the gentlest setting. Biting her lip, she remembered the feel of his muscular hand over her mouth. How hard his cock was. The gentle vibrations gave her a pleasant, little orgasm, and it was enough to shut her brain down, and a part of her took delight from the fact that he didn't control her orgasms anymore. She used to think she could soothe his angst, that D/s turned it down and gave it focus. Now she wasn't so sure.

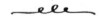

Even with the interrupted sleep, she had slept better than she had in months.

Grabbing the first piece of clothing she found, which was a t-shirt of Gabe's from over the chair, she made her way out into the kitchen, blinking at the light. She had missed this bright and warm, cheerful, open space.

Her space. With her photos of sunflowers on the wall, her sunray mirror above the couch, the kitchen cabinets she had upcycled into bookcases against the back wall, with her collection of multi-coloured vases. So little in this space, Gabe had changed. Missing were the photos of them from their years together.

On the counter sat her French press and her favourite coffee. Ivy shook her head as she started to make the coffee. What did this mean? Was this an offering? An apology?

He was angry with her but left her coffee.

When the coffee was ready, she poured a mug full and opened the doors to the balcony, her favourite iron chair and table waiting for her.

She had missed this, looking out towards the ocean, the sun on her face as she sipped her coffee. It was such a little thing, but she couldn't find this space on her own in this overpriced city. The apartment she shared with Holton had the smallest balcony, and they couldn't fit a chair on it, never mind a plant stand and a table for six.

She had worked so hard to buy this condo, rising in the ranks at Metric. With one post, it came crashing down.

Emery was right. She needed to get herself together because she couldn't rely on Gabe.

Ivy sighed. She had to get on with it, and she had spent too much time wallowing in her hurt.

Picking up her phone, she dialled her mom.

"Ivy! Hello, honey. How are you this morning?"

"Hi, Mom." Ivy took a sip of her coffee. Her mom's voice made her feel as if she could cry and let out all her pent-up emotions, and she didn't want to do that right now. "What are you doing today?"

"I'm going to help Dad with cleaning the south field. He's already been out there for almost four hours. I have a rehearsal later tonight."

"That's good." For a moment, Ivy wanted to be back there, helping her dad clean the fields and helping her mother get all her stuff together for the rehearsal.

"Ivy, what's going on?"

"I think I'm ready to look for a new job."

CHAPTER TWELVE – IVY

A pause where she could hear her mother smiling. "Honey, that's wonderful! Someone out there is going to see how talented you are."

"My last client. I mean, it didn't work out."

"Ivy, I know Metric firing you shook your confidence, but posting pictures for a social media influencer isn't what you wanted to do. It's okay that your foray into personal PR didn't work out."

"Yeah, I know." Her throat felt tight. She was so lucky to have caring, supportive parents. She hadn't told her parents about the breakup between her and Gabe, but she had told them Metric fired her, skirting around the reason.

"It's weird to look for jobs. I don't know what Metric will say or if they'll give me a reference."

"You got really lucky right out of school, Ivy. Maybe your bosses at Metric won't give you a reference, but your coworkers will."

"Thanks, Mom."

"Anytime. And don't be afraid to go out of your comfort zone. I know you love Vancouver, but look everywhere, even in Calgary."

Ivy laughed. "You just want me closer."

"Can you blame me?" She could hear the smile in her mom's voice. "Call me later. Let me know how it went."

"I will. Tell Daddy I'll call him tonight." Ivy said.

"Better tomorrow. You know he isn't going to stop working until the job is done and then come in and crash on the couch."

"Yeah." Ivy's throat grew tight. Her parents had been together forever, and she wished her relationship could have that kind of familiarity.

"Break a leg, Ivy," her mom said.

"Bye, Mom." Ivy clicked off, feeling lighter, determined. She finished her coffee and packed her laptop bag. Her cell buzzed as she stepped out the door.

"Well, hello, roomie. You remembered me."

"I am a horrible, *awful* person. Can you ever forgive me?" Holton asked.

"You're not awful," Ivy said as she stepped into the elevator.

"Yes, I am. You didn't have to leave, and they aren't moving in right away. You have until the end of the month, even longer if you need it. I did the same thing Gabe did to you."

Ivy sighed. That thought had crossed her mind. "Not samesies at all. You didn't promise to love me, take care of me, and protect me. You had a break you've been longing for and got caught up in a whirlwind."

"Cake tonight?" Holton offered.

"Yes, you can bribe me with cake."

"See you at seven," Holton said.

Shaking her head, Ivy smiled, pushing open the doors to the bright sunshine.

Taking her time, she wandered through the neighbourhood, stopping at the fancy clothing store. The woman inside recognized her and asked if she needed anything.

"Just browsing today," Ivy said, fingering a well-cut pair of pants with a beautiful matching dove grey blazer. She loved buying clothes from this place and had many pieces from the high-end store in her closet.

She waved on her way out. Maybe she'd get a callback and then buy that suit for her interview.

As she rounded the corner to her favourite coffee shop, she stopped as she caught a flash of red hair through the window. Ella Riddell, Zee's wife, was sitting at a table in the corner, next to a woman with curly black hair and glasses. Ivy bit her lip. She couldn't go in there and face Ella, not after that interview with Zee.

Ivy recognized the curly-haired woman as Josie, the caterer who made fantastic bread and catered a few dinners for the Bandit Brothers.

She started to turn, to head home.

CHAPTER TWELVE – IVY

"Excuse me." A woman with a stroller was trying to get through the doorway, right where Ivy stood.

Ivy moved back, opening the door, so she didn't run into the woman. Because that's all she needed, to run over a baby. She snorted.

Standing in line, she focused ahead, not looking over at the table.

She ordered a decaffeinated ice tea and a blueberry scone.

"Ivy! It's so nice to see you. Would you like to join us for a moment?"

Ivy swallowed. Ella's warm eyes held no judgement.

She bit her lip. "Hi, Ella. Okay, I would love to join you."

Grabbing her stuff, she followed the red-haired woman over to the small table in the corner.

"Josie, do you remember Ivy?"

"Yes! You gave me great advice about my logo."

"I did?" Ivy's voice came out high-pitched.

"Yes, right after I dropped food off at Ella and Zee's?"

Ivy frowned. Her life had been divided into two halves, before the post and after the post.

"At the labour day party almost two years ago. Ella and Zee ran out of alcohol, and Jordan knocked on their neighbour's door, asking for a drink in exchange for a song?"

"Yes," Ella smiled. "I had never seen so many people in the neighbourhood out."

"He brought people together," Ivy said. She missed the always upbeat, always there man. Jordan had a way of making people feel more relaxed in their own skin. The Bandit Brothers weren't the same without him.

"Sorry to bring it up," Josie said.

"No, it's good to remember. And it's nice seeing you again." Ivy smiled.

"I should go. I have a dinner order to finish. Ella, I'll see you next week at the soup kitchen." Josie grabbed her crutch, stood up from her chair and waved.

"Now I remember. I told her to use a different font and drop the white bread basket from her logo because she did more. I think I told her just to use her name."

"You did. Josie's catering business is booming. Your suggestions gave her a lift. Ivy, how are you?"

Ivy took a sip of her drink, searching Ella's face. She still saw no sign of judgement. But she didn't know how much everyone knew. When the other members that went to Club Bandit stopped talking to her, she assumed everyone knew the details. And though not all of them were on social media, many were, so how could they not see the post she made?

"I'm okay. The roommate I was staying with got a new gig. I needed somewhere to go. So last night, I went home to the condo I shared with Gabe."

"Did that go as you hoped?"

Ivy shook her head, pressing the heels of her palms into her eyes. God, she was tired of shedding tears over this. "In part. But not really. Anyway, what are you working on here, Ella?" Ivy peered over Ella's laptop screen.

Ella gave her a gentle smile and turned her laptop so she could see the front page of her website. Ella made and sold fetish wear and corsets and donated the proceeds to a foundation she and Zee had.

"I want to increase online sales directly through the website. I'm not having a great amount of luck with it."

"May I?" Ivy reached for the laptop as Ella nodded.

"I think you need warmer colours, for starters. Also, there is nothing here about all proceeds being donated to the foundation."

"I thought that would detract people," Ella said.

"Nope. People like causes. You need to give people an option to buy directly from your social media, too," Ivy said.

"Good idea. I didn't think of that," Ella said.

"It gives people something to scroll to when they click your posts." Ivy passed the laptop back to Ella.

CHAPTER TWELVE – IVY

"I'll mull over your suggestions, thanks."

"Let me know if you need any help. Your online store interface could be more current, too."

"I can take all the help, but I don't want to take advantage of your time."

"I'm not doing much with my time right now," Ivy said. "I'm happy to help."

"I can't do anything about club business. That's Zee's department, not mine. But I have a friend looking for a co-host of a podcast. It's paid."

Ivy pushed her hair behind her ears. "What's the podcast on?"

"Sex and kink and things like that," Ella said.

"I don't know. I've done nothing like that before."

"Julien is a great guy. This is a pet project of his."

"I'll think about it. I came here to start the job search. It's time I find something or try to."

"I don't think you'll have a problem, Ivy. Sometimes things are bigger in our head than in reality."

"Maybe." Ivy shifted in her seat.

"Can I give Julien your name?"

"Yes, sure," Ivy said.

"Perfect. I need to get to physio, and my girls are home tonight for dinner, and I have a hundred more errands. Talk to you soon."

"Bye, Ella. And thanks."

Eating her scone, she brought her laptop out of her bag, set it on the table next to her phone and plugged in her headphones. She flipped open the screen and logged into her social media accounts for the first time in seven months. After Metric fired her, she locked down all her accounts and stopped posting online.

Scrolling through her notifications, she saw she didn't miss much. Opening her messages, she saw a few messages of support from her co-workers. A couple of them told her that she was too good to be fired and let her know if she needed anything. There were a couple of troll messages and one that seemed a little creepy, a message saying she better stay out of it if she knew what was good for her. Out of what? Ivy frowned. That message seemed very specific. She clicked on it, and it led to a blank profile. She hit the block button and kept scrolling.

Emery and Ella were both correct. This had blown up so huge in her head that she had disconnected from the reality that people didn't care that much about it. Other than her bosses and Gabe.

She smiled, seeing a picture of her cousin Alice's baby in Alberta. Though her cousin had sent photos to her phone, it wasn't the same as the daily posting. Ivy liked a bunch of them, then sent her cousin a private message saying she was on the job search and asked if she knew anyone who was hiring.

She laughed, seeing her dad post pics of her new truck. Ivy commented, "You're right. Dad, the red does look good on you."

How could she be nervous about making a post? But as her fingers flew over the keys, she was. For the first time in seven months, she was putting herself out there. She made a post, telling everyone she was looking for work again, ready to take on a new PR role and let her know if anyone knew anything. As soon as the post went up, she logged out and spent the next half hour going through the online job postings.

She knew she should take anything, but she had worked so hard to get up the ladder that she didn't want to take a step down.

Her phone buzzed. Glancing at the number, she bit her lip. He was the last person she wanted to talk to. But she answered. "Hi, Cole."

"Hey, Ivy. Look, I just saw your post, and I think I might have something. I'll swing by later and check it out? I could bring beer and pizza."

She didn't like Cole. He was rude and arrogant, and she hated how he joined their father in putting down Gabe. After she had convinced him to sign on with their client at Metric, she saw too much of his personality to trust him fully. He would yell at the camera crew and the make-up people on the commercial set, and he was a complete ass to work with. Ivy had never been so relieved to have a file taken from her when Flint told her he was taking over all celebrities on that client's list. Gabe didn't need her to gain up on how awful Cole was, so she tried to keep the peace.

"I'm not sure what happened, but I've missed you, Ivy. Let's hang out together."

She was being silly. It was like the nerves she felt while making the post; she was just nervous about interacting with people again.

"Fine, Cole." He wasn't her favourite person, but he had been around more since retiring, and if he was trying, Ivy thought she and Gabe should, too.

"Great, I'll see you at seven."

Ivy bit her lip and texted Holton, rescheduling for tomorrow night.

She could do this. Taking charge of her life wasn't easy, but it wasn't as hard as it was in her head. Ivy fired off one more resume, closed up her laptop, and left the coffee shop.

Walking down to the beach, she checked the chime on her phone. She frowned. It was another weird message. "Saw that you're posting again. You need to stay quiet."

She wondered if it was from Bethany. The influencer was paranoid, and maybe she was worried that Ivy would share some behind-the-scenes stuff. She scoffed. Her meltdowns weren't that interesting. She called her former client and left a message, reminding her the last invoice was overdue. Walking up to the condo, she wondered where Gabe was and if he knew she had posted online. She wondered what he would think. *Maybe if he sees that I'm trying to get it together, he'll continue to unthaw.*

Last night had been intense, rough, and left her wanting more. It wasn't the action of a man who didn't want her.

She still loved him. But she wondered if Gabe could let her love him.

CHAPTER THIRTEEN – GABE

"You got to admit, it looks good," Nick Laurent said, his dark eyes peering through his steel wire-rimmed glasses.

Gabe shrugged at his best friend and fellow Bandit Brother. They were standing on the newly opened staircase in Club Bandit and had a direct view of the stage and the entire club, except for the hallway beside the bar that led to the private rooms. The new space had a playroom with a large window. People could stand outside and take in the scene, and there were plans for four private themed rooms up here.

"I'm surprised Zee didn't add more bedrooms," Gabe said.

"There are enough morning after rooms in the hallway. This was an excellent compromise."

When Zee took Club Bandit from the founders' only private status to open to the public, he hadn't been a fan of the decision. He liked private spaces where he knew everyone, and though Gabe didn't know every founding member well, he knew them on sight. The biggest problem that had come out of making Club Bandit open to the public was the cry for more morning-after rooms. But Zee didn't want to run a hotel, so those rooms were reserved only for founding members, whose fingerprints could open the locks. The increase in demand is what brought Zee to open up this third level and create extra space.

CHAPTER THIRTEEN – GABE

"I guess. What is Marrock building down there?" Gabe gestured to their friend.

"Some kind of new torture contraption," Nick said.

"Going to get a close-up."

As Gabe came down the stairs, it looked like a metal privacy screen. "You're building a gate?"

"No," Logan said. "It's going to be a cage around a bench."

"It's kind of weird." Gabe crossed his arms, peering at the contraption.

"Going to stand there or just offer commentary?"

Gabe jumped on stage and held the frame steady while Logan screwed in a padded leather board across the frames.

"She can sit here. There will be a rail midpoint," Logan explained. "So I can tie her to it. I can't wait to dole out punishments on this thing."

"If it holds weight," Nick commented. "It looks like something that belongs in my Grand-Mère's garden."

"Just wait until it's done," Logan said.

"Some punishment," Zee said. The owner of Club Bandit came from the stage's wings, dropping a toolbox by Logan.

"*Funishment*, whatever, a thing to torment my submissive on," Logan said.

"Hey, Gabe. Seen Ivy lately?"

Gabe ran his hand over his face. Guess he could tell them. "She's been at the condo for the past couple of nights."

"You came to your senses." Logan grinned.

"I don't know. We're not exactly back together."

It had been hell to stay away from her. She left him stir fry in the fridge and a ready-made protein drink.

He enjoyed seeing her towel on the towel rack. He liked smelling her shampoo in the bathroom and the lingering scent of French-pressed brewed coffee when he came home.

He had been on another job for Stone Security the past two nights and must have just missed her. Though he wanted to feel her, to touch her again, it was easier to not be in the same room with her. At least that's what he told himself.

He wanted her, but he knew that night had been a mistake. He couldn't look at her without feeling angry, without being reminded of the hurt she caused him.

"I wish I could punish her," Gabe said.

"Why don't you?" Nick clapped him on the back.

Gabe's hand curled into a fist. Except for that one time when he punished her for missing dinner at his dad's. Punishment wasn't part of their dynamic. He and Ivy kept their kink to the club or in the bedroom.

He was a Dominant, but he never thought of himself as the strict Dom who needed control over all things. But Ivy had asked him for more. If his father wasn't so controlling towards his mother, Gabe might not have had the fear that kept him back.

"We don't have punishments as part of our relationship."

"To give a punishment, there has to be established rules," Zee chimed in.

"Or she could agree to it as a way of wiping the slate clean?" Nick suggested.

"There's no one way to do D/s." Zee shrugged.

Logan placed his drill back into the open toolbox. "I don't know if you can let your anger go, Gabe. The thing about having punishments is it's done and over. You can't hold on to it after."

Gabe avoided meeting Logan's eyes. His friend knew him too well, and Logan was the only Bandit Brother who didn't seem as bothered by Ivy's behaviour as the rest of them. But then again, Logan Marrock believed in living life in the moment. That was a freedom Gabe envied.

"But what if it would help you agree to let it go and give her a second chance?" Nick pressed. "You've been miserable and broody since the summer."

"I don't know. She's not sorry," Gabe said.

"Do you *need* her to be sorry?" Zee asked. "Or do you *need* her to realize her behaviour wasn't acceptable? Or like Nick said, is it a one-time and done thing?"

"Ivy knows what she did wasn't acceptable to you, Gabe," Logan said.

"I don't want to be angry with her, but every time I look at her and remember what happened last summer, it all comes back. We were happy, and she ruined that."

"Yeah, I thought you were going to be married before I was," Logan said.

"You're not married yet," Nick said.

"Close to it. Living with Harper is sweet."

"And Xander and Ares? You're not feeling crowded?" Gabe spat out the words.

"Nope. I get to see my submissive every day and have her all night long, and sharing has its perks." Logan grinned.

Gabe scoffed. "I still can't believe you share with our boss."

Logan grinned. "That has its own perks."

Zee laughed. "You make it look so easy, man."

"If you want to work it out with Ivy, go for it. Ask her if she would accept punishment and agree to what that would mean," Nick said.

"She came and applied for membership," Zee said.

His shoulders tensed up. "What did you say?"

"I told her I wasn't sure how comfortable you would be with her here, and unfortunately, we know about her history of outing someone."

"That's harsh." Logan lifted his contraption, his thick biceps budging. Nick stepped up to help him.

"You don't think it's true?" Nick said.

"I think people make mistakes," Logan said. "Ivy tried to talk to you. You ignored her. She tried to reach out to each of us, and we didn't listen. This was something really important to her. She lost a lot after making that post. You lost one contract."

"Yes, I feel like an asshole. What are you trying to do, make me feel worse?" Before he knew it, he was in Marrock's space, standing chest to chest.

The giant man towered over him and stepped forward, placing his hands on Gabe's shoulders. "I think there's a punching bag in the office if you ask Zee nicely. Otherwise, you should probably leave now and figure out what you're going to do with your girl."

"She's not my girl anymore." Gabe shook off Logan's hands, stepping back.

"Then why does it bother you so much?" Logan raised an eyebrow.

"I don't have time for this, anyway. Good luck with your device."

"You can borrow it for Ivy when she's wearing your collar again." Logan grinned.

"Sorry to drag you out. It wasn't meant as a confrontation," Nick said.

"It's fine. Ivy showing up tilted my world a bit."

"I want to see you happy again, Doc. And I think Ivy is good for you."

Gabe shook his head. "There's no going back, right?"

"Nope," Nick said.

"Find a girl to play with, have your own fun." Gabe clapped him on the shoulder.

Nick gave his one-shoulder shrug. "Are you working for Stone tonight?"

"Yeah. I haven't heard from Axis Management."

"Go talk to them, Gabe. Tell them you need in. I'm sure they would rather have you than you moonlighting."

"Okay. See you." Gabe gave Nick a man-hug, got in his car and drove to their condo. He had hours before his gig with Stone Security tonight.

CHAPTER THIRTEEN – GABE

He wanted to see Ivy. Wanted to see the light in her green eyes, see that sly, sexy smile.

Ivy had been the only person who encouraged him to play his guitar, to take his music seriously. When she came across a band needing a new guitarist, she urged him to go audition. But he didn't have the nerve. His father's voice telling him he was okay, but Cole was better than him, was a loud echo in his head he couldn't shake.

His past wasn't Ivy's fault. She had embraced him, despite it. Despite only being a medic and before the offer came from Axis Management, she didn't comment on how much money he made.

Hell, they were so young then. Pulling into his parking space, he shook off the memories. Maybe it was possible to start over.

He hoped Ivy was there; he smiled as he rode the elevator up to his floor. Turning the corner to the hallway, he stopped.

He stopped in his tracks. Cole was leaning on the doorway, crowding Ivy. But it was the expression on his face that had Gabe curling his hands into fists. Ever since they were kids, Cole wanted what Gabe had. If Gabe got a new pair of jeans, Cole wanted them, even if they didn't fit him. Gabe went to science camp one year, and Cole begged their dad to let him go even though he hated science.

When Cole got serious about hockey, the relief Gabe felt about his brother's attention being off of him was like breathing clean air after inhaling smog.

Cole did nothing other than belittle Ivy. Gabe's stomach churned. But did Cole want her? He shook the thought away. Cole had been with his girlfriend, Chantal, for over a year, and she came with money and connections, not the kind Ivy had.

Gabe marched over to them. His brother turned, the easy much-photographed smile flashing across his face.

"Hey, Gabe. What's up, man?"

"Cole. Didn't know you were coming by."

Ivy's eyes darted from him to his brother, and Gabe wondered why she was acting so nervous. She leaned against the wall beside their door.

"Ivy posted that she was looking for work. I came by to talk to her about a job. There's some pizza if you're hungry.'

His brother might be taller, but Gabe weight trained three days a week and had muscle on him.

"Not hungry," Gabe said.

"Okay. We should go for beers this weekend." Cole slapped the doorframe.

"Sure," Gabe said.

"Ivy, good catching up with you," Cole said. He waved and strode down the hall, whistling as if he didn't have a care in the world and Cole Arthur didn't.

"Tell me. What was he doing here?"

"Exactly what he said," Ivy murmured.

"You know I would rather not see him." Gabe held the door for her.

"I didn't know when you were coming home."

"I'm supposed to tell you now?"

Ivy flinched at his raised voice. He put a hand on her shoulder.

"Look, seeing him always makes me tense up. Sorry."

"Don't worry about it."

"Thanks for leaving me dinner."

"It's no big deal," Ivy said.

He cursed. So much for coming home with ideas for making it work. His brother had screwed it up. No, his angry reaction to his brother screwed it up.

"Damn it." Gabe grabbed Ivy's wrist and pulled her close to his chest. He planted his mouth on hers, his tongue plunging into her. Yes, he needed her taste. After seeing Cole, she wasn't his target. She was his balm, just like she used to be.

CHAPTER THIRTEEN – GABE

Her hands roamed around his back. Her mewling noises made his cock hard. He stalked her to the edge of the kitchen table. Hooking his leg between hers, he lifted her onto the table as she squealed.

"It's a very big deal to see you with that asshole," Gabe said. He quickly threw her shirt over her head, revealing a dark red lacy bra. God, her beautiful breasts. He pinched and twisted while kissing her, taking off her bra. Dominating her mouth, biting and nipping her lips. Her legs came around his, and he nudged them down with his waist.

"I didn't mean anything by it," Ivy said.

"I don't want to talk right now." Gabe's hands went to her skirt. He shoved it down, rolling down her leggings, ripping off her panties. "I want to fuck you hard and fast. I hope your cunt is wet and ready."

Ivy grabbed his arms, pulling him towards her. She kissed him hungrily.

Talking was the problem. He wanted to fuck her senseless and see if he could drive out the anger he had for her.

He fumbled with his belt buckle, trying to get his jeans off. Ivy lifted from the table, her hands at his waistband, and he didn't stop her.

His cock throbbed in her hand as she stroked him; he groaned.

Her tongue poked out, a sly smile of triumph on her face

Nope, can't have that.

He removed her hand from his cock, directing her down, so she laid flat on her back on the table.

"Spread your legs wide, you greedy little sub."

She squealed and held her legs wide open for him.

Dragging her to the table's edge, he settled her knees over his shoulders.

He slid in, inch by inch, feeling the warmth of her pussy, feeling how needy she was for him. He gritted his teeth and slowly dragged his cock through her wetness.

"Gabe!" Ivy drummed her heels on the back of his shoulders.

"Did you want something?"

"Yes! You in me! Now!"

"Demanding girl."

His fingers parted her labia while his cock eased in and out, and her hips came off the table in protest.

"Now, you bastard."

"Oh please, I can make you wait all night long," Gabe said.

"You want to fuck me."

"Yep, I do, and I will on my own time," Gabe said. He thrust once, staying buried in her heated pussy.

She groaned, her fingers dug into his shoulders, trying to speed him to action. He laughed, her frustration and impatience so damn cute.

"You could be my little cockwarmer. I can stay in you just like this."

She leaned on his chest, turning her face from him. Her lips grazed his nipple, setting off sparks of heated desire. Fuck, this girl lit him up.

"Please," she whispered against his chest. A wall of heat separated them by inches. Her passion and his anger were a combustible combination. He slowly started to thrust right to the hilt and then stopped.

She protested, drumming her heels on him, her fingers digging into his biceps. "Sir."

His mouth came over hers as he slowly dragged his cock through her heat, pulling in and out.

She cried and bounced on him, a fine sheen of sweat starting to break on her brow. Her body hot. It was a different kind of undone, and it suited his mood.

Ivy sat up, deepening his angle, her hands on his forearms, her nails scratching him. He slanted his mouth to hers and kissed her hard, biting her lip.

"Put those claws away," he said.

She made her hands into fists and thudded them on him.

"Now, Princess, that's no way to get your way." He used his sternest Dom tone.

CHAPTER THIRTEEN – GABE

"Sir, please fuck me." She nipped his shoulder. "Like you mean it." Her green eyes glowed, the words gritted out, angry and frustrated, desperation clear in her voice.

Holding her hips, he drilled into her. She gasped. Her tits bounced against his chest, and he fucking loved it. He went harder, pounding her, and she grabbed him with every muscle she had, her softness against his hardness.

Her expressions flicked from pleasure to pain as he bit her shoulder slightly.

"Yes! Fuck yes," she cried as his hand wrapped around her, rocking deep into her, melding their bodies as close as possible, so there wasn't even an inch between her skin and his. Sweat covered his back and rolled down his sides. Right here, right now, he was fucking owning her.

"*Babylon.*"

Her pussy clamped so tight around his dick that he couldn't hold off another damn second. His balls drew up tight and heavy, ready to explode now.

In his arms, her body tensed, her eyes closed, and with no more energy to fight it, she laid her head against his chest. His orgasm came fast, catching the end of hers, and he held her as the aftershocks rippled through her body.

Damn.

He couldn't let go. He didn't want to leave her warmth. He kissed her neck, her eyelids, and her lips.

"So more fucking less talking?" Ivy said.

Gabe gathered up her short hair in his hands, kissing her sassy mouth.

"Yes," he said. He helped her off the table. She walked away from him, but he grabbed her wrist and pulled her back.

And she didn't push him away like usual. Instead, she rested her head on her chest.

"Good girl," he murmured, stroking her back. He lifted sweaty strands off her face, loving how dewy and soft she was right now.

He held her as she let out a shaky breath. She kissed his bottom lips and tapped his arms. "I need to pee."

He let her go and washed his hands in the kitchen sink.

"Where were you tonight, anyway?"

Her question made him feel heated. Turning, he saw her face open and curious, her arms at her side.

"I stopped by Club Bandit. Logan was working on a new piece of equipment."

"Oh. I miss that place." The wistfulness in her tone was so thick.

"I heard you applied for membership."

"Don't mention it," Ivy said. "I guess that part of my life is over."

"It wouldn't have to be." Gabe strode across the room. "Every time I fuck you, my anger seems to drain out."

Ivy laughed. "So you just want to be play partners or fuck buddies?"

He traced her neck where his collar used to sit. The thought of other people touching her made his skin crawl. He knew it made him a possessive asshole, but no, this was his girl.

"What if I took you to the club and punished you?"

"What if?" Ivy bit her lip.

"Would you agree with that?"

"Why?"

Gabe kissed her forehead. "We would start fresh. It would be a clean start."

"Gabe, I don't know. I'm not sorry for making that post."

He closed his eyes, kissing her lips softly. "I know that other Doms and subs who have punishment as part of their dynamics feel punishment is a way of wiping the slate clean. It'd be punishing you for not listening to me. I asked you to stop posting anything about me on social media."

Ivy shook her head. "I was desperate, and I feel that post saved your life. And I don't know if I can trust you wouldn't be angry with me after the punishment."

"You can trust the sparks between us. The sex is good still."

Ivy laughed. "Yes, the sex is good. "

"And this would be you saying sorry."

Ivy patted his cheek. "Gabe, we've been over this. I'm not sorry."

His hands came around hers, and he threw them off of her.

"Why? Why can't you just be sorry you hurt me?"

"Because I didn't hurt you, I saved you. I don't love the consequences of that post, but even with losing my job, I'm not sorry I made it. I wish you would accept that."

She still couldn't see how wrong she was.

"Don't you want to stay together?" The words croaked out of his mouth.

"I want that more than anything."

"Then we have to move past this. If you were to agree to a punishment scene at Club Bandit, it would go a long way in putting it behind us."

Ivy bit her lip, not meeting his eyes.

His breath caught in his throat. He was sure she'd say no.

"Fine. I'll do it for you, Gabe."

"Yes! Thank you!" The stored tension left his body. He kissed her deeply, savouring her taste.

She hugged him, laying her head against his chest.

"You need to get going, or you'll be late for your shift."

"Okay, Princess. Don't stay up too late. I'll see you tomorrow."

"Okay." Ivy kissed him on the cheek. For a moment, they hung together, caught between their past, before she hurt him, and it felt like things always had between them, solid and comfortable, somewhere he could be without pretending or being compared.

CHAPTER FOURTEEN – IVY

Ivy paced around the luscious rooftop garden as the ship's horns blared from the harbour.

She pushed her hair behind her ears, wishing she had worn a different pair of shoes. Checking her watch, she gritted her teeth.

Trying to calm her nerves, she walked over to the picnic table, running her hand through the planter box of daffodils set in the middle of the table. She pulled out her phone and scrolled through her feeds.

Alice had messaged her, asking her to call her, her dad sent her a bunch of memes about cats, and her mother posted new photos of her latest stage set.

Looking good, Mom, she typed.

She paused on a message. The message read, *Keep your mouth shut, bitch.*

"You look like you just read something horrible."

Ivy startled, pausing to delete that message and quickly tucked the phone away, smiling sheepishly at the tall, well-built Black man striding towards her. She quickly put her phone down.

"Girl, look at where you are and post something about this." He spun around in a circle with his arms flung out to either side.

"Sorry. Your receptionist told me to wait up here, and the time kind of lagged on and I..."

"Used your phone as a distraction. Of course. Can you believe this weather? It feels like a summer day up here. Seriously, take a photo of this and make a post. Shut up, the haters." The man's dark eyes roamed over her as if he could see her insecurities, and Ivy felt her fingers shake.

Was this some kind of interview test? Did he really want her to post about it, or was he joking? Taking in his crossed arms, his searing expression, he absolutely was not kidding. *Great, a Dom.*

"What should I post?"

"What about this magical spot in the middle of Railtown where industrial meets new modern? About to have the best interview of my life. Smile and snap that selfie."

Ivy laughed, her cheeks growing warm. But she did and pressed publish. "Julien Innes?"

"Yes, indeed. Ivy Powell. Nice to meet you. You come highly recommended by my great friend Ella. I've asked around about you."

"You have?" Ivy flushed.

"Yes, it's a small town. Lots of people at Metric thought you should have taken the spot of Fitzgerald junior. Other people thought they gave you too much too soon that you didn't earn your stripes."

"Some of those people thought a fat girl wouldn't look good in the company photo." Ivy spat out the words, surprising herself. She hadn't voiced that out loud to *anyone*. It was in the background, and she tried not to let it get to her, but her not fitting into the company's image was there.

Ivy looked down, twisting a ring on her finger that her mom had given her for her last birthday. "I put in the long hours, I made friends with editors and writers and all the ad agencies I could. I worked tirelessly on the phone. They did me no favours."

"Especially when they fired you and lost three accounts you were handling."

"Really?" She couldn't help the slow smile spread across her face.

"Yes, really." Julien steadied her with his calm gaze, and Ivy pushed her hair back behind her ears. She had heard a rumour of that from Emery but hadn't dared to believe it.

"I'm good at what I do, Mr. Innes."

"Julien is fine. So, here at Quest Media, we have numerous publications and content creation avenues. We're always striving to push boundaries. We have a new show coming up, called *Speak Darkly*. This is where I need you. I need a co-host for the podcast, which will be streamed. This co-host of *Speak Darkly* will also write a weekly column in *Wild*, an advice columnist on sex, on kinky sex."

Ivy's face paled. "I haven't done any broadcasting, well, not since university. I don't think I am the right person for you."

"You know how to craft a good story. My source tells me you're the one who handled the pieces for the Sawyer divorce."

Ivy couldn't help the prideful smile that spread across her face. The celebrity divorce had been one of the biggest scandals, and she had managed that narrative.

"I can't say what I worked on, Julien." Her lips quirked, and she blushed as he raised an eyebrow at her.

"Fair. I found recordings of your university days. You have a perfect radio voice. And you seem comfortable with your sexuality."

"I don't know about that, Julien. I made one post, and it destroyed my life."

His eyebrow raised. "Did you delete the post? Because I'm not sure what you are talking about. But going through your social media accounts, I see pictures of you wearing a collar."

"The collar wasn't that noticeable," Ivy bristled, wondering why she was suddenly feeling shy with someone who was so open about it. Isn't this how she wanted Gabe to be? Was it because this was the last thing she expected to come up in the interview?

"Ella says you are very patient with new submissives." He raised an eyebrow at her.

"It's been a long time since I've been to one of Ella's submissive nights. And we were all new once."

"Here, tell me what this is and give me a couple of lines." Julien reached into his bag and held out his palm to her, the sun hitting the two small orbs.

Ivy took them, spinning them around on her palm. "These are magnet clamps. Usually used for the nipples or the clit but can be played anywhere on the body between the flesh. Even on lips."

She knew she was blushing. And she so wanted to go home tonight and ask Gabe to use their pair on her. Damn, she had missed kink.

Julien smiled. "Personal experience?"

"Is that part of this? Do I have to share my real-life experience?"

"To a point. Telling readers about who you are and what you've enjoyed and tried would be a draw. I want someone people can connect with. And sponsors would send you all kinds of products. What about this?"

Ivy stared at the hollow silicone tube in Julien's hand. She swallowed, took a breath and met his gaze.

"It's a hollow butt plug. During anal penetration, it keeps you more open than a standard anal plug. A penis or toy can be inserted into the sleeve. For deep anal penetration."

"What does it feel like?" Julien raised an eyebrow at her.

"It's made of body-safe silicone. It's smooth. The silicone heats up to your body temperature." Ivy took the toy in her hand, running her fingertips over the midpoint of the plug. "On the inside, the hollow plug is ribbed, adding texture. You might want to use some desensitizing lube with it."

"Good," Julien nodded.

"Julien, I'm not a sex educator. I don't know if I am the person you're looking for. I don't know how comfortable I am with this."

"You don't need to be a sex educator. Just comfortable with the subject, and I need to know if you have familiarity with different toys. What about this?" He handed her a small square pillow.

"It's a pillow," Ivy said. "A wedge. To put wherever you need support. You could just use pillows, but this is firm and small."

"Ivy, I would love for you to consider this position. If you're not getting traction in your field, maybe it's a sign you need to pivot. Sometimes we have to make lemonade out of unexpected lemons. You have a week to decide."

"That's it?" Ivy ran her fingers through her hair.

"That's it." Julien smiled.

"Wow. Okay, thank you. Nice to meet you."

"I'll walk you out." Julien waited for her to step in front of him and led her out of the rooftop garden down the stairs to the street level.

"Thanks for meeting with me," Ivy said.

"Thank you for considering the position. You'll be great." Julien gave her a wave and disappeared back into the office.

Ivy waved and jumped as she heard breaks squeal and a flash of silver turning left. Yikes, that was close to her.

Taking a deep breath, Ivy started walking through the neighbourhood, stopping at a ramen noodle place for takeout. She took her lunch over to a bench by the port and called Alice.

"Ivy! How are you?"

"I'm good. I just left an interview. How's Josh?"

"He's good. Getting bigger. Are you coming home for your mom's birthday?"

Ivy swallowed. She was due for a trip home. "I'm going to try. What's up?"

CHAPTER FOURTEEN – IVY

"So I asked a friend of mine if there was anything in your field. She works as an event planner, and she heard that the Stadium Agency is hiring. I have contact details. I'm going to text you over."

"But that's in Calgary." She hadn't considered leaving Vancouver, no matter what she told her mom.

"Yes, but Calgary is a city too, and you would be closer to your parents. Closer to me," Alice said. "We miss you, Ivy."

For a moment, her head swam with homesickness. Ever since she had left home for university, she had kept going. Kept achieving, determined to leave her childhood home on the berry farm behind.

"I'll think about it," Ivy said.

"Good. I'm about to take Josh in for an appointment. Let me know what you decide."

Ivy hung up and sighed, her stomach a mess of knots. She couldn't believe how much her life had changed from having one erratic client to barely making rent to having two potential jobs. Having Gabe in her life was better, and he was the only person she wanted to talk to about this.

But did she have to talk to him about this sex show? He hadn't been the most supportive of her last promotion at Metric. He didn't always like the hours she worked. Ivy bit her lip, but she had a hard time with him in the army, not always knowing when he would call. And when he left to work with Axis Management, she never knew the details of his job.

He never asked her what she thought about him being a private security operative. Determination ran through her fingers. She loved him, but the last half of the year taught her she had to look after herself.

Steeling herself, she took out her cell phone.

"Well, Miss Powell, that was fast."

"Yes." Ivy looked across at the docks and sighed. She couldn't leave this city.

"What can I do for you?" his rich voice purred.

"I've decided to take the position. I would love to be the co-host of *Speak Darkly*."

"Fantastic, Ivy. I'm going to email you a contract, and then I need a bio and for you to give me five pitches for the first five shows. I have a rough layout, but I want to hear your ideas. Let's meet in a couple of days. Let me know if you have questions. Looking forward to working with you."

"Thanks, Julien."

Satisfied, Ivy scrolled to the message Alice sent her and just to put another resume out there, she followed up with Alice's contact. If this radio show sex columnist gig didn't happen, she wanted a back-up plan.

Logging into her messages again, she saw Emery had sent her a link to a posting in Edmonton. And because she was on a roll, she fired off her resume to that one, knowing she wouldn't get the senior executive position advertised. And she blocked the troll. Throwing her phone in her bag, she grinned, eager to tell Gabe the news.

CHAPTER FIFTEEN – GABE

"What the hell is this?" Fury rolled through his veins.

Ares Montague crossed his arms over his chest, leaning against the windows of the sleek black cave-like office of Xander Montague, as his brother glared at him from across the desk.

"Something we should have done long ago. No more moonlighting. With us getting rid of the bodyguard side of the business, Team Stealth are all the assets we have in terms of personal security, and we haven't launched a recruitment campaign yet."

"Team Stealth isn't personal security; your reasoning is flimsy."

"Yeah, I know, but I want you to sign the fucking paper, and it's the best I could come up with for now."

"So I have to sign this if I want to stay on the payroll?" Gabe dropped the thick bound contract on the desk.

"Yes." Xander raised an eyebrow at him.

Gabe rocked back and forth in his chair. Xander was downright scary with his *'I can see right through you'* look.

"Okay, so when is the next job?"

"Not so fast. You need to go see Dr. Laktur first," Ares said.

"What?"

"Yeah, we're trying to be concerned about everyone's mental health so we don't burn through our assets."

"Besides, I looked back at the calendar, and I should have pulled you sooner," Xander said.

"Is this because I fell asleep on Harper's couch?" Gabe's stomach twisted, thinking about how he had guarded Harper and his friend Logan got hurt that night.

Xander snorted. "No. I talked to you about taking down time months ago, and you said okay, and then we needed you in, so this is for both of us to be committed."

"We think you overworked yourself in the summer," Ares said.

"Quinn wasn't around, and you said go."

"And now I am saying bench. After a month of sessions with Dr. Laktur, you're back in when she gives you the all-clear."

"But in the meantime, I can't work?" Gabe thumped the wall with his fist.

"You got it," Xander said.

"Did you pull this with Quinn?"

Ares's mouth quirked. "You can ask him. I hear you and Ivy are back together. Go spend time with her. Get your head straight."

Gabe stood up, threw his chair back and paced back in front of the desk. "This sucks. I feel ready. You trust me, right? That's why I'm on Team Stealth."

"It's not a matter of trust," Xander.

"Did you sign yet?" Logan pushed through the door of the conference room.

"What are you here for?" Gabe asked.

"Going on a job. Have to go fetch an asset, I hear. You'll be glad to sit this one out. It's a helicopter ride."

CHAPTER FIFTEEN – GABE

Gabe glared at his friends, his hands clenching into fists. "Even if it's jumping out of a plane, I'll take it right now. Come on, Xander. Give me something to do."

Erik Knight was the next man to push through the door. He glanced at Gabe, at his bosses, and joined Logan against the wall.

"Sign it." Xander held offered a black pen to Gabe.

"Yeah, too bad I don't have a girl to rescue." Gabe shook his head. "I can't just bail. I told Stone I would take jobs for the next month."

"River Stone isn't known for his loyalty. A contract makes things super clear."

He held Xander's glare for a moment before he looked away and scrawled his name. He got the hint. He had to fix his stuff.

"Fine. Have fun. If you need a medic, I'll still answer your call."

"Glad to hear it," Xander said.

Gabe stormed out of the conference room, out of the front door of Axis Management. He wouldn't put it past Xander to act as if he was trying to be subtle while not being subtle at all. A lot of D/s couples had contracts. He and Ivy fell into kink together, and to be honest, he thought they were kind of dumb. He wondered if a contract would solve their communication problems. But did he really have to write 'Don't out your Dom' in a contract?

His security gig didn't start for six more hours. He stopped at Ivy's favourite bakery and got that napoleon pastry thing she liked. He was slipping the key in the door as his phone buzzed in his pocket. "Dad, I can't talk right now."

"God forbid you don't spare me a second or two. I am calling to invite you to dinner."

"I don't think I can come." He turned the door, put his keys in the bowl on the hall table and slid his shoes off his feet.

"Get over here on Saturday. Your brother asked Chantal to marry him, and she said yes. That's more than you've done. We're going to have a nice dinner at Chops. Bring Ivy. Cole said she was trying to find work, so no excuse."

"Fine, Dad. We'll be there." He poured himself a glass of water, catching sight of Ivy's blonde hair shimmering in the sun. She was sitting on the balcony, her feet stretched out in front of her.

Damn, it felt so right to have her home.

He grabbed the pastry box and went outside to join her. "Hey, how was your day?"

Her sensuous mouth slid into that genuine shy smile of hers. Gabe reached over, running his fingers through her silky hair and dropped a kiss on her sparkly pink mouth.

"My day was incredible!" Ivy said. "Oooh! Is that box for me? I can use a refresh." She grinned, skipping by him into the kitchen.

"What made your day incredible?"

Ivy strode over to the French press and poured herself a cup. "I got a job offer!"

"Hey, cool. Where?" Gabe set the box down on the patio table.

"I'm going to be a new co-host of a show called, *Speak Darkly,* and I'll also write a column for it. I can't believe it!" Ivy kissed his cheek.

"Co-host of what?"

"It's a radio show that talks about sexy and kinky. It's going to be so much fun. Julien Innes thinks I have what it takes to be their person for this. I think I'll be good at it. I did that radio show for a while in school. Julien found the evidence of that if you can believe it."

"No, not really," Gabe said. He felt like someone had punched him in the stomach. "And Julien?"

"Yeah. Ella suggested my name to him. You know him?"

"He's one of the founding members of Club Bandit. He's a bit of a player, with both men and women."

"So? I'm not going to sleep with him." Ivy put her mug against the pastry box.

CHAPTER FIFTEEN – GABE

"He's a little intense, that's all. Since when do you want to become a radio host?"

"Since that's the job offer I got." She put her hands on her hips. He looked away, his hands curling into fists at his sides.

"So you're going to talk about sex every day? And kink shit?"

"That's the idea." Ivy crossed her arms over her chest. Her eyes darkened, and her lips pursed.

"Haven't you learned your lesson? Nothing good came from the last time you did that."

"Yeah, for me, because my boyfriend kicked me out and left me with nothing for months. However, he's alive to tell the tale and still pissed off about it. This is a space where they *want* me to talk about the kink shit."

"Ivy, I don't think you should do it," Gabe said. "You didn't even ask me."

"Just like you don't ask me when you leave for wherever Axis Management sends you, and you didn't ask me about going to work for the contractor. Since when do we ask each other about our employment?"

"I had to work, Ivy. What did you want me to do? Go get a job as a security guard?"

"I never said that!"

"But you didn't want me to keep going that last year. You thought signing on with Axis Management was a good idea." Damn, this was ancient history he was flinging around.

"You were excited about Team Stealth. I thought you were burnt out. I didn't suggest you quit, though, just that you look at other options."

"Options that would have me out of the action." He grabbed her arms. "I loved being a medic, and you didn't want me to continue."

"That's not true. And regardless of what I thought, you did!"

"So you're going to be some kind of sex host, regardless of what I think?"

"Yes!" Ivy shouted. She turned from him, marched down the hall, slid her feet into shoes and grabbed her purse.

"Where are you going?"

"Out," Ivy said.

"Fine. Go," Gabe spat out the words. He couldn't take this. How did she not see that he was hurt by her taking a job without talking to him about it first? She knew that being out with the kink stuff made him uncomfortable.

"Didn't ask your permission!" Ivy slammed the door closed behind her.

Gabe turned and punched the wall. His bosses were correct. His head wasn't in the greatest place to do this. Thinking back to Xander's steely look, he knew he had to get his head together. He picked up his phone and called Nick. Maybe hitting the weights with his friend would clear his head, and he would wait to show Ivy just how pissed off he was when she got back in bed, where they ended all their arguments.

CHAPTER SIXTEEN – IVY

Spinning the cool glass of double whiskey on the coaster, Ivy glanced at her friends, Emery and Natasha, a co-worker from Metric who didn't hate Ivy. She'd called them after being in the bar for an hour, tired of hanging out alone.

"Ivy, you okay there?" Natasha's cool hand covered hers, stopping her from spinning the glass.

"Yeah." Ivy blinked, pushing the image of Gabe's expression of disbelief out of her mind. Her stomach churned, thinking about it. Was there any hope for them? "Thanks for coming out with me."

"It's good to see you." Natasha smiled, brushing her long highlighted hair off her shoulder. "I'm sorry I didn't call. I didn't know if you wanted to hear from me."

"I did. Sorry, I was so shocked at everything that happened that I didn't call people. Well, except for Emery."

"Only because she needed somewhere to live," Emery draped an arm over Ivy.

"Metric hasn't been the same without you. It's not as much fun," Natasha said. It was weird, but the comment stirred up pride in Ivy. She had been responsible for looking after the junior associates.

"There are other agencies out there. Go somewhere else if you don't like it," Ivy said.

"Yeah, but you know, few are hiring right now," Emery said.

"I meant for Natasha. Lots of junior positions out there." As Natasha glanced away, Ivy drowned the last inch of amber liquid in her glass.

"You got a promotion? Oh. Well, I'm happy for you," Ivy said.

Natasha blushed. "I got lucky and followed your advice of trading for a better story. I kept a caught-with-your-pants-pulled down out of the press."

"What was the trade?" Ivy asked.

"A tip-off for a story about the lead singer of Drill Strikes sleeping with the lead guitarist *and* drummer."

Ivy laughed. "Good job!"

"She learned from the best!" Emery's dark eyes glowed.

"Another round?" Natasha asked.

"Please!" Ivy raised her empty glass.

"Be back in a sec." Natasha headed off to the bar.

"So, you and Gabe?" Emery asked, her eyebrows shooting up to her curly bangs.

"Don't want to talk about it." Ivy glanced out the window.

"Okay." Emery squeezed her hand.

"Here we are, ladies, cheers!" Natasha set the drinks down. Ivy threw the glass back in one swallow and winced.

"I'm going to be late!" Natasha drowned her white wine. "Thanks for inviting me, but I got to go. I'm meeting someone for dinner."

"Oh, a new love interest?" Emery teased.

"Yes, a hockey player." Natasha grinned.

Emery caught Ivy's eye, and the women laughed. Both of them had been hit on hockey players over the years, and the experiences were always memorable.

"Have fun," Ivy said.

CHAPTER SIXTEEN – IVY

"Oh, I plan to. While it lasts." Natasha waved.

Ivy envied her carefreeness and the bounce in her step. "That woman is going places."

"Yeah, but she's not as good as you. They needed to hire two junior associates, one senior PR person and a guy who worked in advertising to take on your list."

Ivy grinned. "I need to order food to sop up all this alcohol." She waved a server over.

"What can I get you?" The server swept up their empties.

"Appetizer sampler, please. And another."

"Sure." The server smiled and left.

"Going a little hard?" Emery asked.

"My day kind of sucked." Ivy put her head on the table.

"You need days that don't suck. What's going on?"

Ivy sighed. She didn't want to get into it, but Emery's dark eyes filled with concern, and Ivy knew she could trust her friend.

"I got a job offer," Ivy mumbled on her arm.

"Ivy! That's great." Emery clutched her arm.

"It's with Quest Media, for their *Speak Darkly* show, where they talk about sex. I got a job as a co-host of a sex show." Ivy giggled.

"Wow. Are you going to take it?" Emery grinned.

"I said yes, but I'm having second thoughts. Gabe doesn't like it."

"Does he have to?" Emery raised her eyebrows.

"I don't know." Her head buzzed a little from the alcohol, and she twisted in her chair. "I'd like him to be supportive of me. Maybe the time apart was better as much as it sucked."

"You and Gabe have been together forever. Can you imagine your life without him?"

"I mean, we spent months apart," Ivy said. She missed Gabe every day they weren't together. Her heart had been broken. And even though she had been back living with him in their home, the distance between them felt too wide to cross. Except for when they were having sex.

"I don't know if things can get back to normal." Ivy smiled at the server as she placed the appetizers down in front of her, with plates and cutlery and a fresh drink.

"Maybe it can be better," Emery said. "Because both of you know what you want?"

"I don't know." Ivy shook her head and dipped a spring roll. She had hoped some of his anger had simmered, and she had hoped he had found contentment in working with Axis Management.

"Let me rephrase it a different way. When you weren't with Gabe, did anything positive happen?"

"Emery, you know how my life was. I was struggling to get by and crashing with your brother." Ivy picked up a nacho chip, crunching it. She shook her head, trying to wave away the self-realization.

"But?" Emery pressed.

"I realized how good I am at what I do. I know I had only one client, and that ended terribly, but I didn't put myself out there as much as I could have. I found I like watching movies on the couch on Sundays, and I love going to see live theatre by myself. I love rollerblading. And I wish he was supportive of my work and small things, like going to see my family."

"Did you tell him all this?"

"No. I'm almost afraid to talk to him. He'll take it too personally if I say anything, or he'll just explode." Ivy bit her lip.

"He isn't a mind reader. Maybe he didn't think you needed support with your parents because your family is so normal."

"It is not!" Ivy said.

"Please. Your parents have been together since the dawn of time. You guys took a vacation every year."

"So?" Ivy sipped her drink.

"That's not how a lot of us grew up. Your parents never tried to stop you from doing something you wanted to do."

"Okay. I know, they're great. I suck for not going home." Ivy whipped out her cellphone and texted Alice.

Going home for my mom's birthday.

"Good." Emery smiled.

"Now I have a date." Emery slid off the barstool and patted Ivy's shoulder. "Hang in there. And if you need it, I have a couch."

"Thanks." Ivy waved to her friend and glanced at her phone. A text from Julien and a rare text from Gabe.

Where are you?

Ivy called for another round and flipped through her social media. Her dad had sent her a message asking if she was coming home for her mom's birthday. Ivy grinned as she accepted another drink and replied to her dad, telling him she was booking her flight.

Maybe Gabe would come home with her this time. Glancing at the couples in the restaurant, Ivy shook her head. Tears gathered in her eyes.

If Gabe loved her, he would be happy for her with the job. And if he loved her, he would forgive her. But Ivy knew he needed more than words. Gabe needed to cement it with action. The room suddenly spun. She put her head in her hands.

"Miss Powell."

Ivy lifted her head off the table at the calm, deep voice, meeting a pair of laser blue eyes under dark, wavy hair. Quinn Walsh had his arm around a petite honey blond woman, and a man wearing a ball cap, just a little shorter than Quinn, stood next to him with those same piercing blues.

"Hi Quinn," Ivy said.

"Dad, could you and Simone go to our table? I'm going to talk to my friend here. And maybe take her home."

"Sure. We've all had nights like yours." Quinn's dad smiled at her. Ivy blushed.

"I'm fine, Quinn." She gripped the tabletop with her fingers.

"It doesn't look like you are. I'll take you home." Quinn offered her his arm.

"I don't know if Gabe will be there."

"Doesn't matter if he is there. What happened?"

Ivy glanced at Quinn's face, trying to read his impassive expression. She knew Quinn to be a solid guy.

"I got a job offer today. Gabe didn't like it. We argued, and I left."

"To get drunk?" Quinn cocked an eyebrow.

"To meet friends," Ivy said.

"Just asking," Quinn said, guiding her out of the restaurant. "From where I'm sitting, it looks like you and Gabe need to work it out."

"I don't know if we can," Ivy whispered. She wiped furiously at her eyes.

"Are you going through with that punishment scene?" Quinn's lips pressed together in a thin line.

Great, he probably still hates me. "Yeah. Why?"

Quinn gave a one-shoulder shrug. "Heard about it. Gabe's been pretty miserable these last few months, Ivy, and if this is what he needs, then I'm glad you said yes. It sounds like you guys are working it out."

"I don't know about that," Ivy said. She sniffled and stumbled against Quinn as the room tilted on her.

"Let's get you home." Quinn led her outside, and Ivy leaned against the restaurant, taking big lungfuls of air.

"Does Gabe know where you are?"

"No."

"At least you only live a block away. My truck is over here." He walked her over to his truck and held the door open.

"Sorry, you don't have to do this."

"It's the least I can do." Quinn closed the door.

Ivy leaned her head on the cool window, closing her eyes.

CHAPTER SIXTEEN – IVY

"I'll have you home in a moment," Quinn said.

He didn't speak the short distance to their condo, and Ivy wondered if he hated her, too. She missed the Bandit Brothers. When she and Gabe had been apart, she had missed Quinn collaring Simone and Logan getting together with Harper and Xander Montague.

"Here. I'm going to walk you up," Quinn said as he parked the truck in visitor's parking.

"Not necessary," Ivy said.

Quinn stared into, and she sighed.

"Okay, thanks."

"That's better," Quinn said. Ivy leaned on him, feeling the earth spin as she stepped out of the truck and grabbed onto Quinn. God, she felt like she was going to throw up.

The reverbing of the car tires caused Ivy to jump. Quinn grabbed her, pulling her onto the lawn. "Asshole driver. He could have hit you."

"Glad you were here," Ivy mumbled. The car looked silver, reminding her of the one she saw coming out of Quest Media's building after her interview with Julien.

In the elevator, Ivy closed her eyes against the light. Quinn held her arm the entire way until it stopped. He all but marched her down the hall. He knocked on their door while Ivy tried to find her keys.

"Walsh." Gabe opened the door.

"This belongs to you. Take better care of her."

Ivy stumbled in the front door. "Hi."

The glare Gabe gave her made her stomach lurch. The steely look he gave her cut like a blade through her. Ivy bit her lip but returned his glare coolly. While the men talked, Ivy poured herself a glass of water.

"Thanks, man, good night." Gabe closed the door. He glared at Ivy, crossing his arms over his chest. "Did you have a good time?"

"I needed out. I was tired of arguing." Ivy shrugged.

"There's no more arguing." His sharp tone made her feel small. She put the glass in the sink as he stood next to her.

"I wanted you to be happy for me." A lump formed in her throat as Gabe laughed.

"Princess, I'd be happy if it was a different job." His palm pressed into the base of her spin. Ivy shivered as his hand slid to cup the back of her neck, turning her so she faced the windows. He pressed down on her body until she leaned on the counter, her cheek cool against the marble. She swallowed, gasping out short breaths. *Yes, this is what she'd asked for.*

She shivered as she felt his sock-clad foot run along her nylon-clad legs. He toed off one of her heels, then the other.

He hiked her skirt, folding it into her waistband, and she yelped as his palm came down hard across her ass.

"We have to stop going in circles." Gabe punctuated his words with another slap to her heated flesh. "Enough. When you ran out the door, Ivy, I was afraid you wouldn't come back."

"I didn't mean…"

Gabe's hand came around her mouth, covering her nose. He squeezed. "Not one word. You're going to stand here, silently, and take it."

Her pulse raced. She closed her eyes, stilling herself in his hard caress.

Against her thigh, she felt Gabe's knuckles brush her thigh as he worked his belt loose. She swallowed at the sound of leather swooshing through the air.

She jumped as his belt landed on her calves.

"You don't need a job, at least not right away. I can take care of you like you kept a roof over our heads. If you want a job, you'll wait until one comes along that matches your impressive resume."

Ivy's stomach tightened as his belt slapped her other calf. It wasn't until Gabe started working for Axis Management that he had any real money. She made almost twice as much as he had as a medic.

"What you will not do is be some kind of sex talk personality." The belt scored across her ass. She jumped, gasping as he struck her other ass cheek.

"I am not the kind of man to live my life on display, Ivy. I *care* what people think of me. Maybe I shouldn't, but I do. At some point, I might want to do something with my qualifications. I cannot have my girlfriend talk about how to give a guy good head."

"Gabe!" She shrieked as his belt snapped across the underside of her ass, harder than before. So hard, tears sprang to her eyes. The slap of the leather felt like flames against her skin. He sent the belt to her ass again. Ivy pushed up from the counter. He pushed her down.

"Hate you," Ivy said.

The leather stripe landed again, and then Gabe paused, squeezing her ass, digging in his fingers until her head came off the counter, and she pushed at his hand. Her ass blazed. She hated the tears running down her cheeks, and she had enough.

"I said to be silent. Get back to where I put you."

"Make me." She glared at him. A thrill raced through her veins at the words. His slow, sultry smile and how his eyes zeroed sent her nerves buzzing with anticipation.

His strong arm came across her back, pinning her in place, his fingers digging into her fleshy sore ass.

She squealed and kicked at him. His leg wound around hers, pinning her down. His muscled chest against her ass and back was damn delicious. She knew she was soaked between her legs.

"There. Better?" He pushed his arm into her, his breath hot in her ear.

"Fine," Ivy gritted out.

He removed his arm across her shoulders, placing his hand on her ass.

"I find it disrespectful that you took this job without thinking about it. Without talking to *me* about it. I want you, Ivy, and I want to rebuild what we had. I want to make it better. But I need you to be on the same page about this." He rubbed her ass in slow circles. Ivy closed her eyes, feeling the tears roll down her cheeks.

"Tomorrow is going to be a fresh start for us. I made a contract. You can look it over tomorrow and add anything you want or take away things. But after the punishment at Club Bandit, you need to decide if you want this, want us, and want us as something more than play partners." Gabe pulled her up from the counter, hugging her.

Her arms remained at her side. She sniffled.

"Come here, Princess." His gravelly voice made her heart thump.

She wrapped her arms around him, and he kissed the top of her head.

"I want you to be happy. But I want us to be happy too, and I know I can't be happy with that job. I also realize that you want more than what I've given you before." Her heart leapt with hope. Gabe had listened to her. He had zeroed in on her needs. Ivy lifted her head from his chest, feeling woozy and flushed.

"Thank you." She softly kissed his lips.

He took her hand, walked her to their bedroom and helped her undress. Ivy laid back against the pillows, her head reeling.

She didn't know Gabe would feel this strongly about the job with Julien, and what did he mean that he wanted to do something with his qualifications?

"Here." Gabe sat down with a glass of water and two aspirin. He reached over and turned out the light and kissed her cheek. "We'll talk tomorrow."

As he turned and walked out of the room, Ivy sighed into her pillows, feeling scrambled. She wanted him to talk more. She wanted to explain.

No, she realized, she wanted to justify. But a bigger part of her liked this calm and relaxed dominant that took her in hand, giving her thoughts peace.

CHAPTER SEVENTEEN - GABE

"Where did you go last night?" Gabe handed her a mug of coffee.

Ivy pulled a throw blanket around her, her feet stretched out on their patio table. Summer was taking its time in arriving. Their view this morning was a cloudy grey landscape.

"I met Emery and Natasha. I had a couple of drinks, maybe one past my limit."

Gabe ran his hand over his beard. "I didn't like that you stormed out on me. I don't like that I told you to go."

"I'm sorry. I didn't know what else to say." Ivy bit her lip.

Gabe sat down across from her and placed a hand on Ivy's knees. "I think communication is our downfall. I know I made fun of it a couple of years ago when you brought up the idea of a D/s contract."

Ivy's mouth quirked into a smile, showing her dimple. "You said it was 'trendy bullshit.'"

"Hey, we kind of fell into kink. Or at least I did. You always knew you were submissive in the bedroom. I had to get my head around it, and because we were already a couple, the idea of a contract seemed like we were trying to be something we weren't."

"And why do you feel differently now?" Ivy's emerald eyes met and held his.

"I like the idea of putting it all on the table." Gabe rapped on the table with his knuckles. "I think we stopped talking about what we wanted and just took each other for granted."

"You said I only wanted kink in the bedroom." His heart lurched as she touched her throat, where his collar used to be.

"I know. And if I had listened to you, maybe I wouldn't have said that. I'm working on managing my anger so it doesn't spill into everything."

"You took care of me last night. Thank you." Ivy sipped from her favourite coffee mug and pulled her sweater tighter around her.

"Ivy, what's wrong?" Gabe raised an eyebrow at her.

"Nothing." She didn't know how to give voice to her thoughts.

He reached out and turned her chair so that she was facing him. He put his hands on the top of her thighs.

"Tell me. After tomorrow night, we sign this and consider it a new start."

"I just wanted you to be happy for me. I got a new job. Julien could have asked anyone. Ella knows lots of people, but she recommended me to him. After months of everyone ignoring me, it meant something to me."

He brushed his hands through his hair, wincing at the pain in her voice. Even though her actions caused him to freeze her out, he could have checked on her, *should* have checked on her, and made sure that the others weren't freezing her out.

"I know. I'm sorry you were so alone these past few months."

"Are you, or do you think it was my fault?" She turned away from him, looking out over the balcony railing.

He took his hands off her knees. "No, it wasn't your fault you were alone. I don't like what you did, but I didn't want you to be harmed by it."

"Are you sure? Because you didn't do anything to make sure of that."

"I know. I got tied up in my head, Ivy. I should have checked on you. I should have called you. And I shouldn't have let you keep paying for this place."

She set her mug down and looked away from him. "Being here with you is just hard, sometimes. It's hard to trust that you won't throw me out."

A lump in his throat swallowed. He didn't want to be without her. She was one of the only bright spots in his world.

"Ivy, I get that your emotions are high, too. The thing with a contract is they set out expectations and responsibilities. This contract is also a sign of commitment that we both agree to stay in the bonds."

"Okay." She wouldn't meet his eyes. "What did you put in the contract?"

"Things like speaking respectfully to each other at all times, not walking out the door to end an argument. Playing at Club Bandit once a month. Not posting our kinky life on social media." Gabe picked up the bound pages and handed them to her.

"Gabe I-"

"No, Ivy. I'm not comfortable with it, sorry. Maybe you can make up an alternative identity or something. But I can't risk kink being linked with my professional life through you."

"So, it's either you or the job?"

"I wouldn't put it like that." Why couldn't she see he was trying here? He wasn't asking her to give up anything but to deepen their commitment to each other?

"No, you wouldn't. I don't share a lot at work. I'm good at what I do and work hard, but I don't share much personal stuff there. When

Julien offered me this job, I felt free. I felt like I could be all of me. I love French pressed coffee and the beach. I love the colour pink, and I like being spanked. I like crops and leather. I love sex. Why can't I talk about those things?"

"Because I won't get hired, Ivy! Because people will know you're my girlfriend, and they won't trust me as a medic or someone with battlefield experience. They'll just see me as a pervert."

"Then you're not letting me be who I am."

Gabe sighed. His ask wasn't unreasonable.

"I'm trying to protect us, to protect our future. You can be who you are. Start your own podcast on body positivity and kink. Write about how you love the colour pink and how people can better brand themselves, but you could do it under a different name."

"What if I don't want to?" She drew her legs up to her chest.

Dammit, her words crushed him. What was the point if she didn't want to put the time and energy into this relationship? How could he make her safe if she couldn't bend a little for him?

"I don't know, Ivy. We can put that aside because we aren't getting anywhere on it."

"How mature of you," Ivy muttered.

"I'm trying!" Gabe picked up the bound pages and dropped them on the table. "What do you want out of this? What's the most important thing to you?"

"That you're my solid, calm place you once were. That you don't look at me with hatred in your eyes. That you let me be who I am."

"Ivy..."

"No, it's true. You asked. That's the answer. I made what you consider a mistake. I don't think I deserve to be hated for it. You can't hate what I did and love me."

CHAPTER SEVENTEEN - GABE

"I can, though. I will always love you, Princess." His voice hitched on the words, but it was true, and he needed to make her feel cherished and safe.

"I want to try, but I'm afraid maybe we're not right for each other."

"Ivy, don't say that." He traced her lips with his finger. "Cole called me a kept man."

"Gabe, that's not...."

He shook her words away. "Listen, Cole called me a kept man. That ruffled my feathers because he was being an ass when he said it, and he couldn't imagine caring for someone. Ivy, I like taking care of you. I don't mind doing most of the laundry or making sure there's food in the house because you'll forget to go to the store because work will call you." He ran the back of his knuckles against her cheek and tapped the contract between them. "You are so strong out there. So powerful. Here, with me, I love that you are soft. You giving me control of your orgasms is so heady because, out there, you never give them an inch. Look," Gabe picked up the contract again, "I have things in here we've tried but didn't stick to. Asking for orgasms. Asking permission to come to bed. Kneeling when you get home. Your submission means so much to me. I was afraid to put structure around us. To want it because it's more commitment from both of us, but when you submit like that, you give me the reassurance that I am the Dom you need, the man you need. You're not going to leave me."

She stared at him, shook her head, and closed her eyes. "Gabe, you asked me to leave. How could you be worried about *me* leaving you?"

Yeah, it sounded incredulous. "Maybe that's why I asked you to leave, Ivy. I don't know. I know I have been miserable with you gone ever since you made that post. Maybe I was afraid you would leave. Like my mom." He bit the words out. His voice was hoarse.

She reached over and took his hands in hers. "I wish your family treated you better. I'm sorry I did something that made you think I was like them."

He stared at her for an entire moment. That was exactly it. She had. Just like his fucked up family, she had hurt him.

"Tomorrow is the new start. Just hang in here a little more with me, okay?"

"Okay," she whispered. "I'm going to shower and get ready for dinner." Ivy took her coffee cup and his water glass from the table. As she cleaned up the kitchen and her silky blonde hair fell against her cheek, Gabe knew she wasn't happy about the state of things. He didn't know what to do to fix it.

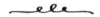

"Damn, woman." Gabe took her by the hand and pulled her against his chest, kissing the column of her neck. "You look too beautiful to be in their company."

"It's armour." Ivy giggled.

Her eyes, framed in black, perfectly applied mascara, glanced up at him wide, and she patted his cheek.

"You clean up pretty well yourself, Mr. Arthur. You could skip this, you know."

He let her go and watched as she smoothed out her black skirt that just hit her knee, pulling down her red top. She loved well-made clothes, and Gabe knew these had come from her favourite designer store.

He reached for his suit jacket and put it on over his dark navy dress shirt as Ivy slipped on her long dangly earrings.

"You know, if I skip it, I'd never hear the end of it. I wish I could just write them off and not bother with them."

CHAPTER SEVENTEEN - GABE

"They're your family." Ivy kissed his cheek, her heels almost putting her at eye height with her.

He hated that he couldn't give her a decent family. Her family was wonderful, right out of a storybook. His family played games like, "how much can we hurt each other tonight," but Ivy always tried to get along with his dad and brother.

"Remember we went to Chops late the night before our anniversary one year?" Ivy wrapped her arms around him, putting her head on his chest.

"And we got the best table," Gabe said. He put his hands around her waist and kissed the hollow under her ear.

"That was the night you brought out the wide crop. I like that thing."

Gabe smiled. "Then we'll have to get it out of the closet. I like how the wide part slaps, and the handle can be used as a small cane. Are you ready for what I have in store for you tonight?"

"Let's just survive this dinner. If I can get through this, I can get through anything you have dreamt up." Ivy took his hand.

Gabe smiled at her, and for a moment, it felt like old times between them. They were united against his father. Gabe sighed, knowing how unpleasant this part of the evening would be. On the short drive over to the restaurant, he glanced at Ivy in profile again, thinking how lucky he was to have her. She was worth trying to set his hurt aside. She was worth trying to make a new start.

His father, Cole and Chantal, were already seated inside the restaurant. "Did we say seven-thirty? I thought we said seven?" His dad slapped him on the back.

"Yeah, got a little caught up," Gabe said. "Cole. Chantal." Chantal flashed him a smile of perfectly cosmetic teeth and held out her ring finger.

"Wow, Cole, that's a pretty rock," Gabe said.

"It's lovely," Ivy said. "Congrats, Chantal. Cole, you're lucky she said yes."

"Don't I know it." Cole slid an arm around Chantal.

With every small topic his dad brought up, from his stocks to the latest repair on his sports car, Gabe wished he was anywhere else but here. "So did you see the write-up they did on me? Take a look." His dad shoved a phone in his hand.

Gabe snorted. "'With his son, Cole Arthur, the Arthur family continues to be a successful family to be envious of. What these two men have done with very little resources is an inspiration to all'. Didn't want to mention me?"

Cole smirked. "You don't like the spotlight, Gabe."

"It wasn't up to me what to print, son. Any time you want, you could go to business school and then have a position at the firm."

Gabe couldn't imagine being in a suit all day, lying to people and selling them insurance. "I'm good, thanks."

"You couldn't hack it, Shrimp."

"Did you go to business school?"

"Didn't need to. I became a successful business guy without it, right Ivy?"

Ivy smiled thinly at Cole.

"So, what are you doing with yourself these days?" his father asked him.

He was saved by a server. "Have we decided on appetizers?"

"I'll take an order of calamari. Salad for you, Ivy?" his dad said.

Gabe ground his teeth and took Ivy's hand under the table. "She'll have the shrimp cocktail. I'll take the clam's casino."

"It's a celebration, right?" His father grinned at them.

Ivy wasn't bothered by their comments. He tried not to be.

Chantal and Cole ordered, and the restaurant din roared in his head. Ivy ran her thumb along his clenched knuckles, and he exhaled.

CHAPTER SEVENTEEN - GABE

He was supposed to be looking out for her.

The thought landed like a stone.

She had always taken his dad and his brother's rudeness.

And he had been shitty to her.

He knew this punishment tonight wasn't just for her but for him. A reset that would reboot their relationship to where he wanted it.

"Gabe, what are you doing with yourself?"

"Keeping busy," he said. He couldn't talk about what he did for Axis Management, so he kept all his answers vague.

"See, if you were a real military man, you could have work up the wazoo with the private contractors. Too bad you couldn't go through with it, right Chantal?" Cole said.

"Yes, my father always takes well-trained men. They have new jobs frequently." Chantal smiled at Gabe.

"Your father?" Ivy asked.

"Yes, I'm Reid's daughter." Chantal sneered at her.

Throbbing started at Gabe's temples. Chantal Reid, daughter of the bigwig who bought out Ribbon of Aid and made it into a private contractor.

"Gabe, I'd invite you, but you didn't make it last time," Cole said.

"What do you mean I didn't make it?" Gabe frowned.

"Last time you bailed on them." Cole shrugged.

Gabe clenched his fist. "I did not. They told me they didn't want my service."

"Gabe, it's all right. You don't have to hide your failure," Cole said. "Chantal's right, though. We always take men with experience in combat."

"What do you have to do with it?" Ivy asked.

His brother shot daggers at her. "I'm learning the family business." He pulled Chantal close to her, and she giggled.

"Ivy, what about you?" his dad asked.

"Peter, I'm about to start a new job."

"It's a shame you couldn't hack it at Metric. There's a company with some prestige," his dad said.

"I'm excited about new opportunities." Ivy beamed at him, and Gabe wanted to applaud her.

Finally, the plates were cleared, and they were standing outside in the parking lot.

"Nice to see you. Go get a job or something," his father said.

"Or something, yes," Gabe said.

"Ivy, it's nice to see you coming out with us again." Cole kissed Ivy's cheek, and Gabe clenched his hands.

"It's nice to see you," Ivy said.

"Bye, Chantal."

His brother and Chantal waved. He gave his father a manly hug and then turned to his girl.

"Thank you," he said.

"For what?"

"Putting up with them."

"Gabe, it's no problem. I love you."

He kissed her hard, the taste of her easing his frustration at his family, the taste of her reminding him of home.

"Princess, tonight it's a new start for us. Let's go get it."

She hugged him, laying her head on his chest. "I can't wait."

CHAPTER EIGHTEEN – IVY

Ivy lightly squeezed Gabe's thigh as he drove from the restaurant. "You don't have to prove yourself to them."

He glanced at her, his eyes shaded with hurt, his knuckles gripping the steering wheel so tight they were almost white. "I know."

Ivy studied his profile, his Adam's apple moving up and down as he swallowed, the tight set of his jaw.

"We don't have to go to Club Bandit tonight," Ivy said.

"Are you having second thoughts?" He raised an eyebrow at her.

"No, of course not, but if you aren't in the mood...." Gabe glared at her, and Ivy turned to look out the window. She pulled out her phone and fired a text to her dad through the wave of homesickness she felt right now. Being with Gabe's family always made her miss her own.

"I have a degree in biology. It's like my service and what I've done with my life means nothing to them because I don't have the flashy car or...."

"Wife?" Ivy supplied.

"No, *job*. As if that's the only thing that matters. What if I want to sit on the beach and play guitar for the rest of my life?"

"Then I'll bring you cold beers." Ivy smiled.

Some of the tension left Gabe's shoulders. He took her hand in his. "Thanks for putting up with them. Don't you think Chantal and Cole moved fast?"

"I don't know. The last time I knew, Cole wasn't with anyone. The last time I saw them was at your dad's in the summer before...."

Before she hit publish on that post and ruined what they had.

"Tonight marks the beginning of our fresh start. I can't wait to have you on the cross on stage."

"Is that what you have planned?" She chewed her lip.

"Yes." He smiled, but it didn't reach his eyes.

"Okay." Ivy shook out her wrists, trying to dispel her nerves. Gabe seemed like he was a whole planet away from her.

At Club Bandit, Ivy forced herself to relax. This was a place she loved. Gabe wouldn't push her past her limits, and she wanted this to cement a new beginning.

Her phone rang, her mom calling. She turned it off to call her later.

"Hey, I wanted to ask if you would come home with me for my mom's birthday."

Gabe's eyebrows raised in surprise. "When is that?"

"Next week. I already booked my ticket home."

"I don't know, Ivy. I don't want to leave if I get called on a job."

"Okay." Ivy pushed her hair back behind her ears. Gabe came around and opened her car door for her, took her hand in his, pulled her against his muscled chest, and kissed her until her lips felt bruised.

"I'm so lucky to have you, and I'll try to come to your mom's birthday, okay?" His eyes darkened as he kissed her again, and when he let go, Ivy's head spun. She hadn't eaten much during dinner.

At the entrance desk, Gabe turned her towards the dressing room, swatting her on the behind. "I'll see you in fifteen minutes."

Ivy sighed, walking into the dressing room. She wasn't sure this was the right night for this scene.

CHAPTER EIGHTEEN – IVY

"Hi Ivy, haven't seen you for a while." Clara smiled at her.

"Hi, Clara!" Ivy returned her hug, her stomach a mess of nerves. She went into a stall and quickly got changed.

"Wow! You look amazing. Something special planned for tonight?" Clara said.

Ivy styled her hair in the mirror and glanced at Clara. Clara looked stunning in her leather halter and matching boy shorts.

Ivy buttoned the lacy see-thru shirt that showed off her black lacy bra and her short leather burgundy skirt.

"Kind of. It's a return to Club Bandit for Gabe and me."

"You've been missed," Clara said, putting on lip gloss.

"I don't know about that." Ivy frowned, pulling her hair out of the clips and shaking it loose.

"I didn't know what happened and didn't want to pry. I should have called you." Clara hugged her.

"I could have called you," Ivy said.

"And Gabe has barely smiled. He seems so down, sometimes."

The words boomeranged into her chest, and Ivy's hands stilled. She didn't like thinking of Gabe being unhappy, and she knew ever since the summer he had been. But she felt she was the only one who noticed.

"Are you all right?"

"Just nervous about being on stage."

"You'll do fine," Clara said. "Just focus on your Dom. Its member's night, so only founding members and their guests."

"And founding subs," Ivy grinned.

"Yes," Clara said. "Ready?"

Ivy squared her shoulders back and nodded. "Yes."

In the main room of Club Bandit, she relaxed a little. It wasn't too crowded tonight, with a few scenes going on throughout the place. Ivy noticed the staircase going up to the newly opened third floor.

"We can go up after if you want." Gabe wrapped his arms around her waist. Ivy closed her eyes, breathing in his familiar spicy cologne.

She missed his arms around her, missed hearing the uncensored cries only found at Club Bandit, missed seeing the subs and Doms in their interplays.

"Thanks for bringing me here." She turned in his arms and kissed him, hoping to soothe some of his frustrations from earlier.

"I've missed having you here, Princess. Shall we start?" His eyes scanned the room.

Ivy's stomach pulled tight in a knot of tension. Gabe didn't seem connected, but she nodded, and Gabe took her hand and led her through the stage. He stepped up the three steps behind the black curtain.

"I'm going to make you earn it." Gabe gestured to the wooden cross in the centre of the stage.

"I don't think that will hold me." Her voice wobbled.

"Of course, it will. Come on over." He patted the cross.

Ivy ran her hand over the smooth wood of the cross.

"Are you excited?"

"I think I'm nervous."

"Ivy, we've played on things like this lots of times. There's no difference. Just pretend it's you and me. Face it, and I'll strap you down." Gabe's mouth came around hers so quickly that Ivy gasped. His tongue danced with hers, and Ivy melted against him, feeling reassured by his insistent kiss.

"Yes, exactly like that. Good girl." Gabe slipped the restraint around her wrist, then did the next to the other side and then did her feet.

"Circulation is good?"

"Yes, fine." But she bit her lip. This didn't feel fine. Generally, in a scene, she would be anticipating what was to happen. She would be feeling turned on and ready. Here she just felt apprehensive. And even though Gabe kissed her and his hands massaged the back of her calves

CHAPTER EIGHTEEN – IVY

and shoulder blades, there was something distracted and quick about his movements.

It's just been a while for both of us. Ivy tried taking a deep breath.

"Ready?" Zee asked.

"Yes, this is going to be good." Gabe flashed her a smile, but it didn't quite reach his eyes.

From beside the cross, he opened his toy bag. Ivy gasped as she saw the small cat o'nine tails. It was her least favourite toy, the leather was stiff, and she didn't like how it landed.

Swooshing the whip through the hair, he tapped her calves with it.

"After this one scene, it's over," Gabe whispered, his tone thick and gravelly.

"Yes, Sir," Ivy said.

Gabe stood back, and god, she heard the implement sing through the air half a second before landing on her ass. She yelped. That hurt. Gabe swung again, and Ivy jumped. Hot tears slid down her face at his third strike, and she gulped for air.

"Say you're sorry," Gabe whispered to her.

Oh god. He wasn't going to let up. No matter what she said or did, it wouldn't be enough.

He raised his eyebrow at her, and she shook her head. She couldn't give him what she wanted. Stepping behind her once more, he struck her calves, and Ivy screamed. He swung the short whip through the air again, and it came down on the top of her thighs.

"Come on, Ivy, remember this is a new start for us. Just say sorry."

Gabe circled her neck with his hands, pressing on the hollow of her throat, his steely eyes boring into hers. She wanted to give this man anything he wanted, but she couldn't. Maybe too much time had passed. Perhaps they would never get over her making a desperate post, but she couldn't give him something untrue.

"Ivy?" Gabe let go of her neck, brought the flogger down hard on her other thigh, and Ivy yelped as the heat of the impact travelled up her leg to the base of her spine.

"Say you're sorry." His stare bore into hers, and she couldn't.

No endorphins were running through her system to keep these strikes from hurting. As he brought the flogger across on her ass, *holy hell*, she jumped.

It was pain, fire hot through her body, and she wanted out of it, *right now*.

"*Red*," she whispered.

She closed her eyes and heard Gabe curse.

He stared at her as if she had stabbed him. Her mouth went dry, and her pulse raced. Where he hit her with the trails stung. She gasped, gulping in mouthfuls of air, clutching her hands into fists. The room seemed to tilt.

"Get your sub off the cross, now." Zee's calm voice took on a tone Ivy had never heard before. Gabe unlatched her arms and her legs, barely looking at her.

"I need air." Gabe turned.

Ivy stared at his back, wiping away her tears. *What the hell was that?*

"Ivy, here, come over here." Ella took her hand and led her to a chair by the wall.

Ivy bit her lip, the tears flowing. That was unlike any scene she had been in before. There was no connection with them. The spark they had fed over the last couple of weeks was suddenly gone on that stage. Gabe didn't move them forward tonight; he moved them back.

"It's okay." Ella patted her knee.

"I couldn't say what he wanted me to say," Ivy sobbed.

He promised her this was about wiping the slate clean, not making her apologize.

The compassion in Ella's eyes made Ivy look away.

CHAPTER EIGHTEEN – IVY

"We all have limits," Ella said. "Whatever he asked of you, it was too much, at this moment anyway."

Ivy laughed hollowly. Could it be considered a limit? The unwillingness to offer a fake apology to ease something in him? Something that was broken? As his sub, shouldn't she be able to give him what he wanted?

"Ivy." Ella rubbed her fingers over her hands. "Take it from me. Sometimes saving them from being in a ditch is the best act of submission you can give."

Ella stared at the older, kind woman, then she let out a shuddering breath, put her head between her legs and cried. For the first time, she felt seen.

CHAPTER NINETEEN – GABE

She wasn't sorry.

His blood roared in his ears. He paced back and forth, sending pebbles flying with his steel toes.

Fuck. Her face when she called red, he'd never forget the pain in her expression.

The door swung open, bringing him out of his thoughts.

"What's going on, Gabe?" Quinn strode over to him.

"I was about to ask that," Zee said, pushing through the back doors. "Gabe, I don't know what's going on with you, but you got to get it figured out before you come to my club again."

"I can't believe this. Don't the new rules say we need to call a vote or something?" Gabe kicked the wall.

"Hey man, are you all right?"

"Did you all show up tonight?" Gabe asked as Logan came through the doors.

"Your submissive is being looked after by Ella and Clara. Simone's showing Harper something on her phone. The girls aren't in the mood to play tonight," Logan said.

"This is unreal," Gabe muttered under his breath.

CHAPTER NINETEEN – GABE

"Gabe, your job as a dominant is to take care of your sub. To protect her," Logan said.

"My head was not in the right place tonight. I know. I'm going to take Ivy home and forget this happened."

"I'll get her," Zee said.

"What, you won't let me go in?" Gabe stared down at the older man, his muscles taut with tension, ready to uncoil.

After a moment, Zee nodded. "Go in, get your girl, and stay the fuck away."

Gabe brushed by Logan, who glared at him and shook his head. They didn't have the whole story, and they rushed to a conclusion. He didn't want to go into details about his family or how he had just come from that dinner where his dad and brother made him feel like he wasn't measuring up. He wanted to be known as the guy who fixed problems, not caused them.

He found Ivy sitting next to Ella, her head in her hands, her shoulders shaking softly.

How vulnerable she looked there. So completely lost. He wanted to wrap her in his arms, take her home, throw her on the bed and never leave the house again.

"Ivy." He crouched down in front of her. The look in her eyes was like cold water being thrown at him. He was a prick.

Her tear-streaked face shattered his heart. "Come home with me. I know that was bad. We can talk about it and work through it."

He caught the raised eyebrow from Ella before she glanced away.

"You're welcome to stay here or even at our house tonight if you need some space."

"I'm not going to hurt her, Ella," Gabe sneered.

"I didn't say you were, Mr. Arthur," Ella said. "I was only offering space."

Ivy shook her head. "Ella, thanks. I'm okay. I would prefer to go home."

"Call me if you need to, Ivy, anytime." Ella patted her shoulder.

"Thanks," Ivy said.

She took his offered arm, and Gabe led her through the club, ignoring the attempts at small talk from the Doms he knew, glad that maybe not everyone had seen their scene. No one mentioned it.

He waited for Ivy to change and grab her bag.

"Want to go for a beer tomorrow night?" Nick clapped him on the shoulder.

Gabe shrugged off his touch and shook him off. "No."

"Okay, you know I'm here if you need me."

Gabe ran his hand through his hair, exhaling. "I had dinner with my brother and father before coming here tonight."

"Oh man, Gabe. You should have gone to the gym, not here."

"I'm tired of people telling me what I should and shouldn't do," he muttered.

"Hey, you can jump out of a helicopter if you want." Nick raised his eyebrows.

"Fuck you," Gabe said. Nick knew how he felt about helicopters. "But maybe I do need to do that."

"Let me know about that beer," Nick said as Ivy came out of the dressing room. "Ivy, take care, eh?"

"Thanks," she mumbled.

"Let's go." Gabe held the door open for her, and they stepped into the rainy night.

"That's the first time that he's spoken to me."

"Yeah. I think he took your betrayal hard."

"Betrayal?" Ivy spun around, her voice rising in disbelief.

"That's what it felt like, Ivy. Not just to me, but to all the Bandit Brothers. Your post could have harmed us all."

CHAPTER NINETEEN – GABE

Her face scrunched up, and her hands came into fists. "But it didn't, Gabe. This... tonight was supposed to cement our fresh start, and instead... I don't know what that was tonight, but it wasn't a scene."

Gabe swallowed. "It was a scene, Ivy. Maybe I could have done more or better or made it longer, and yeah, I got mad for a moment, but we did it. Isn't that what counts?"

Ivy shook her head. "I don't know if I can do this."

His heart dove to the ground. He hugged her, kissing her forehead. "You were right, okay? Tonight wasn't the best night for us to do this scene. Let's go home. We can talk more about the contract."

"Gabe, I don't know if I can sign it," Ivy whispered. She glanced at the ground, hugging herself.

"Hey, Princess, you don't have to think about it now." He pressed his lips to her forehead, breathing in her magnolia scent.

He opened the car door for her and paused before opening his door.

He fucked up. She had to sign the contract. It's what they agreed on; more than anything, he just wanted them to return to normal.

As they drove through the neighbourhood, with its mansions and sprawling properties, Ivy checked her phone.

"What's up?"

"Just letting Dad know what time my plane gets in on Thursday. I can't wait to see them. They would love to see you."

She was too good for him. That was the truth.

"I said I would think about it, okay?" He didn't mean to snap. But Ivy's parents were great as on TV, and he always felt uncomfortable around them. Like, he didn't know how a typical family acted.

Ivy didn't say anything until they were at the door of their condo. Her hurt expression pulled at his heartstrings. He had fucked up this night so badly.

"Ivy, thanks for coming to dinner with me. And I'm sorry."

She nodded, grabbed his hand, and smiled. "I know you're trying, Gabe. I just want to go to bed."

He's trying? Shouldn't it be her that's trying? He pushed away how irked her comment made him feel.

"I'm going to take a quick shower, okay?" Ivy kissed his cheek.

"Okay." Gabe smiled at her, wanting to restore their earlier harmony.

While Ivy took her shower, he paced around their condo, finally calling Xander. He left his boss a message, saying he was ready to be back in the field and asking if Xander would reconsider.

Work gave him focus. It gave him that feeling of having a purpose; without it, he was one unfocused, angry mess in a hardened shell. It sucked.

He made Ivy's favourite nighttime tea and brought it to her as she finished her shower.

"Peace offering?"

"Thanks." Her big eyes took him, and she shook her head. "Gabe, I don't feel up to talking or doing anything tonight. I feel like I haven't processed what happened."

"That's okay." He twirled a piece of her hair around his fingers. "Your hair is always so silky. I've missed your hair."

"Just my hair?" She smiled slightly.

"No, I've missed you. Seeing you in our bed, finding your books laying on the coffee table, your jacket over the door in the closet instead of hanging it up, the smell of your French press in the morning. You, all of you." He cupped her cheek and kissed her, long and slow.

In that kiss, he pushed into her how sorry he was and how much he hoped he could be better.

"I'm going to bed now."

"I'm going to get in right next to you, okay?"

"I would like that." She put a hand on his chest, leaned her forehead against his, and he took her mug from her, put it on a shelf and hugged her hard. He didn't need anything outside of this room. He didn't need the approval of his father or brother. He didn't need to chase the high of some dangerous work op.

"Baby, I'm sorry." He kissed her with all the tenderness he had. He didn't deserve her. If only he could let all of this go.

"It's okay. We'll figure it out. Maybe you can go talk to someone?"

"Like a shrink?"

"Yeah."

"Maybe."

With her in his arms, his anger had vaporized at this moment. There wasn't a trace of it in the air between them. He took her hand, lacing his fingers through hers, and led her to the bed.

He threw off his clothes and pulled down the blankets.

Ivy slipped in on her side and he on his.

"Hold me?" Her green eyes held trepidation as if she feared he would reject her.

"Yes." Her familiar body was perfect in his hands as he ran them over her soft flesh. He kissed the back of her neck gently. His hands palmed her breasts.

Ivy moaned, pushing against his hands, urging him on. Gabe kissed her as if punctuating his devotion to her, down her arm, along her rib cage, he palmed her pussy, making slow circles with his fingers.

"I love your hand there," Ivy said.

Gabe smiled as his fingers slid into her clit, into her wet folds.

Here in their bedroom, he didn't have to be anyone other than himself. He didn't have to be the team's former medic or the guy who hated flying. Or the dude with the famous hockey brother. He was just himself, who hated messes, loved the Lions, and liked to run each morning and watch the game on Saturday nights.

He wasn't a complicated man, though Ivy always told him he was more intelligent than he believed. He loved playing his guitar. He liked helping people. He knew how to patch people up.

But being with Ivy felt like normal. It felt like it was between them before she made that post.

"You're so beautiful, all heavy-lidded and flushed like that. You're going to come on my hand, aren't you, Princess?"

Ivy moaned, jerked her hips towards him and then pushed his arm away.

"What is it, Princess?"

"Gabe, sorry. I can't keep in the moment. I don't want to do this." Her voice broke and felt like a knife to his heart.

He stared at her and wondered what would happen if he commanded her. If she'd still respond to her cue word. But she was telling him she wasn't in it right now, which was fair. He didn't have to make the same mistake twice tonight.

"It's been a long night," Gabe croaked out. No reason to push her, not now. He kissed her lightly, pulling the blankets up to her chin.

"I'm going to hit the gym."

"I'm sorry. Tomorrow we can talk." Ivy smiled.

"Tomorrow's another day. Get some rest."

He took a cold shower, trying to shed the image of Ivy's teary face at Club Bandit, her being comforted by Ella. How his friends and the other Doms looked at him. He could never get it right.

He threw on a pair of shorts and a t-shirt and filled his water bottle. His phone buzzed on the counter.

"Think I had enough of you," Gabe said.

"Whatever. You're going to want to listen to this. Reid needs bodies for dropping a shipment of medical supplies Friday. Chantal recommended your name to her dad. You got another in with them if you want it."

CHAPTER NINETEEN – GABE

"You're not joking?" Gabe's stomach clenched. Knowing his brother, this could be a prank.

"No. Don't say I didn't do anything for you. Sending you over the details now," Cole said.

Gabe ended the call. *Yes!* This was precisely what he needed.

Gabe went into the bedroom to grab his gym bag.

"What's going on?" Ivy turned on the light.

"You listening to my phone calls?" Gabe demanded.

Fuck. All it took was hearing his brother's voice to change the mood from sweet and sensual to icy cold again.

"Sorry. I'm going on a job for Reid. You'll be rid of me for a few days."

"Gabe, no. You can't be serious." She got out of bed and crossed her arms over her chest.

"Princess, you look adorable, all mad like that. Listen to me, Ivy, this is a second chance, okay? I've been happy because you're here. You're the only thing making me happy right now, but I am better when working. I think we both know that. You didn't tell me about the job with *Speak Darkly*."

"Yeah, I didn't think I needed your permission to take a job interview. You're not even going to talk about this with me?"

"Same thing," Gabe said. "I know what you are going to say."

"It's not the same thing at all. You're going to make the same mistake." Her eyes flashed with anger, making them greener. "I want you to be happy for me. You want me to accept that you're going to do what you're going to do, despite what I say. And what about your contract with Axis Management? You're going to leave Bandit Brothers?"

"I'll always be a Bandit Brother." Gabe stalked towards her. "But I need to work, Ivy. I'm not the guy to be content to sit around while his significant other brings in the dough."

"So that's what this is about? You don't want me to have a job?" Her eyebrows furrowed.

"You leap to conclusions," Gabe said.

"And you don't listen!" Ivy raised her voice, stalking over to him.

"Am I the one who is supposed to listen?" Gabe fisted her hair in his hand. She gasped, her eyes wide, and he pulled. "I thought you liked me being in charge."

"I do," Ivy squealed.

That squeal was so damn sweet. He grabbed her mouth, forcing it open. Damn, her taste was exactly what he needed right now.

She pushed him away, tapping his wrist. He let go of her hair.

"In all these months that we've been apart, did you ever think that 'maybe Ivy was right?' Did you look into Ribbon of Aid's operation?"

"Didn't need to. They disappeared shortly after, probably because of your post. Then Vince Winston and Chantal's dad teamed up to take it from an NGO to a private contractor."

She laughed, the sound startling him. "You think that little post of mine has that much power?"

"I think, Princess, you want to surrender, but not without a fight." He grabbed her wrists and pushed her to the wall. He nudged her feet open. With one hand, he yanked down his shorts as he returned her kiss, just as demanding as his.

He lifted her, holding her legs.

"Stop. You can't hold me." Ivy pushed against his chest, her nails digging into his biceps.

Oh yes, he could. He glued his lips to hers, the heat rolling off her back to his, making his cock throb. He swallowed all the space between them as he shifted her so she was better lined up with him. He sunk his cock in her cunt, pushing her against the wall.

"Keep those eyes open and look at me."

"Damn you," she cried out. She yelped as he rocked deep in her fiery core, an inferno of hot and ready warmth; his spine tingled as he pumped into her.

CHAPTER NINETEEN – GABE

She leaned forward, biting his shoulder, and he pushed her as hard as he could against the wall, driving into her.

"Hell yeah." He thrust hard. "And you're going to stand there and take it."

She clawed at him, and he didn't care, thrusting harder. His hands gripped her thighs so damn tight as he angled her to take him even deeper.

Another deep, diving thrust, her tits bouncing, her short raspy breaths making his cock throb.

"Not fair," Ivy spat out. Her hand ran up and down his biceps, and he groaned.

"What?"

"That you make me feel like this."

"Like what, Princess?"

"Like out of my mind." She kissed him hard, biting his bottom lip.

"Yeah, bring it." He grabbed her arms, bringing them up over her head.

"Going to give me what I need now?" he breathed into her ear.

"I don't know. What's in it for me?"

He laughed against her lips. "My cock is so damn hard for you."

And then he drove as deep as he could in her. She screamed and dug into his skin, and he didn't give a damn. He pumped, staring right into her green eyes, this gorgeous woman who was his, his cock slapping against her wetness.

"Scream again," Gabe growled at her.

"I hate you." She screamed as he rammed into her, holding her soft curves against his hewn muscles, both of their bodies as hot as their tempers, her legs trembled with the effort of being open, and he didn't care.

He kissed her neck, sloppy, angry kisses, her breasts, her ear, every exposed part of her his lips found.

"Damn it," Ivy said from above him.

He kissed those lips until they were red. He grazed his teeth along her ear and rocked, slowing his pace.

She clenched around him, screamed in protest, and he laughed. He held her like that, rocking her, moving her up and down on his cock, almost teasingly. He wanted them as skin to skin as he could get them. Shifting her up and down again, he revved up the speed, drilling into her, each cry of hers driving him on. He could barely see as the haze of desire covered his eyes, and the tightness in his balls was too intense to ignore.

"You are mine." He bit her ear as he came, hard and fast, exploding in her sweet pussy.

Ivy panted against him, her body going slack. He held her, taking all her weight as he eased out of her damnable warmth. He rested his forehead against hers. "Fuck, Princess."

"Not fair," Ivy mumbled, breathing hard. "You can't end a fight like this."

"Yes, I can," Gabe said. He held her for a moment until his heart rate slowed, then he lifted her in his arms, holding her tight. She yelped as he carried her across the room, setting her on the bed. She flicked her feet at him, a mild protest.

"That's what I should have done to you on stage, fucked you senseless." He sat beside her, pulling her head on his chest and nibbling her ear. His hand squeezed her breasts, then trailed down along her stomach, lower, to between her thighs. "Open for me."

Ivy slightly turned her face to his chest as he submerged his fingers in her folds, plunging deep.

"Yes!"

He kissed her brow, still sticky with sweat.

Her eyes bore into his as his fingers kept working in her pussy, and his lips crashed against hers. With insistent passion, he feasted on her, drowning in her taste. His thumb pressed down on her hard nub.

CHAPTER NINETEEN – GABE

Ivy moaned as her lips worked against his, returning his passion with matching energy. "Gabe," she groaned out her name as he pressed hard on her clit.

His fingers dove deeper into her pussy, and he curled his finger high right on that spot.

"Yes!" Her eyes closed.

He worked his fingers mercilessly, hooking a foot over her leg, delighting in how she writhed, her toes curling.

And just because he wanted to, he whispered in her ear, *"Babylon."*

"Gabe!" Her high pitch keens were sweet music to his ear, and he kept his fingers working right through her aftershocks until she gasped, wrung out.

So damn gorgeous, his Princess, coming apart for him.

"Still mad at you."

"I know." Wrapping her in his arms, he curled next to her. "Sleep, Princess."

And finally, for the first time in hours, the anger left him completely, as he slept next to the woman who had his heart.

CHAPTER TWENTY – IVY

Ivy swiped her sweaty palms on her dressy black slacks, giving herself a pep talk like she would before going into a pitch presentation. *I have nothing to lose. I can speak well and stay focused.*

Ivy didn't have a plan. She knew the entrance to the black and glass building was by appointment only, but she figured she could stand there until they let her in, or they must have an intercom or something?

She exhaled as she saw Quinn, with his arms folded beside his black truck, glaring at his purple-haired sister. Ivy smiled to see Kayleigh again. She was so spirited and funny. Ivy had missed her. Next to Kayleigh, there were stacks of boxes.

"Kayleigh, Deidre painted that for your sixteenth birthday. You can at least take that to your new place."

"Please, Quinn. It's better with my other stuff," Kayleigh pleaded.

"If I take all of this, all you'll have is some clothes," Quinn said.

"The new place is being painted. Simone said it wouldn't be a problem storing my things." At the mention of his wife's name, his arms uncrossed. He took the painting and put it in the truck's backseat.

"Fine. I don't like this because it feels like you're hiding something."

Kayleigh looked away towards the traffic and back at Quinn.

"Hi. Need any help?"

CHAPTER TWENTY – IVY

"Hey Ivy! Haven't seen you in forever." Kayleigh hugged her tightly. Ivy smiled, returning her hug, giving Quinn a shy smile over her shoulder.

"What brings you here?" Quinn was always right to the point. Her stomach fluttered under his intense look.

"Obviously, she wanted to talk to you or someone." Kayleigh gestured at the building behind them.

Quinn grunted as he put boxes in his trucks.

"Ivy, do you still get great concert tickets? I want to see Stella Gray, and her concert is coming up next month."

"Sorry. I'm not working for Metric anymore."

"Ahh! That's too bad. What are you doing now?"

"Kayleigh, you're being nosy," Quinn said, picking up the last box.

"It's okay. I just took a new job as a radio show co-host. We'll see how that goes."

"Wow! I would love to do that. How do you get that job? I guess you need to go to school for it." Kayleigh pushed back her hair.

"This one just found me."

"I wish something would just find me," Kayleigh pouted.

"All right, Kayleigh, that's everything. Are you sure I can't drive you to your new place?"

Kayleigh shook her head. "Nope, I'm good. I'm going to walk. I'll see you on Saturday. Ivy, wait, what's your number? I don't want to lose touch with you, even if you don't have concert tickets anymore."

Ivy gave Kayleigh her number and waved.

"I don't know what's up with her, but I feel like she's hiding something."

"She knows she has you," Ivy said. Then her cheeks warmed as Quinn stared at her.

"Yeah. I guess she does. Ivy, what can I do for you?"

"Um..." Where did she even start? The last time she tried to protect Gabe, it didn't end well for her. Suddenly, she couldn't get enough breath into her body, her hands shook, and the world spun a bit.

"Easy." Quinn slung an arm around her. "Here, let's go inside. Kayleigh threw me off there. Do you have siblings?"

Quinn guided her to the austere door of Avis Management. A box beeped as Quinn stared at the retina scanner, and a light flashed green as the door clicked open. He held the door for her, and Ivy walked into the big, open area, passing an empty reception desk.

"In here," Quinn said. He led her over to a conference room. Instead of the usual conference room furniture, it had a kitchen table and chairs. Ivy tried to relax, resting her hands on the back of a chair as Quinn spoke into his phone.

God, what if this was a mistake? What if, when Gabe found out, he hit the roof? What if she was betraying him by being here? Instead of supporting what he wanted to do?

"No, I don't have siblings. I'm close to my cousin Alice though," she answered when Quinn was done with his phone call.

"Sit down, Ivy." Quinn took a bottle of water from the mini-fridge, uncapped it and handed it to her.

Ivy pulled out the chair, gulped down a mouthful of water and stared at Quinn as he sat across from her. "Thanks," she said. "Sorry, I'm nervous."

"Yeah, I get that." Quinn leaned back in his chair.

"I know you guys all hate me after what I did."

"I hate everyone equally." Quinn smiled.

"I know it seems I betrayed Gabe or whatever, but he wouldn't listen to me, and I had to do something to get his attention. Maybe it wasn't the right thing, making that post, but at the time, it was the only thing I could think of."

CHAPTER TWENTY – IVY

"It was a difficult time for all of us. We had just lost Jordan. Maybe we should have been paying closer attention to what you said, and maybe we should have gotten all the details before writing you off."

Ivy's swallowed, blinking back tears. That was almost an apology.

"Also, I didn't realize until recently that Gabe kicked you out of your condo and that scene at Club Bandit? You're one gutsy woman. Gabe doesn't deserve you."

Ivy shook her head, wiping away the sudden tears.

"I love him," she said, and it was true. It was refutable that she loved the man, with all his stubbornness and single-minded focus.

"Tell me what's up, Ivy." His voice turned to warm steel, and Ivy met his piercing blue eyes and felt like spilling her entire life's secrets, like when she hid Alice's diary because she thought it was dumb. Or the time she made a sex blog because she needed to talk about kink, and she didn't have Club Bandit anymore. Her cheeks grew warm thinking about that.

"Ivy?" Quinn raised one eyebrow, and Ivy wondered if they all learned that in Dom school.

"He's planning on leaving tomorrow morning, at like two am or something, joining up with Winston-Reid. Winston is one of the people who were behind Ribbon of Aid. They've given him a second chance. Chantal, Cole's fiancé's father, is a bigwig there. He's the Reid in the Winston-Reid partnership, and they want Gabe in on this job."

"He's a dumbass," Quinn said. "Axis Management just made him sign a no-work agreement."

"I know. But he needs to work. He's a different person when he has a job, Quinn."

Quinn raised his hand. "I know. Ivy, did you hear them say the guys on their mission were disposable?"

She closed her eyes, visualizing that day at Metric. "Yeah, 'these six guys aren't going to come back. They think they are dropping off medical supplies into the hostile territory, but it's drugs. They're great at what they do, and no one will know it's us. They'll think it's an ambush or something from someone not wanting medical supplies though'. That's exactly what I heard the guy from Winston-Reid say. They came to Metric for their recruitment ads. I sat in a meeting with them, and it just seemed like he wasn't on the up and up."

"I don't think I ever got the full story before," Quinn said slowly.

"Can you...I don't know...check what happened on that job? See if those six guys made it back? If they did and it was just a job, I misheard or jumped to conclusions."

"That's a strange thing to mishear," Quinn said. "What made Gabe a great medic is that he didn't take bullshit and did not listen to anyone trying to convince him to go against protocol." Quinn smiled for a moment, his eyes far away. "He was stubborn, and he knew his stuff. He listened to his superiors and the more experienced people in the field, but we all respected him. His single-mindedness out of the field can be a hindrance."

"Yeah. He's like a caged bear or something. So angry with no work outlet."

"Ivy, has he ever-?" Quinn looked away.

Her throat went dry. She was stunned Quinn would ask that about one of his best friends.

"No, not like that, Quinn. Angry, yes, but he doesn't take it out on me." Ivy bit her lip. "At least not in violent, non-consensual ways."

Quinn grunted. "I'm going to repeat what you told me to the rest of the Bandit Brothers, and we'll look into this company more like we should have done in the summer. Our heads weren't right. We didn't take care of you, Ivy."

"I know," Ivy said. "It's okay."

"No, you paid the price for it. Do you need a ride home?"

"No. I'm okay."

"Ivy, Gabe is one lucky bastard to have you."

CHAPTER TWENTY – IVY

"Thanks, Quinn," Ivy said. He walked her outside. Ivy sucked in long lungfuls of air as her head tried to clear. Gabe might hate her for tattling on him, but it was the only way she could think of to stop him from going on this job. *Again.*

Back at home, Ivy didn't think Gabe had come back since he slipped out this morning to go to the gym. He mentioned something about stopping by Nick's. She was about to call her mom when her phone rang in her hand, an unknown number flashing on her screen.

"Yes?" Ivy stepped out onto the balcony.

"Is this Ivy Powell?"

"Who is speaking?"

"Hi Ivy, this is Aiden Markson from the Sunset Corporation, and we would like to schedule an interview with you."

"You would?" Ivy's heart leaped into her throat as she leaned against the railing.

"Yes. You have a very impressive CV, and I want to talk to you about joining our team as soon as possible. Can you be in Edmonton on Tuesday?"

"Yes!" Ivy said. Edmonton was only about forty minutes from her parent's berry farm, much closer than working in Calgary.

"Great. How is one o'clock on Tuesday, then?"

"Sounds great."

"I'll send you directions to our office and the job description. Looking forward to seeing you, Ivy, have a great day!"

"You too!" Ivy grinned.

In the excitement of the phone call, she had forgotten about accepting Julien's job offer.

Ah well, maybe the interview would go badly. And could she leave the ocean, this condo behind? She didn't want to be in Alberta. But she missed her parents and Alice and Alice's baby. What about Gabe? Would he move with her?

Her phone buzzed, and she smiled.

I'm home in ten, picking up pizza from Atteli's.

You spoil me.

It's my job, Princess.

Ivy paced around the condo, grinning. As long as they were apart, texted, or had sex, they were fine. She couldn't wait to tell him about the job offer.

She chewed her lip as she realized she had made another decision without talking it over with Gabe.

Deciding she'd meet Gabe on his way inside, she locked their door, and in the elevator, she moved her flight. Her mother would be thrilled.

A silver car revved into the parking garage and then backed out. Ivy frowned. That car looked like the same one she saw leaving Julien's office, and wasn't it a sliver car she saw the night Quinn walked her to her door? She was just nervous about telling Gabe the news, letting her imagination run wild on her.

She jumped at the firm hand on her shoulder.

"Ivy, hey, come with me. I need to drive over to Gabe." Cole glowered at her, pulling her towards him.

"Cole! What's wrong?"

"Gabe's not himself, Ivy." Cole glared at her.

"Where is he? He just texted he was coming home with pizza."

"Yeah, he's in a bad state. You know how his migraines come on." Cole pressed down on her shoulder, and Ivy took two steps back, shoving his arm off.

"Should I get his meds?"

"Come on, we don't have much time."

Ivy hesitated. She didn't trust Cole. Shortly after getting Cole to agree to the sponsorship while working late one night, he barged into her

CHAPTER TWENTY – IVY

office, closing the door. She glanced away from Cole now as the memory played in her mind.

"Cole, is there anything else you need? I'm just typing up your requests," Ivy said.

"I came to see if you wanted to go for a drink."

"With Gabe?" Her hands were still on the keyboard.

Cole put his hands on her desk, knocking files and papers to the side. He leaned down, so he was in eye contact with her. "No, with just us."

"Cole, I'm still working here," Ivy said. "Maybe another night."

Cole reached across her desk and yanked on her arm.

"Let go! What are you doing?" Ivy pulled her arm away, but Cole was too strong, and he gripped her arm tightly, twisting, so Ivy stood out of her chair to try and get more momentum.

"You are with the wrong Arthur. Gabe is a loser, Ivy. He's going to do nothing for you. I have money. I have wealth. You wouldn't have to work every day. Give me a chance."

Cole pulled her over the desk. Ivy wasn't sure what he wasn't going to do but planting her feet, she pulled away from him, walked around her desk. She opened the door. "I think it's time you leave now, Mr. Arthur."

She held her breath, hoping for once she wasn't the only one in the building, hoping he would stop there and not escalate this any further.

"Fine, you fat cow. Have it your way."

She closed her door, then laid down, sobbing on her chaise. God, he was awful.

Ivy never told Gabe what happened, but every time they got together, Cole piled on the comments about her weight and job and seemed to put Gabe down more. But two weeks before the job that cost Jordan his life, Cole had shown up at the condo, telling her he was sorry. She didn't believe him but accepted his apology, thinking it would have been worse on Gabe somehow if she hadn't. Since then, Cole had shown up occasionally with pizza or beer, or sometimes they went out for drinks.

She tried to bring Gabe along. He seemed genuine in his apology, but Ivy would often catch him looking at her and see him almost sneer at her.

Cole always wanted what Gabe had.

"Look, Ivy, I know I'm not the nicest to Gabe, okay? I can't help it, but he's my brother and in trouble. Will you come?"

"I'm going to call him." Ivy pulled out her phone.

"We really don't have time for that."

Cole grabbed her hand, hurrying to his SUV.

A woman with her husky interrupted them, holding out a pen and a notebook. "Hey, you're Cole Arthur. Would you mind signing this?"

Cole flashed a smile. "Not at all." He scribbled his name and handed the woman back her pen. "Have a nice day, now."

"That's nice you gave her an autograph," Ivy commented.

"Yeah, I got to keep the fans happy," Cole said.

"Where are we going?" Ivy asked as he unlocked the doors.

"I'll get us there, don't worry."

As she was going to text Gabe, she saw that she had a text from Julien asking about the profiles he wanted.

"Whoa." Ivy held onto the grab bar.

"I need to get you to him. You're always good for him, Ivy. You make him calm down."

"I try," Ivy mumbled. "Cole, I think you're going a little fast. This isn't the way to your dad's."

"Leave the driving to me. And I never said he was at my dad's." His lips pressed into a thin line, and Ivy stared out the window. Cole sped up.

"Cole, where are we going? This is the turn for the airport."

"Just relax, Ivy. Everything is going to be fine. I got to get Gabe on this job."

"What are you talking about?"

CHAPTER TWENTY – IVY

"The job for Chantal's father. I can't chance this not working. She comes with good connections, you know? I've got to look out for myself."

"Gabe seems pretty determined to go do this job."

"Unless you talk him out of it. Do you know we had to change our name from your damn post? No one would join after that post! This is a multi-billion dollar business. It took us months to recruit enough ex-military men."

"Cole! You can't be serious. These guys are bad news. My post couldn't have caused that much damage."

"It did." Cole sneered at her.

She shook her head. This was going too far. She had lost everything because of that post, and everyone had blamed her. But it wasn't her fault; this shady company wasn't upfront and Gabe didn't stop to check.

"These guys are money, Ivy. I'm going to get rich. And either my brother is the soldier he claims to be, or he isn't."

Her stomach dropped. "What are you doing to me?"

For long moments Cole didn't answer as they drove along the stretch of highway, pulling onto the private airport access. With a squeal of the brakes, he stopped by a hangar.

"Getting you out of the way, fat bitch. Sorry but you're not going to ruin my plans this time." His eyes were drawn, his expression angry. Ivy's stomach rolled.

"Cole!"

Ivy tried kicking at him, but Cole was strong. He dragged her across to the hangar. She screamed. She kicked, and she felt hot tears spill down her face.

"You're not my problem anymore. Gabe could have done so much better than you. Maybe when this is over, and you've got some sense beaten into you, I'll come back for you." The door to the hangar opened. He pushed her so hard she stumbled, falling.

The cold concrete ground was smooth under her cheek. She screamed as the hangar door shuttered to a close.

This sucked. She heaved a sob and blinked away the tears. No, she wasn't going to let this happen.

Rage boiled in her at Gabe.

Dammit. All these months, he escaped Scott-free from her post; she saved his ass, and if he had just done what Axis Management wanted him to do, she wouldn't be here in a hangar, about to be... who knows what? Her head spun. Shipped? Sold? Ivy stood up, stomped her feet, and screamed all the despair she had inside her. She was going to kill Gabe if she ever saw him again.

CHAPTER TWENTY-ONE – GABE

"What is this, an intervention?" Gabe glared at the wall of Bandit Brothers in front of him. Quinn shook his head, Logan smiled, spread his arms wide, and Nick stepped forward, pulling out a chair across from Gabe. He had been at Atteli's getting the pizza when Nick had strolled in the pizza place, telling them to hold it for later. He said Gabe they needed to see him at Axis Management.

"Yeah, you could call it that. You can't go on this job for Winston-Reid because it will violate your contract with Axis Management."

"Like that contract was real?" Gabe thumped the table with his fist.

The doors to the conference room opened, and Erik strode in, nodding to them all.

"Did you all sign one? Did *he*?" Gabe pointed at Erik. He had no problem with the guy and owed him one for getting him these jobs with Stone Security, but Erik didn't go out of his way to make you feel good. Quinn maintained it was Erik's fault Jordan was dead, even though it was an invisible technology that foiled them that fateful June day.

"You got something against me, Arthur?" Erik was suddenly in his face.

"No. It's just you seem to get all the prime jobs. You seem to always be working, but nobody decided you had to go off rotation."

Erik shook his head at him. "I don't walk around angry and then crash to exhaustion. I can work like a bulldog and not burn out. It's my talent."

"Who said it was?" Quinn said.

"Hey guys, this is about Gabe." Logan leaned on the table. "Look, we love you on Team Stealth, and for whatever reason, Xander and Ares asked you to sign that piece of paper that promised you wouldn't work for someone else. Come on, you can trust them by now."

"Yeah, I don't sleep with them," Gabe said.

Logan slapped his hands on the table and spun away from them, running his hands through his short, spiky hair.

"Easy, Gabe. We're just looking out for you. You got Ivy back. Things are on the upswing. Just take some time off and forget about working for Winston-Reid," Quinn said.

They were all so damn calm, all of them. They probably didn't have nightmares when they closed their eyes. Nick had his hair slicked back and was wearing contacts, meaning he was probably on the job. If they had been taken off rotation, they would feel differently.

He was so tired of people interfering with his business. His brother, his father, Ivy, and everyone had an opinion of how he should work. And how he shouldn't. He stood up, toppling the chair to the floor.

"Heard your opinion. Thanks. I've got to go get a haircut." Gabe walked out the door, and Erik stood to block him.

"Three."

He put his palm on the door, then turned back. "What are you talking about, Quinn?"

"Three guys. That's how many came home out of the six they sent on the deployment of medical supplies. Two wouldn't talk to us. One did.

CHAPTER TWENTY-ONE – GABE

He made it back, but with his arm blown off. They were washing dirty guns and money, Gabe, under the guise of being an NGO."

"You're bullshitting me," Gabe said. "And how did you even know I was going to work with them?"

"Your submissive has more balls than you do," Quinn said.

"Damn it. Didn't she learn from last time?"

"Thankfully, she still gives a fuck about you," Nick said. "We were all too raw from Jordan that we didn't stop to fully investigate Ivy's story. This is big, Gabe. Your brother is an investor."

"He's the one who told me about the job!"

"Maybe he doesn't know they're running dirty," Logan said.

"I don't know. This is crazy. I don't believe it," Gabe said. But he knew it was true. Cole had never done anything for him. And it was Cole who sent him both jobs. The one with Ribbon of Aid and this one with Winston-Reid.

"I need to talk to Ivy."

"You do that and then do whatever Xander and Ares told you to and forget about private contracting. Or if that's what you want to do, find a good one and sign off here," Quinn said.

"Fine." Gabe felt the simmering anger below the surface. Whatever her reasons, he couldn't pass the fact that Ivy didn't go to him first. Thinking back to their argument the other night, she brought up everything his brothers said to him here. They had been hasty, and maybe he had jumped to conclusions, letting his grief and paranoia cloud his rational thought.

"Dammit," Gabe said.

"I'll go with you, okay? I don't have wheels," Nick said.

"I don't need a babysitter," Gabe growled.

"I haven't heard the story from her. I would like to hear it," Nick said.

"Fuck you all, you bastards."

"But you love us," Logan said.

As he walked out with Nick, Gabe gave them the finger behind his back.

"You were on a job?"

"Yeah. I just got back, and Quinn said we were having a meeting." Gabe grunted.

"I know you like to work because you feel you're good at it."

"I am good at it," Gabe said, opening the doors to his SUV.

"Yes, you are a good medic and great in the field. But you're not bad to hang out with. You're okay with dogs. You know how to do stuff. There's more to you than the army, Gabe."

"Doesn't fucking feel like it," Gabe muttered.

"It's because you've always wanted your dad's approval."

"It would be nice if he looked at me for longer than a moment without comparing me to Cole. Your parents are so much better."

Nick snorted. "My asshole father, who still thinks I am going to join the company? He's on wife number four. And my mother, who I can barely have a conversation with without her going off on some cause? Yeah, I won the parent lottery."

"Your parents don't compare you to your sister."

"Sure, but they still think I am wasting my life. Not as bad as yours, okay? But not a cakewalk, either."

Gabe looked over at this friend as he turned out the window. Ever since they met on an army training exercise, Nick had always been there for him. He knows Nick would love to have a girl of his own to care about.

"Seeing anyone?"

"No. Playing a few times with the subs at Club Bandit, but no one serious." Nick shrugged. "Relationships aren't for me."

"Yeah. I don't think they are for me either."

"Yes, they are. You're just being stubborn. You are better with Ivy than without, that is for sure. She's still not answering?"

"No. I want to blaze her ass red and buy her dinner."

CHAPTER TWENTY-ONE – GABE

"Then do both." Nick grinned.

He laughed, and some of the tension eased from his shoulders. Quinn was right. Ivy had balls.

He parked, they got out, and as Gabe unlocked, the front door to the lobby almost got run over by his neighbour's husky.

"Sorry," the woman said.

"Oh, no worries." Nick scratched the excited pup behind the ears. "You're such a good puppy."

Gabe rolled his eyes. His friend needed a pet of his own. Badly.

"Hey, I never knew Cole Arthur was your brother," the woman said.

"Yep."

"He was so nice to give me his autograph." The woman grinned at him.

"He was here?"

"Yeah, earlier this afternoon, he was going somewhere with your girlfriend. He also liked Hughes, here."

"Who couldn't like Hughes?" Nick said, scratching the dog's chin.

"What time was this?" Gabe asked.

"I walked him just before I left, so about two o'clock in the afternoon?"

"Thanks," Gabe said.

"No worries! Hey, do you think you can ask him to sign a jersey for me?"

"Sure." Gabe smiled tightly.

"Okay! Come on, Hughes, let's go!"

"Bye, doggy!" Nick said. "What? We were never allowed pets growing up."

Gabe shook his head. "You're not winning the contest."

Punching in Ivy's number again, they entered the elevator.

"Still not answering."

"Call Cole."

"Yeah, guess I have to. Quinn said he saw her around noon. Ivy said she had some errands to do. I don't know where she went with Cole."

Entering the condo, Gabe looked around. "Her keys aren't here. And the French press is still in the sink from this morning."

"So?"

"She wasn't home for a long time."

"Maybe they went shopping? Something to do with the wedding?" Nick shrugged.

"Guess I have to call him."

"I'll just make myself comfortable." Nick stretched out his feet on the sectional. "You complain about downtime, but I could use a bit of a hit."

Gabe dialled his brother.

"Gabe?"

"Hey, Cole. Is Ivy with you?"

"Why would she be with me?" Cole said.

Gabe gritted his teeth.

"You shouldn't be worried about Ivy. You have to get on a plane in a few hours. You should be napping or whatever you do before a job."

"Yeah, I will. I just don't know where Ivy is at the moment, and she's not answering her cell."

"You know Ivy's unpredictable. Don't worry about her. You just make sure you're on that plane. Chantal put in a good word with her father for you."

"I won't let you down," Gabe said.

"That's right, bro. Remember who got you this gig and gave you a second chance. Talk to you later."

"Bye." Gabe threw his phone across the counter. Ivy was a lot of things. Unpredictable wasn't one of them.

"He lied?"

"Yeah. Why?"

"I don't know, but it is suspicious."

CHAPTER TWENTY-ONE – GABE

Nick got up from the couch and, from his jacket pocket, brought out his tablet, the one with his father's company logo.

"Do you know Cole's plate number?"

Gabe ran his hand through his hair and reeled off the numbers. "You're going to try and find him?"

"You didn't tell him that a neighbour saw him with Ivy. You're suspicious too."

Gabe thumbed his fist on the counter. Damn it, why couldn't he have a brother that gave a shit about him?

"Yeah, I am." Gabe rattled off the plate number, and Nick typed furiously.

"What are you looking at?"

"Traffic cameras."

Gabe whistled but didn't ask how. Nick's tech skills had saved their bacon lots of times.

"Here." Nick showed him the tablet, a map on the bottom screen with a picture of Cole's car.

"Is that the turnoff to the airport?"

"Yep."

"Why is he going there?"

"I don't know," Nick mumbled. "What's Ivy's number?"

Gabe punched it in while Nick opened another screen, typed in long segments of code, and cursed in French under his breath.

"What?"

"Her signal died at the airport."

"What are they doing there?"

"I don't know, but let's go get your girl."

"This has to be a misunderstanding." But his mouth went dry, the back of his neck hot.

"I'm calling Logan and Quinn just in case," Nick said.

Gabe glared at his friend, then nodded. Better to have a backup than not because, with his asshole brother, Gabe just didn't know.

CHAPTER TWENTY-TWO – IVY

"Fuck!" She slammed her palm down in frustration. "Ow."

The world spun for a moment, feeling nauseous and dizzy, but she forced herself to get to her feet.

She had told them.

Out of sheer desperation, she wrote that post, and yes, she wanted it to stop Gabe from going on that job.

And save his ass.

But to know that his brother was behind it? It made her head spin. The business failed because they couldn't recruit enough people after her post, so Chantal's father bought the assets and reconstructed it as another business? It was like a weird fairy tale she'd somehow found herself in because she didn't want her boyfriend dead.

Guess it made her a shitty girlfriend. That's how Gabe treated her and how the rest of them, the Bandit Brothers, treated her too. No one ever fact-checked or followed up or listened to her.

Ivy sucked in a huge gulp of air. Now she was stuck here, just when she had gotten her life together. And she had stood on her own two feet without Gabe. Well, okay, him letting her back in their condo was helpful. But she should have fought him over it. She could have gone home to her family's berry farm and licked her wounds.

With fury rolling through her body, she ignored the throbbing in her knees and head and walked the hangar length.

There had to be an out, right? Or lights? She would feel better if she could see.

And what did Gabe do during this time? He just got angrier. Great, she was angry too. She was mad that he didn't care enough about her to ensure she had a roof over her head. Furious he didn't listen to her. She was angry that instead of celebrating a new job with her, he was more concerned about her not telling him about the interview.

Maybe she and Gabe were done.

Ivy slammed the ground, furiously wiping away tears. Staying near the wall, she ran her hand along, searching for a light switch. Do they even have light switches in hangars?

What is Cole's plan, anyway, to leave her here? He said he'd come back for her… after … *god*, is someone else going to come for her?

Her thoughts jumbled together, and the anger boiled through her veins.

Is this how it was for Gabe? Ivy shook away that thought.

She knew it wasn't like that for him, and to explain his anger was almost impossible. For Gabe, it was always there, under the surface, almost as if it was fuel for him.

For years, she had heard about how calm and quick thinking he was in the field, and she believed it, even if he seemed impulsive and angry out of that environment. It's like he needed a task; he *needed* something to do.

But she wished he didn't feel he had to prove himself to his father and brother.

CHAPTER TWENTY-TWO – IVY

I wish I was enough for him. The tiny voice in the back of her mind made her angrier than she'd even thought that. *Of course,* she was enough for him.

Her hand glided over something smooth and metal. "A panel," Ivy mumbled. She found the lip on the cool metal, pulled it open, and her hand fell over a row of switches, and she flipped them up.

And the hangar flooded with light.

This would be pretty damn cool if she was looking for space for a photo shoot or an event, but right now, it was terrifying because she didn't know why she was here.

Wait, there had to be a door. At the back of the hangar, Ivy saw an exit door. Pushed it. Locked. Of course! Cole took her phone from her. But did hangars have phones? An intercom, some way to connect to the outside world. There had to be a way out.

Ivy tried the exit again and pushed on the door. It opened a little, and a breeze of cool air brushed against her skin.

She kicked the door. "Ow!"

That did nothing other than hurt her foot.

Okay, so pushing it was. She pushed and pushed.

As soon as I am out, I will join the gym and, in the gym, start weight training. As soon as I am out of here, I will call Dad.

She swallowed past the lump in her throat and pushed the door again with all her might.

It sprung open, taking her with it, and Ivy grabbed on to maintain her balance

Yes! Freedom.

Her stomach sank as she saw a silver car and a black SUV parked to the side. Cold sweat broke out over her skin as she recognized that car. It had been following her! It wasn't in her head. She ran, the grass slippery under her feet.

It would be a trek to the main airport, but she could do it. There were people over there. Maybe she could flag down a car or something. She just had to keep walking. Tonight, she was going to pack her bags and fly home.

She would admire her dad's truck and bake a pie with her mother, watch whatever reruns her mom was currently bingeing, and relax on the old sofa in her childhood home, cursing herself for thinking it was better to leave it.

That she had to do everything by herself.

Isn't that why she had a Dom? So she didn't have to take on the weight of the world by herself?

He could have lifted some of that off of me, she thought and stopped, wheezing as she leaned down on her knees.

But Gabe had the same problem. He was wired to do it himself, though he had to. And he did because his father and brother weren't there to help him. They had never been there for him.

She bit her lip, stood, and kept walking. She was mad at them, horrible people who couldn't see the good in their son and brother. He just wanted to help people and play the guitar. Why couldn't they just let him do that and not criticize him for not doing what they wanted him to do?

She didn't want to hurt Gabe; despite how he treated her this past year, she loved him.

It almost hurt to love him, but she did.

He made her feel like a goddess in the bedroom and gave her everything her submissive heart needed among the sheets.

But was it enough?

Were those things enough to build a life on?

She didn't know.

Ivy had been mad at her mother for asking her when she and Gabe were going to get serious. She had meant when Gabe would put a ring

CHAPTER TWENTY-TWO – IVY

on her finger. Ivy shook her off. But they had been together for a long time.

Her mom had a point.

Was he ever going to commit to her?

As soon as she got out of here, she would ask him. Yes, she would. Ivy scoffed, some submissive she was, asking her Dom to marry her.

Well, that was exactly the kind of submissive she was.

And it was time for her to be the confident woman she was when she worked tirelessly at Metric, making a name for herself.

None of the last year was fair, but going forward, it would be different.

She just had to get through this never-ending field.

Shouting startled her out of her introspection. Ivy turned, tasting acid in her mouth as her stomach rose to her throat.

Four big, scary men were running towards her. Whatever it was, Cole wasn't going to come back for her. This wasn't some kind of surprise setup that ended on a tropical island.

What could she do? She ran.

Her arms were down at her side, pumping as hard as she could, cursing herself for not joining Gabe on his morning runs. *When this is over, and if we're still together, I will.* Strange moment to take comfort from a future thought that involved Gabe, but she did.

She wished her legs were longer. Making it to the front of the hangar, she wanted to spin in victory. She saw a black SUV pull into the driveway as she tried to move faster, sweat coating her brow.

Was that Gabe's car? It looked like it.

"I'm over here—" A gloved hand clamped around her mouth.

She kicked back, trying to remember the self-defence course she had taken, but her arms were grabbed from behind.

"Fuck you!" Ivy screamed behind the glove, trying to bite. With all her strength, she leaned back into the grasp. This sucked.

A wave of nausea came over her as the gloved hand was removed from her mouth, and they lifted her off her feet. Four guys, one her.

"Ivy!" He started sprinting towards her, his long legs moving him closer.

The guys dragged her inches closer to the plane, with the open door six feet away.

A black pickup truck and a motorcycle rolled into the drive. The three cars surrounded the plane, the motorcycle parking right in front of the loading stairs.

The Bandit Brothers had come for her.

Ivy screamed as the man holding her punched Gabe in the mouth. Suddenly Nick appeared on her other side, kicking the guy holding her.

And when she started screaming, she couldn't stop. She twisted as Logan planted a round kick to one of the guys holding her and then punched the guy who had hit Gabe.

Quinn tackled the other guy behind her, and it might be four to four, but it wasn't even, not by a long shot.

Fists flew, blood flew, and cracking of bone and cartilage sounded.

One of the men got up from the ground and charged at her.

Erik kicked the man, wrestling him to the ground. He then grabbed her and flung her off to the side. She stumbled, righted herself and sat her butt on the grass.

Her body trembling, she stayed there, frozen.

"Princess, you're safe. We got you." Gabe's voice was filled with tenderness. He took her arm, pulling her to her feet.

"Guys, we gotta book it," Erik said. "I don't think one of them is down for much longer. Let's go."

Gabe jogged, keeping her steady, while Quinn took her other arm.

"Nice and steady," Quinn said. "But fast, let's move!"

Her pulse raced as they ran to the car. She skidded, found her footing and got herself in the backseat.

CHAPTER TWENTY-TWO – IVY

"See you!" Quinn said, closing her door shut.

Nick got in the driver's seat, and Gabe sat next to her with Erik in the passenger seat.

Logan's motorcycle roared past them as he drove towards the plane and the men they left.

"Jesus! One of the fuckers is shooting at us," Erik said.

"Go, Nick!" Gabe yelled.

Ivy closed her eyes as she heard tires squealing on the pavement. "Hope Logan is okay."

"Marrock will be fine," Gabe said. "It's you I'm worried about right now."

"Nice of you all to show up," Ivy spat out.

"That's a weird way to say thanks for saving my life," Gabe said.

Ivy snorted. Nick shook his head, Erik looked out the window, and Ivy glared at Gabe.

"Yeah, how does it feel, asshole? All of you. Not one of you paid attention to me."

"Ivy, that's too simplified. There are many reasons it went down the way it did," Gabe said.

"Fuck you all," Ivy spat. "These past few months have been hell. And you all just let him mope around in his anger bubble? You call yourself brothers? You're not even his friends."

"Ivy, I don't know what happened, but we'll figure it out," Gabe said.

"What happened is your asshole brother set me up, afraid I would cost him money or whatever, wanted to make sure you were on this job tonight so you could be blown up. Now, will you stop comparing yourself to him?"

"Ivy, calm down. Now isn't the time for this." Gabe said.

"What are you going to do? Nothing. You never do anything, Gabe. In all these months, you never checked on me. You never made sure I had what I needed. Obviously, you think I am a partner who will ruin your life."

"I don't think that." Gabe's eyes flared with anger.

"What a way to show it," Ivy snorted.

"Do you want me to call someone?" Nick asked.

"No. I'll take care of it," Ivy sneered. "Just get me home."

"You aren't wrong, Ivy," Erik said quietly. "Gabe messed up. We all did. But he's better with you."

And that was the thing that made her burst into sobs. He might be better with her, but was it better for her to be without him?

CHAPTER TWENTY-THREE - GABE

As soon as Nick stopped the car, Erik jumped out, and Gabe opened Ivy's door.

He loved her so damn much. And his stomach was in a giant knot. His damn brother. How insane was Cole's plan?

"Come here." He pulled her against his chest. She shook her head and threw his arm off of her.

He laced his fingers through hers, squeezing her hand. "I got you." She shot daggers at him, and he exchanged a glance with Erik. Yeah, his girl had fire.

His phone rang. "Yeah?"

"Nick filled us in. I got a crew coming over there to clean up," Xander's calm voice sounded in Gabe's ear. "Okay." He bit his tongue so hard he tasted blood. He knew those men were former military. He wanted to strangle his brother.

"We'll be in touch." Xander hung up.

"Erik, am I taking you home?" Nick asked from the front seat.

"Yes," Gabe said.

Ivy glared at him.

"I'll bring the car back to you tomorrow," Nick said

"Sure. Thanks for having my back."

Ivy snorted, marching ahead of him.

"Good luck," Erik said.

"See you." Gabe waved to his friends. He caught up to Ivy in the lobby and grabbed her hand. She wrenched it away.

Hell no.

Ivy could be upset with him all she wanted, but she was going to walk into their home with him by her side, if she liked it or not. He put the palm of his hand against her back and ushered her into the elevator.

Her mascara streaked down her face, her sleeves were torn, a hole in her pants, her hair tumbled but god, did she look sexy as hell; she was so damn strong. Her posture was erect, her eyes blazing with anger as she looked at him.

Because his asshole brother took her and threw her in the hangar for pick up by who knows whom, to be sent to who knows where, though Gabe could make an educated guess.

He wanted to scream; he needed to punch something, but damn it, right now, he had to take care of his Princess. He hated she was in pain.

But you didn't mind the pain you caused her. But he did, more than anything.

As soon as they were behind their front door, she marched down the hall to the bedroom. He shut the front door and followed her.

"Gabe, I just want to forget this."

"Yeah? You can't. It sucked that it happened." He threw his jacket on the chair. "It was horrible. I will never talk to Cole again."

Surprise flashed across her eyes, and her chin jutted out. "Gabe, I wouldn't ask you to do that."

"Ivy, I should have taken better care of you." His voice broke.

She shook her head, brushing by him.

He grabbed her arm, pressing her against the wall.

CHAPTER TWENTY-THREE - GABE

"I'm fucked up. I've been horrible to you. Maybe I'm more sadistic than we thought. I left you and ran away from you, thinking you had betrayed me like my father and brother had so many times. I didn't view what you did as out of love for me."

And cupping her cheek face in his hands, he kissed her as if he could apologize for all the damn pain he'd caused her. His hand tangled in her hair, pulling it by the root. Her eyes flew open in surprise. She pushed back against him.

"Hell no. Say 'Red.' I will not listen to your protests unless that word tumbles out of your lips. Why did you get in the car with my brother?"

She snarled at him and kicked him, her nails scratching his arms. "Because he said that you had a migraine and weren't right. I tried to call you."

He laughed. Taking her wrists in his hand, he held them above her head. "Most fucking girls would be a wreck right now, crying and shivering. But you, you want to fight, right?"

"No! Gabe, get off of me!" Ivy said.

She looked so damn cute, half-heartedly pushing at his chest.

"Too bad we're not as good outside the bedroom as we are in it." Gabe dropped her wrist, grabbed the hem of her shirt, and threw it off. He knew he should look her over, get some water in her and substance but damn it, he wasn't going to stop.

Holding her in place with his hips, he dropped her wrists and worked the button on her pants, pulling them off. Leaving her standing there in her purple lacy underwear.

"Damn you," she bit out.

His eyes roamed every inch of her, rubbing her shoulders. Other than a bruise on her knee, she was fine. Thank God.

"Stop looking."

"Never, Princess."

A small smile broke on her lips, and needing to taste her again, he kissed her with all the angst he felt while yanking down her bra straps. She pushed him back, and he broke the kiss, taking her breast in his palm as if weighing it.

He squeezed her soft flesh, twisting her nipple, wanting to wipe off that look of scorn from her face. Her mouth relaxed as he kneaded and pinched, then her eyes rolled upwards.

Kneeling at her waist, he grabbed her hips, pulling her against his mouth. He pressed his lips to her soft skin, dropping kisses along her hip bone, over the flesh of her stomach, right to her tits, until his mouth covered her juicy nipple. He sucked on it like it was the best damn treat ever.

"Totally unfair," Ivy moaned as he pressed his tongue on her sweet beaded point.

He loved this strong, stubborn woman, and if he could stay buried in her breasts all day, every day, that'd be enough for him. Her hands threaded through his hair, and she pulled him closer. He roughly pulled her underwear to the side and finger fucked her hard and fast.

"No! Too damn much."

Her hips hit his face. He grabbed her legs, took his fingers out, and stuck them in her mouth.

"Not too much at all, Princess."

Her lips sucked his fingers, glaring at him. He pulled his fingers out of her mouth, spreading her legs wider. Her pussy was so wet, shining with her juices. As his tongue circled her hood, he inhaled the salty taste of her.

"Gabe! Damn you!" She scratched his arms hard enough to break the skin. He didn't care

She mewled above him, her hands softening. Her hips thrust into his face, and he smacked her thigh.

CHAPTER TWENTY-THREE - GABE

The scent of her pussy. That's what he needed. Nothing on the planet soothed his angry vibes like this. And this is where he belonged with Ivy, his submissive.

He twirled his tongue along her swollen wet folds, sucking and teasing.

"Too much. Yes! Don't stop!" She cried from above him, grabbing his hair.

Oh, he couldn't stop, even if he wanted to. He drowned in her. All his senses washed with the smell, the taste of her. The feel of her wetness coating his tongue was heaven.

He felt her muscles clench, her hands tangling in his hair.

Holding her hips, he flicked his tongue as hard as he could over her swollen clit, sucking it as if the salty sweetness was the very air he needed.

"Gabe! God damn you!"

He pulled out and stared at her from kneeling between her legs. She was angry and trying to be in control, and there was nothing sexier in the whole freaking world.

"You want to come for me, don't you, Princess?"

"No." Her hips lurched forward.

He grinned and pressed his thumb to her clit.

"You will come for me. Right on my tongue."

She turned her head from side to side. "Don't want to."

"Going to make you." He put his mouth on her heated deliciousness, biting down on her clit.

She exploded on his tongue. "Fuck you, Sir!"

Man, her anger was a turn-on. His cock throbbed.

Her legs trembled, but he kept sucking her clit, through the aftershocks. She slid against the wall, her hands resting on his shoulder. "I'm a mess."

"No, you're not." He cradled her, bringing her in his lap. He stroked her hair, kissing her softly.

"I wish I could hate you."

Her pain-stricken glaze tore him to shreds.

"I'm going to make it right, Ivy. I don't know how, but I'm going to try." Gabe swept her hot tears away.

"Every single body part is sore," she mumbled against his shoulder.

"Time to get you in a bath and look you over." Gabe helped ease her to her feet.

In the washroom, he washed his hands.

Damn, he couldn't stand looking at himself in the mirror. It was absolutely as bad as looking at Ivy's face

He splashed cold water on his face, then started the tub, setting a glass of water on the edge for Ivy. He shook her favourite salts into the running water and dimmed the lights.

When the tub filled, he turned off the taps and went to get Ivy. She was curled on her side, her eyes glassy, trembling slightly.

"I don't know where my phone is," she said hollowly.

"I'll see if I can do something about that. Do you want to use mine?"

"Please."

He fished his phone out of his jacket pocket, wishing it could all be different.

"It's amazing you came out of that with just a few bruises. It could have been so much worse."

"I don't want to think about it right now."

"Okay. Here, the bath is ready." Gabe took her by the arm, guiding her to the tub.

She closed her eyes as she settled back against the tile.

"Want me to wash your hair?"

"No. I just need...."

"I love you."

"I...know. I love you too."

"Take the time you need." Gabe dropped a kiss on her head.

"Thanks."

CHAPTER TWENTY-THREE - GABE

This was so awful. It's like they both knew it was the end.

He changed his clothes, and from his go bag, he took out a burner phone, calling Xander as he stepped out on the balcony.

"How's Ivy?" His boss's voice was concerned.

"Holding up." Gabe leaned over the railing.

"And you?"

"Could be better."

"What do you need?"

"Ivy doesn't know what happened to her phone. Can you shut down all the important data or do whatever? Xander, I wish you had let me back in the field."

"I know, Gabe. Feel free to be angry at me. I can take it," Xander said.

"I'm an idiot."

The pause was so long that Gabe wondered if Xander had hung up on him.

"We've all been there. Let us know if you need anything. I'll get back to you about the phone."

"Thanks." Gabe ended the call.

Looking at the lights below him, the ocean in the distance, he sighed. So many good things he had, and he threw them away because he wanted to chase the illusionary perfection of his brother. He didn't deserve Ivy.

Inside, he tapped on the bathroom door. "How are you feeling?"

"Okay. I called my mom." Her voice caught.

"Yeah?"

"I have a flight out at noon tomorrow."

"Okay." Gabe kissed her. "Are you finished your bath?"

"Yeah."

He held the towel out for her, and as she stepped out of the tub, he dried her off, wrapping the towel around her.

Reaching behind her, he emptied the tub, then hugged her.

"I'll drive you." He cradled her in his arms, kissing her head.

"Okay."

"I love you."

"I know," Ivy said. "I need sleep."

He tucked her in, then climbed in beside her, wrapped his arms around her and listened to her as she fell asleep, relieved that she finally stopped crying, and for now, she was in his arms.

CHAPTER TWENTY-FOUR - IVY

Ivy pulled on her sweater as she followed traffic flow through the airport. She didn't want to stop, just wanted to make it outside, to get a cab to her parent's house. During the entire hour and a half flight, she had tried to focus on her interview, running through a pitch in her head, but she couldn't shake the image of Gabe, with his sad eyes and how tenderly he kissed her goodbye this morning. It could be their last goodbye.

They hadn't talked much this morning. He had helped her pack. He drove her to the airport, his hand on her thigh during the entire drive. How did they return from his brother, taking her and throwing her into a hangar thing? Could they come back from that?

Ivy wiped her eyes and, finally outside, gulped in the air and shivered. She had just left the warm and pleasant morning breeze to this chilly, just before the arrival of spring, below zero day.

"Ivy!"

A sob caught in her throat. Standing beside his new cherry red pickup truck, his face grizzled, his brown eyes clear, with an Oilers hat on, was her Dad.

"Dad!" Ivy threw her arms around her him, tears flowing down her cheeks.

"There, there." Her dad patted her back awkwardly. "Is this all you brought?"

"For now," Ivy said. Her dad took her rolling suitcase from her, then her carry-on in the backseat.

"You didn't have to get me."

"I wanted to! What were you going to do, rent a car? When's the last time you drove?"

Her dad hummed as he pulled out into the exiting traffic, and Ivy smiled, seeing a picture of their old dog, Groomer, hanging from his mirror.

"I drive in the city, Dad. And I was going to get a cab."

"Waste of money." Her dad gave her a grin.

Ivy smiled, tucking her hair behind her ear.

"How was your flight?"

"Fine."

"Your mom made pie."

"Of course she did."

"You okay, honey?"

Ivy stared out the window at the stretch of highway.

She had wanted to leave so much. And damn it, she succeeded. Her parents never told her to stay. They always supported her, but Ivy wondered now what would it have been like if she had stayed? She could have helped her parents with the berry farm, even helped them expand.

"Ivy?"

"Sorry. Got lost in thought. I'm okay, Dad."

"Where is this interview on Tuesday?"

"Near the arena."

Her dad grunted. "Such a waste of money, that new development."

"You might like it." Ivy smiled.

CHAPTER TWENTY-FOUR - IVY

"We'll see if it ever gets completed."

Ivy shook her head. Her new phone beeped, and she glanced at it. A text from Emery.

"Is that Gabe?"

"No."

"Things between you two, okay?"

Ivy bit her lip.

He knew. "You know, you can stay as long as you like."

"I know, Dad."

"Here we are."

So pretty in the afternoon light. The horses at the McNeil's farm next door were grazing in the pasture. Her parent's whitewashed farmhouse set back from the road, their berry farm like a vast expansive lawn out front.

"Easy, Felix," her dad told their collie, who was yapping at them. "I brought her home. Yes, I did."

Ivy grabbed her carry-on as her dad scratched the collie behind his ear.

The last time she had been home was Christmas. A lump formed in her throat at the familiarity.

Her dad's toolbox was open in front of the garage, a sheet hanging on the line outside in the yard. Ivy reached down to pet Felix, shaking off the tears in the corner of her eyes.

"Didn't you bring a jacket?" Her mother raced down the steps to her, her coat open, her hair loose in a messy bun, her glasses sliding down her nose.

"Mom." Ivy hugged her mother fiercely. Damn it, she shouldn't have let what happened with Gabe and Metric stop her from coming home. To think that her parents would ever be disappointed in her was crazy.

"Glad to see you, love. Get inside before you freeze. The pie has just come out of the oven. Alice, Frank and baby Josh are coming over. I got to clear the table of my notes."

"What are you working on?"

"It's about a broken-hearted ghost who haunts her former mother-in-law." Her mother smiled at her. "I've been told I have to state that it is not inspired by personal events."

Her dad gruffed from the door. "My mother was a saint."

"Yes, she was, dear." Her mom patted her dad's chest. "I almost burned the pie. I was so lost in it. I have a read-through tomorrow night. Would you like to come?"

"Sure, Mom."

The familiar smell of her childhood home froze Ivy on the mat. Their living room, with its worn leather couches, the new geometric artwork on the wall, and pictures of her growing up and her extended family, was home. The hardwood hall led to the white and blue kitchen her parents had redone a few years ago.

"Do you want a coffee? Do you feel any jet lag?"

"It's only an hour," Ivy said. "Yes, coffee."

"You haven't met your potential mother-in-law, have you?" her mom asked as she tidied away her notebooks.

"No. Gabe's not in touch with his mom. I don't think there is a potential mother-in-law in my future any time soon."

"Oh, Ivy." Her mom hugged her.

"No, it's okay. I just, I don't want to talk about it."

"Okay. I like him, you know, Gabe."

"Really?"

"Of course. I wish you came home more, and he was more comfortable around us, but he's a good man."

"He is," Ivy whispered.

She strode to the coffeepot, took a mug from the mug tree, made her coffee, and looked back towards her mom.

"We're just...." Ivy trailed off. She really couldn't talk about it.

"Having a rough patch?"

CHAPTER TWENTY-FOUR - IVY

"Maybe," Ivy said.

"Well, I'm here if you want to talk about it."

"Thanks, Mom."

"Now, look at this pie! We had a bumper crop of raspberries last year, and I have so many frozen in the downstairs freezer I keep giving away pies. I think everyone is sick of them."

"Impossible." Ivy grinned as her mother handed her a plate.

"It's good to have you home." Her mom kissed her cheek, and Ivy sighed. Some kind of weight had been lifted off her when she saw her dad.

I have no guard up here, she realized. She could just be herself here, in this house she so wanted to leave. She didn't have to prove anything.

"Eat the pie, Ivy," her mom said.

"He's so adorable!" Ivy held up Josh and laughed as the baby cooed.

"Yes! And you haven't seen him enough." Alice reached for her son.

"Alice, give her a break. We could have visited too," Frank said.

"Oh yeah, because travelling with a baby is so easy."

Josh put a hand on her shoulder. "No, but we had the time. Ivy's been making a career for herself. I think it's fantastic that Sunset wants you, Ivy."

"Thanks." Ivy smiled at Josh and plucked a cookie off the tray. "We'll see how this interview goes."

"When is that again?"

"Tuesday afternoon, Mom."

"Oh, you're going to be in the thick of rush hour."

"I'll drive her."

"No, I thought I would leave Josh with you, Aunt Wendy and then Ivy and I can have dinner afterwards?"

"I would appreciate the lift in the city, but the interview is going to go late, and I thought I would stay overnight."

Her parents exchanged one of those silent looks.

"That sounds great! I should get a hotel to myself," Alice said.

"You would miss him too much." Ivy reached over and tickled Josh under his chin. He giggled.

"Yeah, you're right." Alice smiled at Ivy. "What are your plans for tomorrow? Want to go ride at the McNeil's?

"I'm going to Mom's read-through."

"The read-through is only going to be two hours. You'll have good afternoon light to go for a ride."

"That sounds awesome," Ivy said. She had missed riding horses. The last time they were here for Christmas, she had tried to get Gabe to go for a ride, but he shook his head at her and insisted he wouldn't be good at it.

Ivy frowned. Gabe had called her twice, but she hadn't called him back, wanting to stay focused on the interview. But she missed him. And somehow, being in this cozy living room with the people she loved made her miss him more.

"Ivy, so it's a plan? We'll swing by around three tomorrow?"

"Yes, great."

"Okay, let's get Josh home. He's getting tired."

Alice and Frank said their goodbyes, and Ivy kissed Josh's fat baby cheeks again.

"Honey, do you need anything for the interview?"

"I brought clothes, Mom."

Her mother raised an eyebrow at her, and Ivy sighed, helping her to clear the plates from the coffee table. "I might need a shopping trip."

"Yes! We could go in about an hour if you're not too tired?"

"Okay." Ivy grinned.

"I'm glad you're here."

"Me too, Mom."

CHAPTER TWENTY-FIVE – GABE

Gabe's fingers hovered over Ivy's number as he sat on their balcony. He wanted to call her, to ask how she was. He selfishly wanted to share what he had learned at his psychologist's appointment.

He consciously took a deep breath, filling his lungs slowly. He exhaled. It had been three weeks since Ivy had left for her parents. She told him she needed space. So he had done what he thought was right and gave it to her. They agreed to talk on the phone and text, but it wasn't enough.

Gabe knew Ivy wouldn't be surprised by Dr. Laktur's findings, that he had PTSD from the army, but it compounded his PTSD from his childhood and was more involved than he ever thought. For the past couple of weeks, he went to therapy to understand his anger and his tendency to emotionally detach.

His assignment for this week was to pick up a guitar and reclaim some interest in a hobby that had nothing to do with the army or his job. Gabe took in a deep, cleansing breath and closed his eyes for a moment. Dr. Laktur, in her soft, lilting accent, also told him that anger was valid. Anger, she said, served him well on the field because it wasn't

CHAPTER TWENTY-FIVE – GABE

the apparent crystal calm or just the calm. The anger gave him the power to see and assess the situation clearly and efficiently.

What did one do when they had their mind shaken? Go for a run. Grab a drink with Nick later. And get through the rest of the day until he could talk to Ivy again.

She needed to figure out what she wanted, as much as he had to put his own head back together.

He hated being alone. Last year, when he had told Ivy to get out, he was so entrenched in his anger that he hadn't realized how lonely he had been, not really. He had longed for her, but he hadn't missed her like he did now. He needed her.

Seeing her French Press machine at the side of the sink made his heart well up. He would ask her what she thought of them starting over. Maybe she could move back and find a job here. He only had one more week of seeing Dr. Laktur before he could resume with Team Stealth. He was just out of the shower when his phone buzzed.

"Ivy, is everything okay?"

"Gabe, sorry! I couldn't wait until tomorrow. Is it all right?"

"You can call me anytime. You know that."

"I got offered the job! Executive PR Strategist. Can you believe it?"

He grinned, picturing her glowing eyes, her hair glowing and her gorgeous smile across her face. Damn, he wished he had his arms around her right now.

"Yes, I can believe it. That's my girl."

"I'm going to go celebrate with some work colleagues here. Tomorrow I have a full day of meetings. I'll call you when I get back to the hotel."

"The hotel?"

"Yeah, it's getting a bit much at my parents. I've been booking myself a room in the city."

"We'll have to celebrate soon." He swallowed, wondering what she'd say.

"I'd like that," Ivy said. "Talk to you tomorrow."

He stared at his phone in his hand as if it could give him some answers, then he looked around their condo.

There was no way Ivy was coming back to him. To this. To them.

He called Nick.

"Hey, can you meet me soon? I need..." He bit his lip. How the hell did he say he needed company? "I just got off the phone with Ivy."

"I'll come over in half an hour," Nick said. "I'll bring the good stuff."

His phone rang, and he had a flash of hope that it was Ivy calling him back. But no, it was another call he wouldn't answer from his father. After Ivy left for her parents, he sent both him and Cole a message saying he never wanted to talk to them. He's sure his dad is chalking it up to Gabe's feeling of being hurt or something, but damn straight, his feelings were hurt. Xander had people looking for Cole but hadn't found him yet.

Ivy was a great girl. She deserved so much better than him. She deserves someone who had their shit together. Someone who didn't have fucked up family.

He had nothing to give her. He reached above the sink, took down a bottle of whiskey and poured himself a drink.

"She's not coming back to this, man. They offered her some kind of senior executive position out there. What is this to her? It's nothing."

"It's just a condo," Nick said. The man had his suit jacket undone and lounged on the chair, shaking his head at Gabe.

"Is it over between you two?"

"I don't know. Ivy said she needed space. I tried to give her space."

"Okay, but it's been three weeks, and she's still speaking to you. Did you tell her what you want?"

"No, she knows. I don't want to freak her out or anything."

"You need to take *charge*, Gabe. Like you used to, remember? And stop this wallowing in indecision." Nick plucked the glass out of his hand.

"What do you think I should do? Beg her to come back?"

"It's a start. But why does she have to come back to this?"

"That's my fucking' point!" Gabe said.

"No, I mean you can go to her. Show her that you want to be where she is. So what, she makes more money than you; do you really care?"

Gabe stood out on the balcony overlooking the vista they both loved. His dad made fun of him, but his dad was a bully and made fun of him for everything, and his brother followed. But he didn't care about money, not really.

He liked Ivy, and she was good at what she did. It filled her up; for the past year, that light in her eyes had been missing, and he had helped put it out.

"So what do I do? Find a job out there? Pack this up and move."

"Yeah. I hear people do it all the time."

"But about Bandit Brothers?"

"Hey, once you're in, you're in. We don't kick you out, ask Erik."

Gabe stared at the ceiling. "Team Stealth, I mean."

"You quit working for Axis Management. Look, Quinn is just about out of fieldwork. Logan will probably be the permanent leader, and I'm still not bored. You could come back when we need an analytical mind with medic training. You don't have to do it full time."

Gabe stood up and started pacing the room.

"Then I could show Ivy I am serious about supporting her. You think it'll work?"

"I don't know, but you gotta take the risk." Nick raised his glass to him.

"Yeah. I do." His mind whirled, making plans.

CHAPTER TWENTY-SIX — IVY

What am I doing here?

Ivy glanced at her phone, hoping Gabe would call, and spun her water glass between her hands. The conversation from the over-packed restaurant was buzzing in her ears.

Last weekend, she and Alice went for a trail ride at the McNeil's, and Alice mentioned she had a reporter friend at the *Herald,* and reporters were good contacts for Ivy to know. Alice casually said that her friend Nate was single while grooming the horses.

"Alice! I'm not looking for anyone, Gabe—"

"I thought you and Gabe were on a break?" Alice grinned.

"We are, but I don't think it's over." Her mouth tasted sour on those words. She didn't want it to be over. Gabe was going to therapy; Ivy felt he was trying to sort out what he wanted to do.

Since leaving Vancouver, Ivy has had nightmares about what Cole did to her. But it wasn't Gabe's fault.

"Then just have dinner. Don't think of it as a date. It's just two people getting to know each other over dinner. I think Aunt Wendy has her improv group over, so if you want to stay home and join in the fun, I know she always needs another actor."

"You're awful," Ivy said.

CHAPTER TWENTY-SIX – IVY

"Ivy, I know you have this new fancy job, but you need to get out and stop hiding at your parent's house. Besides, I am living through you. And Nate's a good guy." Alice waggled her eyebrows.

"How do you know him?" Ivy asked, tidying away the brushes.

"He did a profile on Frank's firm." Alice grinned.

"Oh great, so I can be bored to tears." Ivy patted her mare Starlight's neck and unclipped her from the cross ties.

"There's always improv." Alice laughed.

"Okay fine," Ivy said. "I'm only going to meet another person. It isn't a date."

Alice had smiled at her, and Ivy shook her head.

Sitting here in the busy restaurant, Ivy wished she had said no because this felt like a date. Ivy glanced at the time. Her non-date was twenty minutes late. If it wasn't for her mother's improv, she would have gone home because work had been intense. She loved her new role; she thrived on being in the hustle again. Her new bosses took her seriously; she didn't have to prove herself.

Ivy smiled, proud that she had saved a story from going to live for one of their top clients, a footballer, by quickly discrediting the source. It hadn't been easy, and it took six staff people on the phone and one parked outside the accuser's house, but it had been worth it. She had worked all day on that and just wanted to go home and put her feet up with a chilled glass of wine.

At least she could have the wine here.

"Hey, Ivy?" A short man with nice brown eyes, in a black suit jacket and jeans, extended his hand.

"Yes, that's me." Ivy returned the handshake.

"So sorry I was late. I got caught up in filing." Nate took a seat across from her.

"No worries," Ivy said.

"Did you order? Everything is god here."

Ivy had read a review and was looking forward to trying the cured salmon on a flatbread.

"No, I was waiting." Ivy sipped her water.

"Thanks. So Alice said you've lived in Vancouver for the past few years. How's that?"

"Warmer," Ivy said.

Nate threw his head back and laughed as if that was the funniest thing he had ever heard.

A server came over. "Can I take your drink orders?"

"White wine, please."

"No, that's just empty calories. Why don't we try the mocktails?" Nate said.

Ivy gritted her teeth and smiled at the server. "White wine, please."

"Okay, I guess the lady will have the wine."

Ivy refrained from rolling her eyes. Maybe Nate was just nervous, too. The server shot Ivy a sympathetic glance.

"Did you always want to be a business reporter?"

"Hell no. I wanted to cover sports, but I never found an in. You know the extreme nepotism in journalism, and I'm an only child. Alice told me you were too?"

"Yes, though Alice is like a sister."

"Yeah, I don't have cousins who are like siblings. So I had to take what I could get, but I liked talking to these guys who make a ton of money."

"And women?" Ivy said.

"Oh, sure. Though I must say, the ladies are less likely to meet me for drinks, which is really bad because I could profile them so well. You can send your clients to me, and I'll take care of them." Nate grinned.

CHAPTER TWENTY-SIX – IVY

Ivy groaned on the inside. She wouldn't put her clients in his hands.

"Are we ready to order appetizers?" the server cut in.

Thank god the wine was here. Ivy sipped it, crisp and cool and perfect.

"Yes, we'll have the deconstructed Caesar salad," Nate said.

"All right, two deconstructed-" The server tapped it in on her screen.

"No, actually, I want to try that cured salmon flatbread I've read about," Ivy said, barely keeping her annoyance out of her book.

"It's amazing!" the server said. "You won't regret it."

"I know I won't." Ivy smiled.

"I guess you don't care about calories," Nate said.

"Nope, I don't." Ivy stared at Nate until he glanced away, sitting straighter in her chair.

Nate looked her up and shook his head. "Okay, so as I was saying, if you bring me your clients, I can ensure they get front and centre. My online click-throughs have been up this month by a lot. I'm sure you aren't getting anyone too big, being new."

"I've just accepted the job as Senior Communications Strategist." Ivy hid her smile behind a sip of wine, noticing how Nate shifted in his chair.

"Oh." Nate glanced out the window.

"Where do you live in the city? I need a new place." Ivy set her wineglass on the table, leaning toward him.

"I'm the burbs, actually." Nate's tone lost some of the confidence he had earlier.

"Too bad. I'm looking for something downtown." Ivy flicked her hair behind her ear.

"I guess with the number of hours you're going to work, that makes sense." Nate scrolled through his phone.

"Yeah." Ivy smiled and wondered what Alice thought was decent about this man.

The waiter put her app in front of her, and Ivy dove in.

"That looks good," Nate commented.

"It's delicious." Ivy speared a forkful and almost moaned around it.

Nate stared at her as if he had never seen anyone eat before, then his cell rang. "Oh, that's the desk. I got to take it."

"Go ahead." Ivy shrugged.

He left the table, and ivy exhaled. She wanted to go but didn't want to be rude. Her phone buzzed, and she thought it was Gabe, but no, her mother had texted her a group shot of her improv group standing in the yard in a circle on hale bales.

Ivy laughed. It was good to be home but also suffocating.

"Hey, listen, I gotta go. It was nice meeting you, Ivy." Nate held his hand to her.

"You too, Nate." She shook his hand. *So glad that's over.* Ivy drank her wine and caught the waiter's eye, requesting another glass.

She opened the menu, scrolling down the list of entrees. She didn't mind eating alone, but it made her wonder where Gabe was at. She punched in his number.

"Hey." His baritone timbre made her heart lurch. God, she wished he was here, with his calm steely eyes. He never criticized her for what she ate. Or for ordering another glass of wine.

"Hey. Alice set me up on a date." Ivy smiled.

"Oh," the word was gritted out.

"Yeah, it totally sucked. He's gone now, and I didn't want to, but I wasn't sure how to say no." Ivy took another sip of her wine.

"Alice is a bit of a tornado," Gabe said.

"Yeah. So I'm sitting in this restaurant, having another glass of wine. My feet are killing me, and my mom's improv group is over. I have to be at work by seven." Ivy grinned into the phone.

"You're going to stay in the city, get a hotel room, right?"

"You think I should?" She bit her lip. In this moment, she wanted him to take the decision from her. She wanted him to order her what to do. Ivy closed her eyes, wishing he was here with her.

CHAPTER TWENTY-SIX – IVY

"Yes, finish your wine, then grab the hotel room. You have clothes in your car?"

"Yeah, I have my overnight bag."

Gabe knew she always kept a change of clothes in her car.

"Good. Is it only your feet that's killing you?"

"What do you mean?" Ivy blushed.

"Anywhere else that needs some attention?" That tone of his almost brought her there. It might have been enough to make her orgasm, and maybe if he talked for longer in that sultry, deep dominant tone, she'd cum right in her chair.

"Gabe…yes," Ivy breathed out.

"Once in your room, take off those heels you're wearing, strip out of your clothes and kneel on the floor of that enormous bed. Once you're naked and waiting, call me."

"Yes, Sir." The words slipped out of her mouth, and a part of her brain went on full alert, cursing her for what she was doing. Another part of her didn't care.

She needed this with her complete self.

"I'll be waiting." Gabe's calm tone gave her flutters in her pelvic floor.

Ivy closed the phone, feeling flushed and unsteady on her feet.

If only they could solve the rest of their issues as easily as some phone sex. Taking one more sip of the fabulous wine, Ivy went to pay the cheque and took the hotel next door to the restaurant, hoping they had a decent room. She needed a comfortable bed for what was going to happen.

Ivy's hands sweated as she let herself into the hotel suite. She put her bag down on an armchair and flipped on a couple of lights, kicking off her heels. The carpeted floor was plush underneath her feet. Crazy to feel nerves roll in her belly, she did, as she folded her work clothes, strode into the bedroom, naked. In the darkened room, she flicked those lights on, and as instructed, she knelt on the floor at the foot of the bed, closing her eyes.

How far had they come from this? Their D/s lately had been full of a power struggle, not a power exchange. But this here was her finding that quiet, submissive place. Nerves rolled through her as she dialled Gabe.

"I'm ready, Sir." Her pulse raced as she said the words.

"Switch to video." His commanding tone made her belly contract.

"Yeah. There's my girl," Gabe said. "Princess, grab your vibe from your bag and your phone holder. You're going need to be hands-free."

From her bag, she pulled out her rabbit vibrator with the grooved shaft and her phone stand.

"Got them," she said into her phone.

"Good. Get back to kneeling for me, Princess."

With a thrill of anticipation racing through her, she set the phone just in front of her. She could see Gabe's face, and Gabe could see her body.

"Look at you kneeling for me, Princess. Waiting to hear what I tell you to do. You're going to do it, right?"

"Yes, Sir."

"Everything I ask you to do?"

"Yes." Ivy's eyes found Gabe on the phone screen, and he smiled at her.

"What if I just make you kneel like that? Just keep you here, waiting. I know how impatient you are, Princess. How you hate waiting. But the sight of you on your knees makes me pleased." His rich voice caressed her skin, and Ivy closed her eyes, her hands on her thighs.

"I bet you're wet already, aren't you? Doing what I tell you to do is making those pink nipples of you stand to attention. Just think, hours ago, you were commanding a whole team. Now here you are, taking my commands. How does that make you feel?"

Ivy shook her head and swallowed, not being able to form words. "I like it."

"You like giving me your power, don't you, Princess?"

"Yes," she whispered.

CHAPTER TWENTY-SIX – IVY

"You like being reduced to my willing submissive, my cum-slut." His tone deepened.

Her mind blanked with a rolling wave of heat, her nipples hard points of need. "Yes, Sir."

"Damn, look at your body. If I were there, I would rub my hands up and down your body, caress your throat and put my hand over your mouth, the way I know you like it. Caress yourself, for me, Princess. Slowly."

Her hand shook slightly as she rubbed her hands along her belly, up to her breasts, around her shoulders, and grabbed her own chin with her fingertips, slowly running them over her mouth.

"Good girl. Don't forget about your thighs. Run your fingers along your gorgeous thighs, but you will not touch your cunt."

Ivy shivered and followed his instructions, her hands pressing on her thighs. Wetness pooled between her legs. She shifted a little on her heels, longing for touch on her pussy.

"Grab those breasts for me, cup them and show me and then pull your nipples, just like I do."

The absolute steely dominance in his voice. She couldn't do anything but give over to her wanting, her longing to follow it.

She lifted her breasts, closed her eyes, stretched her neck, her head falling back as she imagined Gabe's rough touch under her breasts. Gliding her hands to the tops of her breasts, she grabbed her nipples between her thumbs and index fingers and pulled.

"Harder. I want to see tears." Gabe's voice broke through the silence, and she tugged them as hard as she could until she gasped.

"Good girl. You can take that pain for me. I bet you're nice and wet and wanting my little slut."

Ivy moaned as she forced herself to keep tugging at her nipples, bouncing on her knees.

"Isn't it nice to obey, Princess? To turn your mind off of all the things you have to do. No pressure here. Just the expectation of your obedience. Correct?"

"Yes, Sir." She closed her eyes as she uttered the reply.

"Give those nipples the hardest tug can and then drop them. Do not touch your needy pussy."

Her pussy wept, liquid pooling between her thighs. Ivy threw her head back as she pinched and tugged her nipples as hard as she could.

"Put your palm over your cunt, but no, do not finger."

Ivy gasped as she did what Gabe said, feeling heat against her palm, wanting to touch herself badly.

"Are you humping your hand, baby?" She heard the grin in his voice, and Ivy shook her head, her cheeks red hot.

"That's okay. You can be a dirty pet. Show me how much you want to touch your hot little cunt."

Ivy shook her head but did as he instructed. Rocking on her knees, a whine escaped her mouth. The flame of desire running through her was so fucking bright and hot, and she wanted to grab it, touch it, get lost in the peak of those endorphins that Gabe, from miles away, was holding above.

"Good girl. Slide your fingers between your cunt lips and hold up a finger, showing me how wet you are."

As she did as instructed, the relief of touching herself was so welcomed that she almost came right there. She held up a glistening finger to the phone screen. Gabe smiled. "That's enough to get my cock hard, Princess."

"Slowly drag your fingers across your clit, stroke yourself to your cunt, to your asshole and back again. I want to hear you whine as your grind against your hand."

She did, her body tight with tension. It was like touching an electric fence.

"Fuck Gabe," she cried out as she grinded, doing exactly as he said. A wave of humiliation crashed on her, but it felt so good. "Good girl," Gabe said. "With your mouth, pick up that vibe. Then, using your fingers, put it in and out of your mouth as if you're sucking my cock. With your other hand, circle your clit."

She would do this because her walls were so far down, and she was zeroed in on his voice. She wanted to obey his directions. She took the vibe in her mouth, licking the wide part, then with her right hand, she dragged it in and out of her mouth as she circled her clit with her other hand.

"I love it when you drool. I know how much you love that." Gabe's voice was growing further away from her, and her eyes closed. She couldn't see his expression, but she heard the pleasure in his voice, and that knowledge tightened her coil of desire.

"Now, take that saliva-drenched vibrator and spread your knees. Slide that vibe into your greedy cunt and beg me to come."

"Please, Sir. God, please let me turn this on and come. I need this *so* bad."

"Tell me you miss me." Gabe's steely tone had a hint of laughter.

"I miss you so much. I wish you were here."

"If I was there, my finger would be in your mouth. My cock would be in your ass. Turn on your vibe."

She did, and her pussy convulsed around it as it hit her G-spot. She threw her head back and rocked as the powerful vibrations swept through her.

"God, Gabe!"

"You are so beautiful, Princess. Keep going."

She bit her lip as another wave of pleasure kept her going. Sliding to the floor on her back, she screamed as the wave of pleasure erupted.

"Again."

"I can't."

"Yes, you can, or I won't let you come for a month."

She was wrung out, her body hovering on the cusp of exhaustion. Spots danced behind her eyes as another orgasm took her under, a weird kind of exhaustion and pain filling her limbs.

"You look sexy as hell. One more."

"Fuck, no."

"Yes. Do it. Get that vibe on the highest setting."

Her fingers obeying, Ivy did. She screamed as another orgasm ripped through her. She couldn't do anything other than lay on the floor for several moments.

"That's a good cum slut." Gabe's voice filled the room, his tone pleased. "Can I get one more out of you? What if I say our word, Princess? Will you still come for me?"

Ivy panted, her toes pointed. Her pelvic floor clenched, feeling hollow. Her pussy was so swollen she ached.

"I can't."

"Yes, you can. Turn that vibe on again."

Her fingers obeyed his command as her thoughts protested. Holding the vibe to her swollen lips, Ivy scrunched her eyes close. It ached so damn much.

"Flick it to high, and scream one more time for me."

"Sir, please!"

"Princess, you will do this for me. I want you rolling on the floor, the pleasure pulsing through your body. Who does your orgasm belong to?"

"You, Sir!"

"Give it to me now, Princess."

She turned, flipped the vibe to its highest setting, and gasped as pain and pleasure shot through her body.

"Gabe!"

Her body shattered, hot pinpricks of pleasure rolling through her. She lay on the floor, panting.

CHAPTER TWENTY-SIX – IVY

"Good girl. You came apart for me, and I wasn't even there. That's my good sub. When you're ready, get up and pick up the phone."

She didn't know if it was five minutes or twenty, but eventually, her heart slowed as her vision cleared and the room returned to focus.

She grabbed her phone off the holder, noticing Gabe had switched off video chat.

"Hello, Sir?"

"My sweet, beautiful Princess. That was so fucking hot. I'm proud of you."

"Thank you, Sir."

"Put the phone down, wash your face and hands, and get some water. I'll wait."

With soft pleasure humming through her veins, Ivy did as she was told.

"I'm back."

"Good, now tuck yourself in."

"Are you going to tell me a story?" Ivy asked as she pulled down the covers one-handed.

"This is our story, and we're writing it."

The confidence in his voice wrapped around her heart like a hug, giving her hope, making her believe they could be together. Ivy closed her eyes, wishing he was here with her. "I love you."

"I love you, too, Princes. Call me whenever you wake up next."

"Okay." She clicked off with Gabe, set her phone on the nightstand and was asleep in minutes.

CHAPTER TWENTY-SEVEN - GABE

"We respect your decision," Ares said, standing beside Xander's chair.

"Fuck that, I don't." Xander shook his head at his brother, causing his long ponytail to fall over his shoulder. He glared at Gabe from across his desk. "Respect it, yes. But I don't like it. You're great for the team, Gabe. You keep them focused and patch them up when needed. I can't find someone these guys will trust with their body as much as they do you."

"I'll take that as a compliment," Gabe said. "Look, if your offer hadn't come along, I was going to go for another position, and Ivy and I probably would have crashed, and I don't know where we are going, but," Gabe stopped and took a deep breath, "Team Stealth, the Bandit Brothers. You know they mean everything to me. So thank you."

"You're welcome. But I refuse your resignation. I want to call you back in when we need you."

"Come on, Xander, let the man move on and go get his life," Ares said.

"I'm not stopping him from moving on or living his life. I want him to know that I value him, the guys value him, and I want him to answer my calls." Xander raised an eyebrow.

CHAPTER TWENTY-SEVEN - GABE

"I know," Gabe said. "And I will."

Xander stared through him, and Gabe wondered what he was seeing. Gabe shifted under his scrutiny and stood.

Xander came around his desk and slapped Gabe on the shoulder. "You can still get in the building. We won't delete your scans."

"Okay." Gabe knew he was grinning stupidly, but he didn't care. He wanted to belong in this private security operative world Xander, and Ares had.

"Got news on your brother today." Xander's mouth quirked in a half-smile.

"He still breathing?" Gabe clenched and unclenched his fist, concentrating on taking slow deep breaths.

"Yes. Winston-Reid doesn't want this in the media. But they won't be funding any other private contractor companies."

"So he gets away with it?" Gabe hissed out.

Xander spread his hands out, turning his palms up. "He's broke. Turns out the star defenseman had a ton of gambling debts. I hear his fiancé left him too."

"No shit?" Gabe grinned hugely.

"Karma takes care of it sometimes," Ares said.

"Karma always comes through," Xander said.

"I'm glad I don't have to worry about the fucker. I've cut ties with my father, too."

"Some people don't deserve us." Xander slapped him on the shoulder.

"Gabe, take care of yourself. We'll see you at the wedding?" Ares gave him a man-hug.

"I'd like to be there. May?" Gabe grinned.

Xander flashed a rare grin. "Got postponed. They keep making the damn thing bigger and bigger. But we thought it was better to wait until after Harper's done her tour. You bring your girl."

"If she'll have me," Gabe said.

"She will. Don't be afraid to grovel. It sucks, but it pays off," Xander said.

Ares gave his brother a light punch.

Xander shrugged. "It does."

"I'll keep that in mind. See you later," Gabe said.

He waved to them, a lump in his throat.

In the elevator, he exhaled. Leaving Axis Management wasn't easy. But he needed to show Ivy he was all in, and he would be there for her. And that meant living a life where she was, moving to Edmonton.

Edmonton wasn't a bad city. His mother supposedly lived there. Maybe he'd look her up and try to reconnect.

He could find another job, doing something. Though his skill set wasn't that great on paper, honestly. He shut out his father's voice, telling him he wasn't good at anything, and he flicked the bracelet against his wrist. His boss had just told him he was one of the few who had entrance to this black and steel castle in the city. He was damn good at what he did.

At home, he glanced around the almost packed-up condo and sighed. He had to talk to Ivy and see what she wanted to be done with the place. For now, he was packing because that's where this was going, and he wanted to be ahead of the game.

He put on some tunes, poured himself a beer and got to work, packing up the living room. An hour later, a knock on his door made him stall as he wrapped Ivy's favourite vases.

The icy glare of Quinn Walsh met him.

"What the hell Gabe? You're going to skip out and not tell me?"

"They gossip like old ladies. No, I just don't know what to do yet. Come on in. grab a box."

Quinn threw his leather jacket off, grabbed a flat box and started folding. "I just missed you at Axis Management. I'm supposed to be

CHAPTER TWENTY-SEVEN - GABE

training new recruits for Team Stealth. We're going to get busier this year."

"That's what I hear." Gabe taped the next box.

"You've had enough?"

"Never, man, you know that. I got to get my girl."

Quinn threw the box down and clapped Gabe's shoulder. "Thank fuck for that. I'm going to miss you like crazy."

"An hour away by plane."

"You hate them."

"Not so bad when I'm not jumping out of them," Gabe said.

From the fridge, he passed Quinn an energy drink and took one out for himself.

"What really made you knock on my door?"

Quinn pointed at him, raised his bottle in cheers and hopped on the kitchen stool. "I'm sorry."

"No, Quinn. It's not on you."

"Listen, my head was so messed up after Jordan, I didn't see how much...."

"Mine was too?" Gabe grinned.

"Yeah." Quinn looked away.

"You did. You talked to me about being too angry, about needing a break. I blew you off."

"Okay. You're right. It's not my fault at all." Quinn grinned.

"Not having Ivy has been torture. I got to give it a fair chance with her, and I don't think it's ever been fair."

"I think we all owe her an apology," Quinn said. "She was there when you got home, every time."

"Yeah. And I didn't realize how seriously she took her career, how her doing this marketing storytelling thing she does, it's like her mission. Ivy risked a lot to try and protect me, and she was right. And I nearly lost her, for good. Who knows what would have happened if they had tossed her on that plane?"

"Has she talked to you about it?"

"Not much. She says she is fine. She took a new job, an executive position."

"Your girl is impressive."

"A couple of times, she's let herself be angry at me, but I don't know, I feel like that's the Band-Aid, you know? I'm not sure what the cure is."

"Being honest, probably or something. I don't know. You got to tell her how you feel."

"I know. At least I get away from my brother and father, as much as I will miss the Bandit Brothers."

"Have you spoken to your dad?"

"I've told my dad to lose my number. I might try to reconnect with my mother. I understand her better now, you know?"

"Yeah. Does Ivy know you're doing this?"

"No. I wanted to show her I was serious about making a new life. I don't know what she'll want to do with this place."

"I know a great real estate agent. You can get the listing ready. Wait for her to sign off?"

"Great idea. Any other tips?"

"Yeah, we're not defined by who raised us, you know?"

Gabe met Quinn's piercing azure gaze and nodded.

"Copy that. You know, Jordan was the first one to call me Doc."

"After you bandaged that kid up."

"He had a metal spike in his shin. Yeah, like I cared I was off duty."

"You're never off duty, dammit. And then we all followed him."

"Yep, that's what we do." Gabe came around the counter. "Got some time to help me with a few more boxes?"

"You got it," Quinn said.

CHAPTER TWENTY-SEVEN - GABE

Damn, he was going to miss this place, but he also felt peace for the first time.

"Hey, does Simone make more than you?"

Quinn grunted. "Right now, she's teaching at one of the art schools, so no. But she makes more than a soldier's pay, that's for sure."

"It's been an issue between Ivy and me. It was the deciding factor in signing on with Axis Management."

"I always thought that was the reason. Why do you care?"

Gabe pounded on his chest. "One of those fucked-up ideas about me being the man."

Quinn laughed and threw a cushion at him. "That's bullshit."

"I know. You've met my father. Money is everything to him. She was making double what I was as a medic."

"Did she ever care?" Quinn cocked an eyebrow.

"No. She thought I was being dumb about it."

"Yeah, you were. You're her Dom, not her banker."

"I guess," Gabe mumbled, packing the box up.

"It wouldn't bother you?"

Quinn snorted. "My mother is an artist, my father is a carpenter, and I was practically raised by the nurse across the street. No doctors or tech gurus in my DNA. Her parents have a farm?"

"Yeah, a berry farm. They do okay. Money never seemed to be a thing when I was around them. They never mention it, you know? My dad always does. I always felt uncomfortable."

Quinn taped up a box, stacked it on another and taped up another.

"Simone's folks had money, and she had the most sheltered life I've ever heard of. People can be dumb with money. I'm lucky to have Simone. It's just her, and I in our four walls and nothing else matters."

"What if she doesn't forgive me?"

"You're a stubborn bastard. She stuck with you through a lot of stuff. Are you ready for what comes next?"

Gabe leaned against the wall of boxes. "I don't know. Maybe."

Quinn taped up one more box, stacked it, and sighed. "You know, I'm not going to like not seeing your ugly mug every day."

Gabe laughed. "Xander hasn't accepted my resignation. So I might be around occasionally."

"Good." Quinn strode over, picked up his jacket, reached into his inside pocket and handed Gabe a folded piece of paper.

"What's this?"

"If you want it, it's yours."

Gabe's breath caught in his throat. It was a posting for a trainer in Edmonton. "Part-time. The pay is awful."

"I hear your girlfriend is rolling in it." Quinn grinned.

Gabe laughed. "Thank you, man."

"You're welcome."

"You got this tonight?"

"Xander asked me if I knew of anything in Edmonton a couple of days ago. I guess he saw the writing on the wall."

"Scary fucker, sometimes."

"Yeah. We're going to need to have a going-away party."

Gabe's chest suddenly felt tight. "We can do that. Thanks, brother."

Quinn wrapped him in a bear hug, patted him on the arm, and pointed his finger at Gabe.

"Call if you need anything. Go get your girl."

"I will," Gabe said, clasping his arm.

CHAPTER TWENTY-EIGHT - IVY

At an empty table again in the restaurant next to the hotel, it wasn't lost on Ivy how for so long, she wished this was her life. Growing up on her parent's berry farm, being in a ritzy hotel seemed like the thing to achieve. And now she could do it without blinking, worrying about paying rent or having a job. Her first six weeks of working with Sunset Corp were in the books, and already Ivy had proven herself. It felt good. But she frowned, spinning the lime and ginger drink around.

It felt lonely.

She could hang out at Alice's, chilling in the family room or helping to clean up Alice's kitchen while Alice rocked her baby to sleep, or she could be at her parents with her mother's theatre friends, noisily talking about what went wrong on stage. But that wasn't the kind of company she wanted; after putting in a twelve-hour day, she wanted quiet. She'd grab a bite here, then go upstairs to the suite she had reserved, put something on the hotel tv and try to zone out, hoping for a good night's sleep.

Ivy sipped her drink. Every other table in the place was occupied by a couple, and she knew why it felt lonely.

It was because Gabe wasn't sitting across from her. And even though he hadn't been supportive in the way she thought she wanted, he was supportive by making sure the laundry was done; he washed the dishes and put them away and never told her she had to eat salad. He pushed her to be better. By demanding more of her in the bedroom, he boosted her confidence. She had wilted a little during their time apart, gone into her shell. When she was with him, she was more of herself. His calm broodiness complimented her outward confidence.

Her phone buzzed, and she smiled.

"Hey, Princess. How was your day?" His warm sultry voice sent heat to her cheeks.

Ivy sat back in her chair and closed her eyes, wondering where he was. She pictured him at home in their condo, wearing his favourite sweatpants in his worn black Henley.

"I had three meetings with clients, pitched to a famous up-and-coming songwriter, and finally caught up on the client list. Oh, and I met my assistant."

"Are you going to keep her?" His voice had a bit of an edge.

"Him, actually, and yes, he's super qualified. He's invited me for dinner with his husband later this week."

Gabe exhaled, and Ivy couldn't help but laugh. He was too caveman predictable sometimes.

"You must be wiped out. What time were you in this morning?"

"Seven-thirty. I'm at the hotel bar, again. I just needed some quiet. I'm going to have to look for a place here."

"I know." Gabe's voice sounded so far away, and Ivy bit her lip. "I've been thinking about that, too. It's time to move on."

"I loved that condo." She fanned herself, suddenly warm from the overwhelming feelings she had.

"Yeah. We had a lot of happy memories there."

CHAPTER TWENTY-EIGHT - IVY

"I wish you were here," Ivy blurted it out. She had been trying so hard to only talk about the present moment, to stay in the conversation. That meant no talking about their past issues. No talking about where they were going with their future. She was torn between keeping their peace of the present and bringing up their future. Gabe had seemed so levelled; she didn't want to bring up the future to upset him. She bit the inside of her lip, knowing that wasn't right either. He wouldn't want her to avoid talking to him.

"I'm happy you said that." The phone muffled for a moment. "Because you're the prettiest woman in the place, and there is an empty seat across from you."

Her hands shook as she scanned the restaurant. Over there by the door, his long frame, wide shoulders, his hair just above his collar because he was tired of regulation, and about two days' growth on his face, for the same reason. Her heart thundered. A flush crept up her neck. She smiled, watching as he looped over to her table.

"Hi," she squealed

He leaned down and kissed her, his tongue teasing hers, her hand came up to cup his familiar face. He deepened the kiss as if he couldn't stop kissing her. She tapped his arms, suddenly aware they were in the restaurant. He broke off the kiss, and she licked her swollen lip.

"Hey." He put his duffel bag on the floor, sat on the chair across from her, and took her hands in his.

For a few moments, they just stared at each other, not speaking. Ivy took in the tightness of his jaw and knew he was stressed.

"You're *here*."

"I had to come. I couldn't go another day without seeing you."

His sultry tone made her blush.

"Can I get you anything?" A server interrupted their gazing.

Gabe inclined his head to Ivy.

"Actually, I'll skip dinner here tonight and call for room service later."

"Much later," Gabe said.

The server grinned and walked away.

"Let's go."

Ivy got up from the table so fast that the glass shook. He took her arm, holding her close as he walked through the restaurant, into the lobby, to the elevator. With her every step, Ivy couldn't believe this was real.

"What floor?"

"Like you don't know?" Ivy grinned.

Gabe pressed the button for the 7th floor. "You know my tricks."

"Most of them."

As soon as the doors opened, his lips crashed into hers, and Ivy moaned, inhaling his sharp, familiar scent, basking in the familiarity of his solidness. Ivy's hands went under his jacket, feeling his tight abs, his strong shoulders.

"Missed you so much." Gabe grabbed her hand in his as the door pinged.

Six doors down, Ivy took out the key card. It flashed green. Gabe hit the lights, hung his jacket up in the closet, and kicked off his shoes as she flung off her heels.

"I missed you too. I'm happy you're here."

"Yeah?" Gabe smiled. "How happy?"

Ivy laughed. Something was lighter about him as his eyes raked over her, assessing her. His hands ran down her shirt, her linen pants. "Damn. You're the only girl for me, you know that?"

Gabe nuzzled her neck and kissed her collarbone, his hands caressing her arms.

She wanted to melt into him. But her heart skipped a beat. "Gabe, I…"

"Yes. You are. It's true. Nothing you can say can make it untrue."

"We're awful together."

"No, we're not. I was awful for a while there. Together we're better. I love you. And I'm so sorry, Ivy."

His voice broke on the last words. It was enough for her to believe him at this moment.

He gently kissed her as if he were telling her to hush.

Ivy laughed as he pulled her into the bedroom. Her hands slid to his belt buckle.

He swatted away her hands.

"Think you're in charge?"

"Show me I'm not."

Her heart beat like a caged butterfly, fluttering in milliseconds, but the heat in his gaze, in his lips as he kissed her, in his fingertips as he slid down her bra, drew her into his fire. Every caress of his fingertips was sure and confident. He didn't look like the broken, angry man she had left, but the confident Dom she knew he could be. His hands gripped around her throat, his thumbs pressing lightly right where her pulse was.

Yes! This is what she wanted from him.

"Down."

She sank to her knees. He pulled her head against his leg, patting her hair. "I've missed you so much. Have you missed this, us?"

"Yes, Sir," Ivy said.

"My cock is throbbing for you. Suck it, baby."

She helped him get his jeans off, her hands sliding up the back of his muscled calf.

He rubbed her nose along his hard cock and pushed her face into his balls. She rocked on her knees, loving the feeling of being directed, of being used. Her lips sucked his testicles gently, and she moaned in pleasure as he grabbed a fistful of hair and moved her back to his cock. She took it all the way in, wrapping her lips around his hardness. She sucked hard, feeling her cheeks hollow.

"Just like that, Princess. Show me how much you like being on your knees." He pulled her hair, and Ivy wrapped her hands around his thighs, moaning as his foot came over her back in a gentle caress. Under his foot is where she didn't know she wanted to be but belonged here, at this moment.

She lapped his cock, sucking and easing her mouth over it.

So big. So familiar, and yet, it had been so long. Slowly, Ivy dragged her tongue up the length of his rock-hard shaft, flicking her tongue around his tip.

Ivy gasped as Gabe's firm hands cupped her face, and he thrust deep, so deep his cock hit the back of her throat. Ivy breathed through her nose, concentrating on relaxing. *Yes! God*, she wanted this. Gabe increased the pace of his thrusts. Finally, her mind stilled, turning off. Only focused on his musky smell, the strength of his hands, and his gasp of pleasure above her. His hands in her hair, pulling her up, and she drowned in his hungry kisses, his possession of her, her whole body softening to him.

She gyrated against him with her hips, grabbing his hard cock.

"That's my slut," Gabe murmured against her ear as he pushed her back onto the luscious sheets. "Open those legs for me."

Ivy giggled at the intensity of his gaze, sending her nerves roaring. She opened her legs wide, and he adjusted her, so her arms were holding her calves. God, it made her feel so raw, so vulnerable, so gushing wet.

"I want your cock in me now."

"Do you?" Gabe rubbed the tip of his penis around her entrance, oh so slowly. Ivy gritted her teeth.

"Yes!"

The slowly sexy smile reminded Ivy of a big cat predator, and he sank two fingers into her, and Ivy felt her muscles clamp around them.

"Seems like you're just a little wet."

"You know, I can't hold this position forever. Can you hurry?"

"You'll hold it." Gabe smacked her ass, hard and quickly. Ivy yelped, clutching the sheets in her hand and lifting her hips off the bed.

"Yes, Sir."

CHAPTER TWENTY-EIGHT - IVY

God, she had missed this. The play between them, the power struggle, but he always took it back because she always surrendered, no matter how much she protested.

His fingers circled around her labia lips, pulled back her hood, circled around her clit and Ivy bit her lip to endure his almost clinical touches.

"Yep, still wet."

"Please."

"I like the sound of that. Please, what?"

"Please fuck me with your hard cock, *Sir*."

"You know I thought you would never ask." He lined up his cock's head at her entrance and entered her with one long delicious, slow stroke.

"Ah yes!"

Gabe grabbed her legs and drilled into her so fast and so hard that her hips shook the bed. The pleasure mounted from her core and climbed up every muscle of her body. The orgasm exploded through her as she screamed his name, her arms coming away from her legs.

Ivy lolled her head on the pillow and smiled as Gabe slowed above her. As his eyes closed, the sheen of sweat on his tight abs glistened. She loved watching how his orgasm took him, finally making him lose control. He collapsed on top of her, kissing her face, her lips, and his arms around her.

"I love you, Ivy."

"I love you too."

Because, for better or worse, it was true: there was no other man but Gabe Arthur for her.

CHAPTER TWENTY-NINE— GABE

The ringing had him up on his feet. It took another few seconds to register that it wasn't his phone, he wasn't reaching for his go-bag, but it was Ivy's phone, from somewhere near the door.

The room smelled like sex and sweat. Gabe ran to the door and found Ivy's phone in her purse. It immediately started ringing again.

"Give it here." Ivy flipped on the bedside light. Gabe passed her a bottle of water from the table.

"Hello? Don't worry about it. Tell me what we got."

As she talked on the phone, Gabe turned the lights on near the round work table in the suite. He brought Ivy's laptop out of her bag, took it out and set it up, and next to it, he set her iPad, knowing this was a work thing and she liked using both.

"Give me ten minutes, and I'll call you back. I need to think for a moment, but I have an idea." Damn, he had missed hearing how cool and in control she was when it came to her work.

In the bathroom, he started the taps for her, running the shower just below scalding hot.

"You're the best." Ivy stepped up on her tiptoes, cupped his mouth with her palm and kissed him.

"You got to be quick, and if you keep kissing me like that, you're not going to make it to whatever crisis it is."

"Damn hockey players. I think I can handle it from here, but we'll see."

She hurried into the shower. Gabe rifled through her bag, set out some clothes for her, then hung them on the bathroom door.

Five minutes later, Ivy came out with kissable light pink gloss on her lips, a swash of blush on her cheeks and mascara on her eyes. The deep purple shirt brought out her warm eyes.

"Do I look okay?"

"You look great. I'm going to shower. Do you want me to see if the kitchen is open?"

"Not until I know if I have to go or if I can stay here."

Gabe kissed her, whispering into her ear. "I hope you stay."

"Me too."

Ivy took a deep breath and marched over to the table. She was so gorgeous as she threw her shoulders back and stared straight into the camera for her face time call. She looked professional and sexy and in control.

But in the bedroom, I'm in control. The thought jarred him. In the shower, he quickly washed up and let the water pour over him. The last few weeks without Ivy had been hell. But also peaceful because he hadn't taken his father's calls, he didn't care where his brother was, though Xander was looking for him, and as much as he hated to admit it, the sessions with Dr. Laktur made his head clearer.

But he knew what he wanted, and it was Ivy. She was strong, intelligent, capable and fully his. And when she came home from a long day at work, kicked off her heels and knelt for him, it was so incredibly sexy and heady and intoxicating because her surrender was so precious. She met a lot of people at those events she went to. She could have found someone in the time they had been apart. But she didn't. That and what she shared last night gave him hope. Out there, she belonged to her work. In here, with just them, she was his.

He hated that he didn't value this before. But he would prove to her that he would worship her dichotomy from now on.

"Yes, we'll give you three thousand dollars. All you have to do is confirm that Miss Perkins is a piano student of yours if the press asks. Just like that, you don't lie. You say, 'Yes, Natasha is a great student of mine.' Keep it short and simple. What do you say, Rachel?"

Ivy spoke into her headset while making notes with a pen. "She really will come and take piano lessons with you. This isn't a lie. Okay, that's a great help, Rachel. I appreciate it. One of my associates will be right over to brief you further. Thanks for answering my call." Ivy smiled, hung up the call, and made a few taps on her laptop keyboard.

"Hey Danielle, okay, I got it all sorted. Natasha wasn't there to see Lane Gibson. The rumours of an affair are false. If the press keeps harassing them, they finally spill that she was there to take piano lessons from world-famous pianist Rachel Ikes. I will meet with Lane and tell him he absolutely has to move apartments. We'll help him handle it. He can't be seen with his high school sweetheart again if he wants to keep his wife from taking most of what he owns and half his salary. Yes, great work Danielle. Thanks for being so quick on this, and you can call me anytime."

Ivy's rich laugh echoed off the walls, and Gabe's heart glowed.

He was proud of his girl.

She hung up the phone, rubbed her temples and smiled at him.

"Hey, thanks for helping me get through that."

"I didn't do anything." Gabe dropped a kiss on her forehead. "Why don't I order breakfast in? Do you have time before you have to meet with the hockey player?"

"Yes. On Monday, I will meet with him to say that meeting with his PR Firm was a routine thing and not a crisis management thing." Ivy yawned. "I could go back to bed."

"I could have you in bed." He wrapped his arms around her shoulders.

"Later. I need another call with Danielle and an update on this before I relax too much. You, Mr. Arthur, have no clothes on."

"I noticed."

Ivy stood, marched over to him and ran her hands along his chest. Her hand swept down to his cock.

"Nope." Gabe stilled her hands. "You're not going to tease me like that, right, Princess? Or I'll make you cum so many times your pussy will be raw."

"Yes, Sir," she mumbled as the sweetest blush coloured her cheeks. "Could you please go throw clothes on?"

"Anything for you." He kissed her forward, grabbing his bag from the door.

Her phone rang again.

While she answered it, Gabe got threw on jeans, called room service and checked his email. He'd have to tell Ivy that he was no longer working for Axis Management.

Team Stealth had gotten him away from the army when he didn't think he needed to. He could still hear Jordan's convincing argument about why he should sign on with Axis Management and shook his head. That guy could sell religion to the most devout atheist. Damn, he missed him, and he always would. But the other Bandit Brothers were a quick plane ride away.

"Everything okay?"

"Yes, Princess. I'm lucky you were at the hotel and not your parents' place."

"It's basically one long stretch of road off the highway."

"Yeah, I'll have to refresh my memory."

"I'm supposed to have dinner with them tomorrow night. You could come?"

"I would like that." He wrapped his arms around her, and she leaned her cheek against his chest. This, right here, was all he needed. He just had to tell her that.

A knock on the door broke apart their embrace.

Ivy shook her head at him, went to the door and brought the cart in.

"Let's move all the dishes to the table. You got me French pressed coffee?"

"I asked. They said they had it."

"This is my favourite hotel."

They got busy, pouring coffee and dishes and digging into the buffet of breakfast Gabe had ordered.

After he cleared the plates, he set them on the cart and wheeled it outside their room.

"Come here." He sat on the couch, pulling Ivy on his lap. "It's nice having breakfast with you. I've missed it."

"Yeah. I know. Gabe, I know you don't like that I took this job, but I couldn't pass up this opportunity."

"Of course, you couldn't," Gabe said.

"Really?" She bit her lip. "I thought you would be mad because I didn't tell you about it. They called me out of the blue."

"Yes. Ivy, I've been an asshole. I forgot how amazing you are at your job. You should be earning the high dollars, and you would have been dumb not to take this position out here. I know the job with Julien was fun, but I doubt he matched the salary."

"No, he laughed and told me he knew it was too good to be true."

"Good. It's nice to see your confidence back. I know I dented it a bit, and I hate that. I'm so sorry, Ivy." He took her hand in his. "From now on, I'm going to support you in anything you want to do."

CHAPTER TWENTY-NINE – GABE

Ivy shook her head, her short blond hair caressing the top of her eyebrows. "But I let my confidence get too easily shaken too. Losing Metric was a big deal for me. It felt like I had lost a person almost. But it was you not believing me. I don't know. I started to get withdrawn. I didn't recognize myself."

"That's on me. And I'm sorry."

"I know. You said it."

"And I'll keep saying it. Move your feet for a sec."

Ivy swung her feet off his lap, and Gabe grabbed his tablet. "Look at this."

He took her coffee cup as she took the tablet.

"Are you serious?"

He grinned at the shock in her voice.

"Yes, that's what our condo will fetch us. Quinn's mother-in-law thinks she can sell it quickly."

"What are you saying, Gabe?"

"I'm saying I'm ready for something new. Something new, with you by my side, Ivy. I'm all into us."

"Wow, my parents are going to freak out if I tell them how much our condo is worth."

Gabe laughed. "They'll be proud, though."

Ivy nodded. "What about your job?"

Gabe sighed and ran his hand through his hair. "I love the Bandit Brothers, but Ivy, I love you more. And if this is where you need to make your home, then this is where I have to be. It's that simple."

Her eyes lit up, and she kissed him, long and slow, her tongue entwining with his. He ran his hand along her arm, pulling her into his lap.

"I can get another job. Quinn gave me a lead on a part-time job as a medic trainer. The pay is awful."

"I don't care. I can support us. As long as you don't mind?"

"No, I don't mind being a kept husband." Gabe cupped her face and kissed her, biting her lower slip slightly. Her mouth parted for him, his arms tightened around her and under her, and he grew rock hard. The scent of her favourite magnolia conditioner filled his nostrils, and he kissed her neck, then took her hand and kissed the pulse at her wrist. "You are all I need, Ivy."

"You already have an advantage, not being fully dressed."

"In the bedroom, Princess, I will always have the advantage."

Ivy stilled her hands on her thigh. "That's the compromise?"

"It's not a compromise. It's what works for us. We got lost back there, trying to be a certain thing or at least I did. You were always you. You being a boss lady out there and then kneeling for me the minute you get home? Yeah, that works for me."

"Oh, it's like that?" Ivy asked, a huge grin on her face.

"Yes. And asking my permission to get in our bed at night. And never forget that when it comes to this," he grabbed her hair, pulling her back against him, as his hand slid down to palm her mound, "I'm in charge."

Her eyes dilated, the pleasure blushing her cheeks, her gaspy breath going straight to his cock. He feasted on her mouth, nipping at her lips until they were swollen and bright pink. He let go of her hair and kissed the column of her throat, right down to the swell of her breasts.

"Yes! Please."

His hands gently worked the buttons free on her blouse as her cell phone rang from across the room. Ivy collapsed on his shoulder.

"No."

"You got to answer, Princess." He helped her to her feet.

"Hello?" She sounded perfectly composed. "What? She can't do that. She absolutely can*not* talk to the press. I'm on my way. I'll be there in thirteen minutes."

Gabe chuckled. "Need to put out a fire?"

"It's what I do."

"Then go. I'll be here when you get back, and then maybe we can look at some real estate listings."

"Yes, okay," Ivy said. She was distracted, putting her iPad in her bag, sliding on her shoes, and grabbing her jacket.

"Want me to drive you over?"

"No, I'll just... Yes! Hurry, though."

Gabe grinned. He quickly threw on a black t-shirt and slipped his feet into boots. "Let's go."

"I love you."

"I love you too."

CHAPTER THIRTY – IVY

"More." Ivy pushed against Gabe's punishing thrust as his arms came around her. Her body still heavy with sleep, her thoughts still quiet. They were huddled under a nest of blankets. Gabe's hands palmed under her breasts, down over each of her rolls, kneading and exploring with his fingers. His hot breath along her neck sent shivers up her spine.

It was so perfect to be here with him. And he was there for her at eleven this morning when she finally prevented the crisis of the hockey player and his high school sweetheart from spilling onto the front page. She had a few more details to wrap up, and she laughed, remembering the girlfriend's reaction to actually needing to take piano lessons.

"You're thinking, Princess." Gabe pinched her nipple between his fingers as he strummed the other one with her thumb. Ivy closed her eyes and tipped her head back against his chest.

She gave over to his firm touches, his insistent kisses. His kiss blazed heat through her, arrowing right to her clit. Reaching back with her hand, she stroked his hard, thick cock. She smiled as she heard Gabe suck in his breath and then laugh when he suddenly pinned her down, his weight on top of her. He kissed her neck, her lips, her nose. Ivy giggled.

CHAPTER THIRTY – IVY

His callused hands swept over her belly, his fingers teasing along her thighs.

His gaze heated her, and there was nowhere else she wanted to be right now than in these tangled sheets, in this fabulous hotel room with him. Her hips rose off the bed. He held open her thighs, capturing her mouth.

Ivy moaned low and urgently, pressing herself into him. His fingers hovered around her pussy but not touching it, anticipation making her hungry for his touch.

"In me, please," she said through the kiss.

He guided her legs so her knees were bent wide open. And then dragged his cock along her entrance, slowly teasing her. He smiled, but his gaze was still intense. He made her feel cherished.

"Little more."

Gabe leaned down on top of her, bracing his arms on either side of her and with one thrust, entered her. Ivy gasped as her pussy walls stretched to accommodate him, and slowly, he glided in and out of her, his abs rippling, his stare filled with love piercing her heart.

"Gabe, yes!" she cried out as he drilled into her, deep and sure, and suddenly the blankets were off of him. He grabbed her shoulders and rocked deep in her as her legs came up around his waist.

"More, please!" His smooth chest abraded her breasts, he bit into her shoulder, just a little bit, and the orgasm overtook her, causing her to see dots behind her eyes, wave after wave of pleasure making her come apart.

"Holy hell" Ivy wrapped her arms around him, opened her eyes to see his expression tight, feel him inside her, thrust once more and then felt his hot seed in her core. She bit her lip as he collapsed on her, kissing her cheeks, brushing her lips, holding her.

"You're not the only one who missed morning sex," he said. Ivy laughed and rested her head on his shoulder, trailing her fingers along his muscled chest.

"Yeah?" She brushed her hand along his unshaven face.

"Yeah. Why don't you clean me up?" He raised an eyebrow at her, pushing her down. A murmur escaped her lips, a swell of need and want rising in her as her hands came down over his leg.

"What are you waiting for, sub?"

"Nothing Sir," Ivy breathed out. She scooted down, kissing his hard abs, palming his stomach, then lifted his limp penis off his thigh and took it in her mouth, licking it and sucking it gently.

"I give the clean-up lady five stars."

She giggled around him, then her giggle changed to a yelp as his two fingers slid into her anus. He fingered her, setting off firey sensations in her body. She hummed, low in her throat from pleasure. His two fingers slid into her anus. "Gabe."

"Yes, Princess?"

She shook her head, letting her teeth graze him a bit. He slapped her cheek gently. She got the hint and went back to licking and lapping as his fingers explored her most intimate place. It had been a while since he had taken her there; a shudder went through her at the thought. She could not get enough of this man. She sucked and lapped, smiling in satisfaction as his penis lengthened and became hard again.

"Asking for something, sub?"

"No." Ivy hid her face on his chest, with his cock in her fingers.

He covered her mouth with his hand, pinching her nose.

"Try again."

She murmured against his hand as he let up. "Please, take me in the ass, Sir."

"I thought you'd never ask." Gabe turned her, dropping kisses along her neck. Beside him on the nightstand, he grabbed the lube. He took her hand and poured some cool lube on her palm. "Get ready for me, Princess."

Ivy stared at him, and he sat back with one eyebrow raised.

She didn't know where his Dominant confidence had come from, but she wanted more of it. Reaching behind her, she lubed up, put her face down on the bed and spread her ass cheeks.

"Do you like preparing your asshole for me?" Gabe whispered against her ear.

"Hmm."

"That was not an answer." He pulled her hair, and Ivy bit her lip. "Answer me, Princess, or I'll make you wear a butt plug for the entire day."

"You wouldn't."

"Try me," Gabe said.

A thrill of excitement ran down her, and her ass came up high off the bed. He struck her ass hard, laughing.

"Yes," Ivy said. "Yes. I like lubing myself up for you."

He kissed her, long and deep. Ivy closed her eyes, clinging to his familiar taste, his scent.

"Why was that so hard?"

"Making me all vulnerable."

"You're holding your spread ass cheeks, waiting for me to enter. I don't know how much more vulnerable we can get. Unless we were to take a picture of this and post it?"

Her breath caught in her throat, and she grinded against the sheets. He spanked her once, twice and laughed.

"Is that the kind of thing you fantasize about?"

She felt his heat behind her, and she swallowed, trying to make words.

He put a warm palm on her back. She glanced behind her and saw him stroking himself.

"Sometimes," she whispered.

"I'm just a simple man. This is enough for me." He slowly slid into her back entrance; Ivy let go of the breath she was holding and pushed back against him.

"That's it, Princess, relax and let me fill you and pleasure you." His arm came around her, his fingers skirting her pussy lips, and Ivy closed her eyes, lost in the pleasure of his weight against her. His cock, deep in her, she could feel every ridge; every slight movement sent her nerve endings blazing. God, it was so good. Gabe took his time, stroking her, easing himself fully in and out, all while fingering her clit.

Had it ever been this good between them? She didn't think so. Maybe it was because they were more honest with each other? She only knew right now between them, this moment. The D/s connection was more intense. She thought it was lost, broken, something they had to give up. She pushed against him, following his rhythm, and she whimpered as he took his time, slowing down his pace.

It turned out they needed more D/s. She liked knowing that when she walked through the door, she was his. That she didn't have to make another decision for the day. That she didn't have to give the orders; that was his job.

"Now, Princess." His fingers hooked deep inside her, and he found her G-spot expertly, and she shrieked as he pounded into her from behind as his fingers took the edge of the pain off. The sensation was splitting her focus, and she screamed, "Gabe," as another orgasm came over her, shattering her. Another moment, she clenched her ass cheeks as his hot seed emptied into her, and she purred like a cat. He kissed her neck, brought her to him, and hugged her.

"Shower, breakfast and then?"

"We can go look for a place to live," Gabe said. "I got two listings from a real estate agent. One is outside of the city, and one is right in the core."

"That's what I want." She didn't want to commute, she wanted to be close to work, and she liked the amenities of the city.

"I don't know. A little space would be nice." Gabe kissed her mouth.

"A little space adds to my commute, and I miss time with you, with this." Ivy kissed his fingers.

CHAPTER THIRTY – IVY

"Can we look at the one twenty minutes out of the core? It's tree-lined."

"Okay," Ivy said.

"And also a few thousand cheaper."

Ivy shook her head. Yes, it would be cheaper, but she loved the city.

Her cell rang from the bedside table, and her stomach clenched, hoping she didn't have to go to work.

"Hi, Mom." She pushed away from Gabe, wrapping the sheet around her.

"Ivy, are you coming to dinner today? We haven't seen you for a couple of days."

"Sorry, I got caught up at work since Friday. I'm here with Gabe. We would love to come to dinner."

"Gabe...oh good," her mom said.

"Yeah, he surprised me by showing up here." Ivy fluffed her hair and bit her lip.

"Okay. It'll be nice to see him. See you both at six."

Ivy clicked off and looked across at Gabe, who was sitting beside her, his arm around her. "Your parents don't like me," he said deadpanned.

Ivy tickled his ribs. "Remember that time they invited you to Dad's birthday when I was away for that conference? They love you."

Gabe smiled, but his expression turned stony, and he rubbed his hands through his hair. "Ivy, I don't have a lot to offer."

"Shut-up. We're not going down this road again, okay? I love you. I don't care about your family. Well, I care that your brother tried to do something horrible to me, but you saved the day. I have family, Gabe. I just need you."

He stroked her hair; his amber eyes bore into her. As a shiver raked her body, she leaned back into him as his knuckles slid down her cheek.

"You're my family, Princess. I love you."

And as his lips lashed onto hers, her heart exploded. God, she was glad they were together. That they had grabbed his second chance and ran with it, that he held them up, led them forward when she wanted to let go.

Ivy held her phone up and snapped a picture because it was totally social media-worthy. Though she wouldn't post it until she showed Gabe first.

On the McNeil's farm, with the sun setting in the background, strong and tall Gabe was nuzzling the mean old grey stallion, stroking its usually pinned back ears.

"You're a good horsey orsey, yes you are. Thanks for letting me ride you today."

Ivy snorted, covering her mouth.

"What? It's true. Look how majestic he is."

If she had known the way to Gabe's gooey centre would be through horses, she would have insisted on going for more trail rides.

After dinner, her mom pulled her aside while doing the dishes and said, "You seem happier with him, Ivy. But make sure this is what you want. You've spent a lot of time invested in this relationship."

And it was true, almost a decade of her life had been spent with Gabe. From when she was a young professional, trying to prove herself, to when she climbed the ranks and always missed dinner, to her losing her making that post, their separation and her lost confidence. But with Gabe back, she found herself again. Because he brought out the best in her, that couldn't be denied.

"You should have come trail riding with me before." Ivy rested her foot on the crossbar of the gate.

CHAPTER THIRTY – IVY

Gabe gave Menace one last pat. The horse snorted at them and then turned away, grazing on grass.

"Princess, there are a lot of things I should have done. A lot of things I wish I had done. I can't change them, Ivy, but I can promise you, you matter to me and going forward, I am going to make every decision with you in mind."

"Does that mean living downtown?"

Gabe shook his head. "You know there's a place for sale here up the road. I like the country life."

Ivy hesitated, unsure if he was being serious, baiting her or honest. She decided it was a mixture of all three. "Gabe! No, I can't live this far outside of the city and this close to my parents."

"Did you just say 'no' to me? I thought we agreed we would listen to each other." Gabe's mouth crashed into hers. He pulled a strand of her hair tight. "Ivy, what am I going to do with you?"

"Agree to buy the place downtown."

Gabe laughed. "Got to weigh all options."

The downtown house was super cute with two floors of sleek contemporary living, and though the footprint was small, there was a small bonus room upstairs off the main hallway, a rooftop patio and a garden in the tiny backyard.

"I want to see it again," Ivy said.

"Then we'll view it again. Want to see the neighbourhood one again?"

Ivy frowned. The other house was four bedrooms, in the suburbs, in a great school district, but it came with the commute she didn't want.

"No."

"Okay, Princess. You know I will give you anything." Gabe kissed her long and slow.

"That was a great ride today, Gabe. Thanks for being brave and trying out Menace." Mrs. McNeil came down the steps, her keys in her hands.

"He's a great horse."

"You're a natural with them. You know, I'm always looking for help around this place, if you're interested."

"I have time," Gabe said.

"Perfect, maybe we can work something out. Ivy, I got to go and pick up Jenny from her clarinet practice. Can you guys make sure the lights are off before you leave?"

"Sure, Mrs. McNeil. Thanks for today."

"Anytime. It's nice having you home. Take care." Mrs. McNeil waved. Gabe slipped his hand in hers.

"You want to work around here?"

"Dr. Laktur said I needed to explore new hobbies. It's not stressful, I don't feel angry around the horses, the nightmares have been gone since I've quit Team Stealth; I think this is the fresh start we needed."

Ivy's heart lurched. She slipped her hand in his as they walked back through the stable, Ivy making sure the lights were turned off.

"Do you mind having a stable hand as a Dom?" Gabe whirled her against the door of the tack room. His intensity sent her pussy gushing.

"You know I don't. I might even buy you a horse."

Gabe laughed. "I don't need a horse, Princess. I do need you." His hands slid down her hips. Going to her waistband, he unzipped her jeans, his fingers underneath her panties. He rolled them down as Ivy breathed in his masculine scent. They were surrounded by leather and hay, sweat and dirt, and Ivy couldn't think of a better place to be.

The hotel room was great, but this was purely them, the spontaneity that had been missing for so long. Gabe's mouth pressed on hers until she opened for him, giving him all the access he wanted. His hand pushed down her jeans; Ivy felt the cool air on her ass as Gabe grabbed her, kissing her neck.

In two minutes, Ivy had his pants off and down, his cock free in her hand, as she stroked his hard length.

"You are so gorgeous," Gabe said.

"So are you," breathed Ivy, as his hand squeezed her ass, his hand coming around to her mound, spreading her pussy lips wide.

He lifted her up and held her against the door. "Reach up and grab the hook."

Ivy did, hoping it wouldn't come down on her. "Hold on, baby girl, this is going to be fast and serious."

As his lips crashed into hers, Ivy breathed in his musky scent, felt the ridges of his cock slide into her, and out and in again, long and slow, and then he was all serious as he arched her back, adjusted the angle just so, and Ivy screamed as he thrust deep in her.

God, with every deep stroke, Gabe stole the breath from her. Somewhere, an animal scattered, the cat, and the wind whipped against the barn doors; the roughness of the door ate into her back, but she didn't care.

Gabe pounded into her. "You are mine, Princess, and you'll live where I am, do you hear me?"

"Yes, Gabe," she said.

"And I can buy my own horse," he whispered into her ear as he slid deep, so damn deep inside her. "But I'll be generous and let you do the honours."

Ivy giggled as the coil of desire tightened as he rammed her hard against the door of the tack room. Sweat broke out on her back. She gasped for air as the wave of pleasure broke, her nails pressed in on his shoulders.

"Gabe, I love you."

"And I love you too, Princess," Gabe said into her ear. He wrapped her in his muscled arms, holding her and as long as he was there with her, there was nowhere else she wanted to be. Even if it was a house in the suburbs or the back of a tack room door, she needed this man. He had her heart again.

EPILOGUE

The warm breeze ruffled the palms above him. Gabe inhaled, taking in a whiff of the salty ocean and exhaled, trying to stop his galloping heart. Damn, he was a lucky bastard. Beside him, Nick clapped his shoulder. Gabe grinned at his fellow Bandit Brother and man-hugged him. Sitting in front of him, on white chairs, were Ivy's family, the Bandit Brothers, friends of Ivy's. Their guests were mostly on the bride's side. Gabe swallowed a lump in his throat. Then he caught sight of Ares, sitting next to Xander, with Harper beside him and Logan beside her. Gabe smiled. Xander was the only person in the place in a black suit. Everyone else dressed to match the Hawaii beach.

The flautist stood up, and as soft notes floated in the air, Gabe clenched his hands. He couldn't wait.

But wow, it was worth the wait. His bride, his submissive, his soulmate, was right there, like six feet in front of him, walking towards him, on the arm of her father, who was grinning. Gabe smiled. He couldn't recall Mike, Ivy's dad, smiling so much.

The bodice of Ivy's dress hugged her breasts, and the barest of cleavage showed. Her skirt was simple and elegant and flew out from her hips.

Gabe couldn't wait. He left the altar and met Ivy and Mike halfway.

EPILOGUE

"You take good care of her," Mike said. "You take good care of each other."

Gabe nodded, his throat tight. They would take good care of each other from this point out. It would no longer be rife with any competition, but they would support each other, keep each other buoyant.

The kind officiant smiled at them, and as the words to the ceremony started, Gabe tuned them all out, his eyes only for Ivy, her eyes big with the gentlest of eye makeup, her lips a soft pink colour.

So many memories flashed through his mind. The moment he first saw her, waiting outside the backdoor of the arena, the first time they ever played at Club Bandit, her body red and rosy from the flogger, the biggest grin on her face, and her cries of pleasure in the bedroom.

His girl lived life with her entire self, and he couldn't wait to see what happened.

"Gabe," Ivy nudged him.

"Yes, god, yes! I do," Gabe responded, and before the officiant even gave her blessing, his lips were on hers, his tongue gliding over hers, and his arms encircling her where he wanted her, forever.

***

To read a bonus scene of Gabe and Ivy, visit here: https://BookHip.com/KRLZHSW

Have you read *Flame For Two*, the second book in the Bandit Brothers Scene? Below is an excerpt. You can buy Flame For Two, here: https://books2read.com/u/mZZ082

CHAPTER ONE - HARPER

Harper's heart pounded so hard against her chest that she
heard its roar in her ears, even above the chatter of a hundred other dancers.

She took a deep breath, trying to clear her mind, but only inhaled the heavy scents of baby powder and hairspray. She couldn't believe she was going through with it.

She had waited in line for four hours, all the while telling herself that this was a terrible idea. And on the walk over to the theatre this morning, while feeling eyes on the back of her neck, convinced someone was following her, she nearly ran for the safety of her office. Here she was, despite this being a terrible idea. Dancing had been absent from her life long enough. Oh, she had her adult ballet classes, and she kept in shape with her CrossFit training sessions, but it wasn't the same as being on stage. The anticipation made her palms sweat.

Her feet were on the stage floor, and she stood straight and tall as the director marched on stage and welcomed them to the audition for *Canada's Best Dancer*. He split them up into groups. She ended up being in group "C," Then the choreographer came on the stage and showed them the first routine.

Committing the routine to memory was the simple part. Getting her body to execute the steps with some artistry was the challenge because it wasn't in a studio where she spent her days but in an office, following her boss from floor to floor, making sure everyone had what they needed from Team Tech needing special wristbands to Team Stealth having the newest non-military Kevlar coated tactical pants that they could get their hands on, the cost not being an issue. She was good at her job, but it wasn't where she'd thought she would end up.

She had thought she would be like these other dancers here, maybe with an international company, maybe even as a principal dancer or touring in a stage production as part of the chorus. Dancing on stage was all she dreamed about, following in her mother's footsteps.

After they tried out the routine, they cleared the stage for the first dancers to take their turn.

Pushing down the rise of emotion, Harper waited in the wings with the rest of her group. Her work was interesting and challenging and made her happy mostly, but it wasn't what she was born to do. Life had come in like a wicked tsunami, wrecking everything she held dear.

But she was here now, and she threw her shoulders back, kept her head up, and glided onto the stage with her group. There were a thousand reasons she shouldn't be here, like the TV cameras that panned the room for their promo shots. But when the music started, Harper didn't care. Losing herself in the steps of the contemporary routine, her body knew what to do even out of practice.

Before the tsunami of destruction, dancing had made her feel free, a moving part in something boundless, and for the sixty seconds of this first routine, that feeling infused her limbs again.

The music stopped, and the director walked down the rows.

"Cut," he said to the girl next to Harper, then "Cut" to the girl on the other side of her. As he passed, Harper exhaled. She was still in this.

"Wave at the camera for me," Came the instruction as Harper took her place in the wings again.

Ignoring the churning in her stomach, Harper flashed a grin.

"How does it feel to get through that first routine?" the woman behind the lens asked.

"It feels amazing! I'm so thrilled." Harper offered the woman a smile, twirling on the spot.

"Thanks," the camera moved on.

Three hours later, she was packing up her dance bag in disbelief. She had made it through to the solo round and gotten to perform her routine. Now she waited for a callback.

Other than feeling slightly guilty about lying to the production people by ensuring them she would be available for interviews, she felt great. For the first time in years, she had accomplished something all on her own.

Coming out of the changing room, Harper smoothed down her sunflower-covered pencil skirt and tucked in her black high collar blouse.

Refreshing her lipstick, she pulled her long mahogany hair into a ponytail and

exited the theatre into the grey, drizzling November afternoon, turning on her
phone as she walked.

Immediately, her phone started buzzing. She was never
offline, certainly not for most of the day, and she knew her assistant Claudia
could only cover for her for so long without questions. She sped up, work was
only a few blocks away, and it was easier to walk there than hail a cab.

Her skin started tingling. She checked the windows of the
buildings she passed by, using them as a mirror to glance about her, reassuring
herself that nobody was following her. It was all in her head. Years of looking
over her shoulder made her paranoid.

Crossing the street, Harper looked over her shoulder, but it
was only other people in the crowd going on with their day.

Reaching the street where Axis Management stood proudly,
like a contemporary modern art piece, all in black glass and sleek materials,
Harper slowed down.

"Harper! Harper!"

Harper turned at the familiar voice. "Josie, hi."

"You walk so fast!
Where were you coming from?" Josie stopped, leaning on her crutch.

"I had an appointment," Harper said. "What brings you by?"

"I was hoping to catch Ares, but there is no way into the
building. I tried calling him but couldn't get through."

"They prefer it that way," Harper said with a smile. "Ares
should be on a plane flying home. Do you want to come up with me?"

"No, if he's not in, there's no point. It's just...." Josie looked away, running her hands through her short black hair. "One business he sent my way cancelled their contract with us, and I wanted to know if he knew why."

"Sorry to hear that," Harper said. Josie was sweet as her catering company's pies, and Harper knew it was uncomfortable for her to ask for help.

"Just so I can improve, if something was wrong, I don't want him to fix this," Josie said. "I can get my own business."

"Your food speaks for itself," Harper said.

"Thanks," Josie said, glancing down. "I'll get in touch with Ares later in the week. You should come over for dinner. My mom would love to see you."

"I will, definitely," Harper said. Josie and her mother, Fleur, were two of only a small circle of people who knew about her personal tsunami.

"Take care," Josie called.

Continuing to the door of the shiny metallic glass building, Harper stopped by the seamless entrance and punched in the code to activate the retina scanner. When the lock flashed green, and the doors opened, she walked into Axis Management's smooth terrazzo main floor, the security firm that did everything from bodyguarding to government contracts and more. The main floor

was empty, the curved front desk clear. She passed the conference room before
stepping into the elevator and riding up to the executive floor.

"Hello," she said to their receptionist, Viv.

Viv raised her eyebrows at her and pointed down the hall.

Yeah, they'd be looking for her. Harper glanced at her watch.

"Harper!"

Halfway to the office, Claudia flew towards her. "You need to check your messages. Ares's plane is delayed, and there's that fundraiser
tonight. My sister thinks the baby is coming but I can stay if you want."

"Go! Keep me updated!"

"Thanks!" Claudia smiled and waved.

Harper sighed. She did not need this after the rehearsal; she wanted to go home, curl up with a book and tune out the world.

Entering the executive wing, she smiled. Her desk sat outside her boss's office. His door was closed. Putting her bag away, she
sighed. He was going to need a suit.

She waved bye to Viv, who was shutting down her system and walked down the hall, hitting the elevator's up button while rearranging the schedule for tomorrow in her head. When the elevator opened, she strode to
apartment number one, the biometric lock opening to her touch. This was a
ridiculous hassle.

"Totally
unnecessary," Harper grumbled under her breath. From the closet, she

took out a suit and folded it over her arm. She made a couple of quick phone calls and returned to the executive wing. Passing her desk, she paused at the door.

But interrupting came with the territory of being the executive assistant to Xander Montague, billionaire and genius extraordinaire.

She knocked once. Her phone buzzed in her pocket. If he didn't get a move on, they would be late. He hated being late almost as much as he hated wearing a suit, so she did the whole swipe her hand over the lock thing again.

When the door whisked open, she wished she hadn't interrupted.

"Hey," she said, leaning against the door like it was no big deal she had walked in on her boss getting a blow job at five-thirty in the afternoon.

There he sat on the black leather couch in the lounge area with his head resting back, his curtain of dark hair flowing along his arm, his hand guiding the woman's head, while Harper acted like she was just passing through to drop off a file or wake him from a nap. Like it didn't make her heart twist in a pang of jealousy because she wished it was her between his strong, muscular legs.

Xander's eyes flew open, and the brunette woman between his legs startled. Xander swore, and his hands came around the back of the woman's neck, pulling her off.

EPILOGUE

"Sorry, Cindy, I'll make it up to you."

"You could tell her to go." Cindy pouted.

"I have business," Xander said, his voice firm. He had already thrown on his boxers, guided Cindy up from the floor, and smoothed down her dress.

"Bitch," Cindy murmured to Harper as she walked past her.

Harper flashed her a smile as wide as her lips could stretch. It didn't matter how many women came, they went, and she stayed.

"Cindy." That tone made Harper feel small. He never used that deep baritone voice on her like that, though she wished he did. His tone of dominance sent a thrill down her spine.

He grabbed Cindy's arm and raised an eyebrow at her.

"Sorry," Cindy mumbled, looking at the ground.

"I'll call you," Xander said.

As Cindy exited the office, the doors swished closed, and Harper adjusted the suit bag in her hands.

"No! Not the suit!" Xander said, with a hand across his face, as if he was a vampire, and the suit bag Harper had draped over her arm was the blazing sun.

Harper sighed. He refused to keep suits in his office, so she had to keep them stashed in a closet up in the apartments Axis Management had above their offices, and they went through this routine whenever she had to get him one. "You know I wouldn't bring it if it weren't for a good reason."

"Nope, I didn't see it. I'm sure I have a meeting somewhere."

Harper shook her head and watched as Xander tapped his keyboard and frowned.

"You locked me out of the system!"

"You gave me executive privileges for this reason. Go shower. The car will be here in half an hour."

"I'm expecting Erik, and there is that meeting with the Martin Group. I have to go paint a wall or fix a fence."

"No way out of this one. I told Erik you weren't available tonight. He's going to see you at one tomorrow. Ares is Zooming with the Martin Group from the hotel." She put the suit in Xander's hands. "And Mr. Montague, you have never fixed a fence or painted a wall."

"Are you so sure?" his voice purred.

Harper smiled. This was the side of her otherwise serious and dour boss that few people got to see.

"*Positive*."

He had created a popular scheduling app that had made him his first million. He designed a sleeker better satellite phone for military operations that earned him another million and other things, but Xander didn't own a hammer.

"Is there no way he can get here?" Xander pulled back his hair into an elastic band. His rock band T-shirt hit the floor in another second, revealing his tight abs and broad shoulders.

"Ares doesn't like you doing these things, either," Harper said. She turned away as Xander's hands went to his waistband and walked down the corridor with the muted, dove grey walls to her inner space.

When they had been going over plans for this building, Xander had insisted she had a space of her own, and Harper disagreed. She followed Xander wherever he went during the day, and when he was in his office on this floor, she was at her desk, just outside. A wholly separate space for her wasn't necessary, but she loved it after having this retreat for a few months.

She'd had this office done in what she thought of as an "ocean light" theme. The walls were light blue, the curtains in soft pink and framed photos of beaches were scattered around the room. A standing desk and a comfy chaise that doubled as her bed when she worked through the night were the only pieces of furniture in the room. She pulled out a red sparkly gown from the closet next to her bathroom and kicked off her flats, replacing them with heels. She hung the dress on the bathroom door and started her make-up.

"Are you sure he can't get here? We can't send the plane?"

Xander appeared in her bathroom doorway with a towel wrapped around his waist.

Harper met Xander's steel eyes in the mirror. The press called him the "Prince of Darkness of the Business World," and with his pale skin, powerful features, and that long black hair, it was a title he nurtured.

"It's a security threat, so the whole airport is closed. He had to do some sweet talking to leave the airport and go to the hotel. He'll be on the first flight out as soon as they have cleared the threat."

While Xander was the Prince of Darkness of the Business world, Ares, his brother and co-CEO, was known as the Archangel, having a reputation for never saying no to a request for a donation or a photo op, never refusing an invitation to a charity function.

"Not this one," Xander said, taking the gown from her and walking out of the room with it in his arms.

As she finished making up her eyes, Harper smiled, being used to Xander's whims. He had a reason for everything he did.

"Wear this tonight." Xander held up a light purple A-line gown. As he dangled it in his hand, Harper saw it was asymmetrical. The front of the skirt would be slightly shorter than the back.

"It's lovely," she said.

Opening a drawer, she selected a pair of earrings and went to put her hair up.

"I saw it and thought of you."

As their eyes met in the mirror, Harper's pulse raced. He continuously surprised her.

"Are you sure there is no way out of this? They don't even feed you at these things."

"Axis Management gave ten thousand dollars to the Firefighters' Foundation. This dinner is to thank their top donors."

"And ask for more money," Xander grumbled.

"Naturally. We'll get through it, and then you can play Zombies till dawn."

"*Outriders*," Xander mumbled.

"Go get dressed," Harper closed the door on him.

"Top donor? That means I need to give a speech?!"

"There's a full bottle of Xanax in the top drawer of your dresser, in the closet."

"Meet you outside in five."

Harper finished her hair and slipped on the gown, running a checklist in her head of everyone she knew who would be there, trying to prepare for the evening, including a plan to get Xander out of there as quickly as possible.

Many competitors and journalists would love to know that Xander Montague, the mighty Prince of Darkness of the Business World, had a severe anxiety disorder. Harper did everything in her power to keep that contained only to people whose fingerprints could open these rooms. Xander was her rescuer and her protector. She owed him a lot. Keeping his secrets was an easy ask.

Before leaving her suite, she admired how the dress fit in the mirror. Xander always chose right. The dusky purple brought out the olive tone in her skin, highlighting her green eyes. The bodice hugged her breasts snuggly. The longest part of the skirt hit just below her calves, showing off her long legs. She touched the *x* pendant at her throat. It was another mark of Xander's protection he had given her. This *x* served as a broadcast in certain settings to talk to her; one had to speak to Xander first. And while only those in the BDSM scene might know what a protection collar meant, it was her touchstone, another way of reassuring herself that she was safe.

She shut off the lights and through the doors to the central executive area. Before she left, she stopped by Claudia's desk, leaving her a few notes for her meeting with Team Tech and telling her she would be in around eight o'clock the following day in case Claudia's sister's baby didn't come tonight.

At the side door of the building, she found the co-CEO of Axis Management, as most of the world knew him to be, pacing back and forth and speaking rapid French into his phone. His raven hair was in its trademark braid, hitting the centre of his back. He had a pair of sunglasses on. He was decked out in a black, light wool suit with a faint but present red pinstripe. Underneath the suit jacket, he wore a high collar black shirt. His black boots shone to a high gloss. His expression was stoic, with no signs of the humour and playfulness that, in private, she knew well. A few feet away from him was the bodyguards for the evening, Asher and Soren; the job was to keep the press away from Xander.

As Harper came beside him, she heard him utter a curse involving a holy sacrament that never translated the same to English. He slipped his phone into his inner suit jacket pocket and stared ahead.

"That good?" Harper asked.

Xander looked at her. Harper stared back, unflinching.

"Benoit thinks he has what I want, but he won't give it to me yet." Harper couldn't help but gasp. Xander had been working with their technology competitor for months, searching for information that would lead to figuring out who was responsible for an attack on Team Stealth back in June.

"What does he want?"

"He wants access to the information we might have on upcoming government contracts. I'm not good at sharing."

Harper kept her expression neutral, but her mouth went dry, and her heart thudded hard against her ribs.

"We know that."

She often wondered if he could share if he would. But Xander was a person-to-person type of guy. He kept his inner circle tiny, his outer circle small. Axis Management might be worth billions, but they were a small operation run on threads of loyalty.

"I don't have anyone I can send to him to soothe his feelings."

Xander paced for a moment. Harper waited with her phone out.

"Laurent. Get him in my office first thing tomorrow. He's also the least scary person we have to send."

As the limo pulled up, Carli, their driver, opened the door, and the two bodyguards got into their vehicle, going on ahead. Xander often had a team of their bodyguards follow them to any public appearance he made. Harper settled into the seat while leaving a message for Nick Laurent, a member of Team Stealth, or as the team was better known, Bandit Brothers. Xander slipped in beside her and looked at the ceiling.

"I hate these things."

"It will be over before you know it."

"You're gorgeous in that dress."

Harper smoothed out the skirt of her gown as she looked down. "Thanks."

Xander wasn't the only one who wanted the evening to be over. It was getting harder to hide how she felt about Xander. Harper knew he still thought of her as the not quite legal enough to drink girl she'd been when he rescued her.

"Here we go," she said as the limo pulled up at the hotel. There was a swarm of press and a crowd out front, shoulder to shoulder people.

"Fuck me," Xander said.

As he offered her hand, Harper's pulse raced when she caught sight of a big man, who stood head and shoulders over the rest with his spikey blond hair.

"Logan Marrock," she breathed.

"I'll have someone besides you to talk to," Xander said, and he almost smiled.

"Perfect," she said, but her stomach had tightened, wondering how she would get through the night with these two men. One who she wished would love her back, even as she couldn't stop thinking about the other.

***

Keep up to date with Raleigh by visiting her links here: https://linktr.ee/RaleighDamson

CPSIA information can be obtained
at www.ICGtesting.com
Printed in the USA
BVHW080934160822
644711BV00010B/619